SOLAR
PLEXUS

A Dystopian Novel by
VICTOR ZUGG

SOLAR PLEXUS

VictorZuggAuthor@gmail.com

CHAPTER 1

Tiffany Conway wound down her workdays by watching the late night talk shows. Sometimes she agreed with what the hosts had to say and sometimes she didn't. But either way, the guests were usually interesting.

'Tiff,' to her friends, on this night sat on the sofa cross-legged, wearing baggy bottoms and a sports top. She cradled a small bowl of popcorn in her lap.

She listened to the monologue as the host ranted about something he thought the president was doing wrong. In this instance, Tiff agreed with the president; although, that wasn't always the case. On this particular issue, at least, she thought the host was especially insulting with his beat down.

After a couple of minutes of his berating, Tiff finally pulled at her close-cropped blond hair with both hands, yelled, "Asshole," and threw a kernel of popcorn at the TV screen.

At that very moment, the screen went dark and then immediately went to a wide image of the president sitting behind his desk in the Oval Office shuffling papers. There were other people in view off to the side.

Tiff sat up. "What the fu…?"

A man wearing jeans, a polo shirt, and earphones motioned to the president, silently counted down with his fingers—three… two… one, and pointed. The image zoomed. The president filled the screen.

"My fellow Americans, I come to you tonight with grave news that will affect everyone on this planet."

Tiff fixated on the screen.

"A few hours ago the surface of the sun released a massive storm of highly charged particles that are heading directly for us. These particles, called a coronal mass ejection, will strike our atmosphere in less than four hours. Solar storms of charged particles are common and strike our atmosphere regularly. Most are small and relatively harmless. But this one is massive. It is the largest and fastest ever recorded, and it is expected to punch through our atmosphere with relative ease. These highly charged particles will cause serious electrical surges in almost all wiring and circuits even if the devices are turned off and unplugged. For most people, this means no lights, no A/C, no phones or any kind of communications, and no running water. Except for very old models without circuits, vehicles, boats, and aircraft will not work. Fortunately, most military vehicles are shielded from the effects of these charged particles. Our troops will be able to operate."

Tiff was familiar with this phenomenon. An increase in solar storm activity had been reported in the news over the last year or so. She didn't think much of it at the time, no one did. She did remember thinking that there wasn't much that could be done if the sun decided to strike. She focused back on what the president was saying.

"Also, several years ago we began taking steps to ensure nuclear power plants would remain safe during such an event. They can be brought back online with only minor repairs. The problem will be the transmission of power. All transformers are expected to be destroyed. Because it takes so long to build a transformer, even in the best of circumstances, we expect it will be many months, possibly years, before power can be restored to everyone. Most other countries will be equally affected, so they won't be able to help."

Tiff wondered which countries would come to our aid with no strings attached even if they could. Canada and Mexico would likely be equally affected. England and Australia would help, maybe Germany and France, but that would be about it. Tiff perked up with the president's next words.

"We don't have a lot of time, but we've already taken steps to preserve as much as possible. I declared martial law an hour ago. All state governors have been notified. I've nationalized all guard and reserve military units. I've grounded all airlines. State and Federal agencies with access to protected facilities such as bunkers, underground compounds, and even caves, are loading them with critical supplies and equipment. I will be moving, along with much of my staff and cabinet, to a secure facility in Virginia. The military command Authority will be moving to a similar facility in Pennsylvania. I will be able to communicate with the military, along with some government heads around the world, and several of the state governors."

This sounds serious, Tiff thought. She picked up her cell phone and pushed some buttons. The phone came to life. She held onto the phone as she turned her attention back to the president.

"We will begin our recovery efforts immediately, but most of you will be on your own for months, perhaps longer. The only thing I can do for you right now is ask and pray that you do not turn on each other. No matter your skin color, culture, religion, or financial status, we're all in the same boat. Protect yourselves and your families. Help your neighbors. No matter what, we are Americans and we will persevere. God bless you and God bless these United States."

The screen went dark again. A few seconds later the talk show host resumed.

Tiff stared at the screen. "Maybe this is a joke," she mumbled to herself. She was aware that decades ago, back when there were only radio shows for entertainment, one radio station broadcasted a war-of-the-worlds scenario so realistic that people actually thought the planet was being invaded by aliens. *Maybe this was simply a similar joke on the public*, she thought. But then the television screen went dark again.

A few seconds later the NBC national news desk popped on the screen. A newscaster sat behind the desk as two other people fiddled with his earphone. They left the newscaster's side, and he looked up. The screen zoomed to his image.

"This is NBC News in New York. I'm Bret Callaway coming to you with an emergency notification. You've just heard directly from the president. This is not a joke. This is a very grave situation and we have almost no time to react. Soon we will be off the air, but until then we will provide as much information as possible. As you heard, a massive solar storm is heading directly for our planet. The consequences are expected to be significantly life altering."

As the newscaster continued in the background, Tiff dialed her cell phone. After a few rings, an older woman's voice answered with a hello.

"Mom, have you seen the news?" Tiff asked, as she stood up and paced the floor.

"No dear, your father and I were about to go to bed," the voice on the phone replied. "What's going on?"

"The president says there's a solar storm coming that will knock out power and water for months—for everyone. It's supposed to even knock out our phones and cars, we'll have no way to talk or travel."

"Honey, are you sure, maybe they're exaggerating like the news always does."

"This is for real Mom, I just listened to the president, it is happening."

"Will it affect us here in Ohio?"

"Yes. Ohio, here in Florida, the whole country. In fact, the whole world. You and Dad need to go to the store right now and get plenty of water and canned food. If what they say is true, the storm will hit in four hours and we won't be able to talk on the phone anymore. And your car may not work. If you don't get food and water right now, there won't be any by tomorrow."

"But what about you, dear, what will you do down there all alone?"

"I'm going to pack some stuff in the car and start driving toward Ohio. If the car conks out, I'll hike. I have all the gear I need. It may take a while, but I'll get there."

"That would be dangerous, maybe you should stay there."

"Mom, if what they say is true, Orlando will be out of food and water in a couple of days. This is no place to be when the people have no food or water. I'll be better off heading out. I'll stay off the main roads."

"Okay honey, you've always been confident and determined. We'll pray for you."

"Okay Mom, got to go. I love you. And tell Dad I love him."

"We love you too."

Tiff ended the call and looked around the room. "Let's see, hiking gear, tent, food light enough to carry, water—"

***

Water bottles and a couple of one-gallon jugs full of water sat on the kitchen countertops of Tiffany Conway's apartment. Tiff was ferrying equipment from the two bedrooms to her makeshift staging area in the middle of the living room floor. She paused for a moment, thought, disappeared into the spare bedroom, and returned with a small nylon bag in one hand and a rolled up sleeping bag in the other. "Tent, sleeping bag, some food, water, hiking equipment, what else… toiletries, first aid," she mumbled.

She added the tent and sleeping bag to the growing pile of equipment, disappeared into the same spare bedroom, and returned with a large backpack. She sat down next to the pile and started stuffing items.

Tiff grabbed two medium-sized nylon bags from the pile, stepped to the kitchen, and began opening cabinets. She went through the cabinets and pulled out food items that were light and compact. She had just opened the pantry when there was a knock at her front door. She ran to the door, checked the peep hole, and then slung the door open.

A slim, athletic woman, about the same age as Tiff, rushed in. "Tiff, my god, what will happen?" The woman glanced at the pile of gear on the floor. "Where are you going?"

Tiff closed the door behind the woman. "Ohio. Mom and Dad will need me there. You're welcome to come. I could sure use the company."

"I can't Tiff, my family is here. How will we stay in touch?"

Tiff stepped back into the kitchen. "I don't think phones will work. I'll be back though when this is over."

"Looks like you're planning to hike the whole way."

"I'll drive until the car stops. Hopefully, I'll be well out of the Orlando area."

The woman inched closer and hugged her. "Tiff, how can you walk to Ohio?"

Tiff returned the hug and then stepped back still holding the woman's arms. "Meg, I was a marine, remember? Two years ago I was slugging through deserts, swamps, and all manner of crap. I'll be fine. Right now I need to get moving, so I'll have time to make it out of town. Can you help?"

***

Tiff stepped off the apartment building stairs lugging the backpack and shuffled to an older white Honda Civic parked nearby in the lot. The muscles in her arms and bare calves down to her leather hiking boots rippled and flexed from the strain. Meg followed carrying two jugs of water and various nylon bags.

"Can you carry all this?"

Tiff tossed the pack into the back seat. "I'll manage."

She turned to Meg, took the items from her and threw them in the back seat. Tiff dug in the front pocket of her shorts and handed Meg a key. "Take the remaining food, water, and anything else you might need from the apartment. Your family will need it. And if you guys stay here you need to stay at your Mom's house. It's well out of town. Don't trust anyone you don't know. And be wary of the people you do know. It's going to get bad."

Meg's shoulders drooped. She started to speak but choked up instead.

"I've got to go, Meg."

They hugged for a full minute and then stepped apart.

"Are you carrying a gun?" Meg asked.

"I'll be carrying my XDs 9 from now on. You should carry too, everywhere you go."

Meg nodded. "Be safe Tiff."

"You too, best friend of mine."

Tiff checked her wrist watch. "One o'clock, I should be able to make it well out of town before the storm hits."

Tiff opened the driver's door, hopped in, and closed the door. She reached through the open window for Meg's hand. "You might want to hook up with Tom from work, he was in the army and he'll know what to do when things get bad, which will be soon."

"Tom Castor! The old guy in shipping?"

"Trust me, he's a good guy, he's alone, and he's not that old. You could even invite him to your Mom's house."

"I don't know," Meg replied.

"Call him now and tell him I said to get in touch, he'll take it from there. I think he likes you. Just do it."

"Okay, okay, I will," she said, as she pulled out her cell phone.

Tiff started the car. "Gotta go."

"I know. Take care Tiff, I love you."

"Love you too."

Tiff stepped on the gas and sped off with a wave out her window.

CHAPTER 2

Sam Pratt shuffled papers and placed them in neat stacks on his desk. It occurred to him that he actually enjoyed paperwork. Being on top of things, being organized, instilled a sense of order. It was a natural form of Xanax. People could eliminate anxiety if they would just get organized. He had been this way his whole life—fifty years—and it had served him well. He often lauded the fact that he could do in half a day what it took most people a full day. That's what being organized could do. Which is why he spent a couple of hours nearly every evening preparing for the next day—generally staying ahead of the paperwork that came with the job.

That's what he was doing this night. Still dressed in his slacks and polo shirt, with no television and no distractions, he pulled more papers from his briefcase and arranged them with the stacks already on his desk. He picked up one of the stacks and tamped the edges on the desk to align the pages. As the stack hit the desk for the second time he heard a loud boom outside. Sam jumped at the sudden noise. He jerked his eyes to the window over his desk and saw sparks rain from the transformer onto the cul-de-sac. Then the power went out, and he was plunged into darkness. That's when he noticed the lights.

He'd only seen the northern lights on YouTube, but there was no mistaking it. This was them. Sam laid the stack of papers on the desk, got up, and stepped to the window. With his thumb and index finger, he separated the open horizontal blinds for a better look. The sky was full of bright bands of green and red, pulsating into different shades of both and arcing from horizon to horizon. *The light show was beautiful, but wrong*, he thought. The auroras should not be visible from Daytona Beach, Florida; they were a far north phenomenon.

Sam picked up his iPhone and pushed the home button. Dead. He picked up his landline handset. Dead. He glanced around the dark room for a moment and then made his way to a credenza. He felt around inside a drawer until he found the cylindrical body of a flashlight. He pushed the switch. Nothing. He sat the useless flashlight on the credenza and made his way to the kitchen. There, he rummaged blindly through a drawer. Finally, he struck a match and touched the flame to a candle wick. The room flickered with dull light. He put the candle on a saucer and carried it to the living room where he placed the saucer and candle on the table next to his favorite chair.

Sam opened the front door and stepped outside. It was dark and unusually quiet—not even normal street noise. No one was about. Of course, that would be expected at two in the morning. None the less, something was definitely wrong. Sam admired the light show in the sky a few moments more and then stepped back inside and closed the door. He glanced around the room at the shadows dancing on the walls. He took a seat in his chair, relaxed, and waited for the power to come back on.

***

A frantic pounding on his front door catapulted Sam from a deep sleep. He stood, rotated his shoulder to get some blood flowing, and shuffled to the door half asleep. At five-ten, one-seventy-five, he might be in great shape, but he wasn't as agile as he once was. He glanced at his silver diver's watch on the way. It had stopped at 2:07.

He checked the peep hole and saw a tall slender man about Sam's age, short gray hair, a full beard. Sam opened the door.

"Dammit Chet, what the hell time is it?"

Chet, breathing hard, his shirt spotted wet from sweat, rushed through the doorway to the middle of the room and spun around to face Sam.

"Don't know," Chet said. "My watch stopped. Everything has stopped!"

Sam closed the door. "What do you mean?"

"Everything has stopped working. Didn't you hear the news and the president last night? He declared martial law."

"Martial law? What's going on?"

Chet followed Sam to the kitchen. "Bud, life has changed in a big way. Our trip to Dallas and the security seminar today is definitely off. The president grounded all flights. I guess he didn't want planes falling out of the sky. The planet was hit by a giant solar storm last night, around two. The northern lights were in our southern sky. All electricity around the world is off and expected to stay off for months, maybe years. Nothing works—no power, no water, no phone, and worst of all, no car."

Sam, with an empty coffee pot in his hand, opened the refrigerator. The light was out. He flipped the wall switch. No light. "Are you serious?" he asked, as he put the coffee pot on the counter. "How did you get here?"

"Rode my bike." Chet looked down at his t-shirt and pulled at the dark spots to separate the wet cloth from his skin.

Sam peered out the kitchen window. "What do you mean, months?"

"The president said months, maybe longer. It's probably around six-thirty, and already it's chaos; people have descended on the grocery stores like locusts."

Sam stared at Chet for a long moment. "What about you? Why aren't you there?"

Chet slapped Sam on the back. "I need backup, and I was thinking—your buggy might still work. It's made from an old jeep and it has no advanced circuits to burn out."

"Wait a minute—you're telling me that a solar storm knocked out electricity around the world and it won't be coming back on for months or years."

"That's right."

Sam walked into the living room and parted the blinds on the front window. Most of his neighbors were standing in their yards or gathered in small groups, talking. He walked to his bedroom and returned to the kitchen pushing the home key on his cell phone. Nothing. Sam stood still for a moment, shook his head, and then stared at Chet.

"If you had heard the president last night you'd understand," Chet said.

"Martial law, seriously, the president declared martial law?"

"That's right, Chet replied. We are currently in a state of martial law. That basically means the military is in charge."

"Does the military have electricity?"

"If their generators were shielded they do. Aircraft are probably grounded, but a lot of their vehicles were built to withstand this kind of thing. And according to the president, they were able to stockpile some supplies and equipment in bunkers and underground compounds."

"Dammit, Chet! You're serious. This is not a joke."

"No joke, my friend."

Chet's face was solemn. Sam could usually tell when Chet was joking, which was often. But Sam couldn't detect any of the usual tells on Chet's face. He looked genuinely concerned.

"What now?" Sam asked.

"Unless you have a large cache of food and water I don't know about, we need to stock up."

Sam stood motionless for a few moments, nodded, and then moved toward the bedroom. "Okay, let me change."

Chet motioned for Sam's attention. "We'll be looking at chaos soon. You should arm up."

Sam paused, stared at Chet for a moment, and then continued padding his way across the shiny wood floor. He entered the bedroom and stepped directly to the window. He parted the blinds and peered into his backyard. His yard looked pretty much as it usually did. All of his neighbors' yards looked pretty much as they usually did. Grass was cut, trees were trimmed, and all was ready for a new day. A regular day. Except according to Chet, this wasn't a regular day. And based on what he saw out the front window—all of his neighbors milling around in their yards and on the street at o-dark-thirty in the morning—they must have also decided this wasn't a regular day.

Sam shook his head and then padded across the carpet to his dresser. He dropped his slacks, stepped out of his boxers, and slipped his polo shirt over his head. He opened various drawers and threw selected items of clothing on the bed. He picked up jeans in one hand and a pair of dark tactical pants in the other. He shifted his gaze back and forth and finally opted for the tactical pants, along with a black t-shirt, boots, and a long sleeve shirt. He put the clothes on leaving the shirt unbuttoned.

He went to his nightstand, opened the top drawer, and pulled out his Smith and Wesson M&P 9 and its holster. He strapped them to his waist with a sturdy black nylon belt along with a fixed blade Buck knife in a sheath.

He returned to the kitchen and found Chet opening cabinets and pulling out food items. He had already placed a number of items on the counter. He opened the pantry and pulled out a six-pack of bottled water.

"You don't have near enough food or water," Chet said.

"Not for an apocalypse, I don't."

Chet stopped what he was doing and turned to Sam. "Are we ready to head out?"

Sam placed both hands on the counter. "I've been thinking. I have the cabin in Tennessee. It's fairly isolated on ten acres, and there's a mountain stream that runs year round."

"Yeah, if you can get there," Chet said.

"We."

"We?"

Sam put a hand on Chet's shoulder. "That's right, we—as in you and me."

"You want me to go with you to Tennessee. What about my house here?"

"Chet, when food runs out in about two days, this entire area will be a war zone. Our best chance for survival will be to high-tail it out of dodge and head for the hills. The land there has food and water. And best of all, it's defendable. Aside from you being my best friend, I need your help."

"I guess there really is nothing keeping me here. I could lock the place up and hope for the best. We'd need to pop over there so I can grab some gear and all the ammo I can carry."

"Now you're thinking."

"What about the grocery store?"

"I say we skip it, take what we can from our two houses, and get a head start on what will surely be a mad dash out of the cities. But the first thing we need to do is make sure the buggy runs."

Chet nodded, and they both headed for the front door.

Outside, many of the neighbors were still standing around in their front yards, obviously trying to figure out what they should do. Most were too old to walk very far. Some were inspecting their car engines. Some were still gathered in small groups talking.

No one paid much attention when Sam and Chet stepped out of the house. They crossed to Sam's detached garage and went inside.

Parked inside was a shiny, brand new, Toyota 4Runner. And next to it was a much less shiny buggy. If it weren't for the well-known Jeep grille, it wouldn't have been recognizable as a Jeep. Most of the body was composed of large diameter steel pipe, some painted dark green and some black. There were yellow doors, a yellow hood, and a yellow canvas top, but the rest was open. No windows except for the windshield. The cockpit included two bucket seats and a standard shift. The bed was open to the sky and contained a short bench seat. And, of course, the tires were massive.

Sam opened the 4Runner door. "Let's see if this will start."

He inserted a key in the ignition and turned. Nothing. Not a dash light of any kind.

Sam slid out and closed the door. "Dead."

Chet slid behind the wheel of the buggy and stuck out his hand. "Key please."

Sam handed Chet the ring of keys and then rubbed the hood for encouragement.

Chet inserted the key and turned. The engine fired immediately and settled into a smooth idle. Chet smiled and quickly turned the engine off. "Don't want to rile the natives."

Sam nodded. "Unfortunately, the gas mileage is shit, but it has an almost full tank which we can top off from the 4Runner. Plus, we can fill the two five-gallon cans I have around here someplace. I say we gear up and head out."

"Sounds like a plan," Chet said, as he slid out of the buggy.

***

Sam and Chet emerged from the back door of the house loaded down with gear. Sam had a heavy pack with a water bottle on each side in one hand and a short canvas rifle case in the other. Chet had the six-pack of water, a large nylon bag stuffed full, and two military spec OD green ammo cans. They hurried to the garage side door, entered, and loaded the gear into the buggy's bed next to two metal jerry cans already sitting on the bed floor.

Chet grimaced. "Not a lot of room."

"It will have to do," Sam replied.

"Wait till you see how much stuff I need to bring," Chet said with a snicker.

"Be right back," Sam said, as he headed back to the house.

Sam looked around each room and checked all the kitchen cabinets and the pantry for anything they wouldn't be able to live without. Due to weight or size, he left a lot of food items behind. Sam locked and double checked the front door, closed all the window blinds, and exited through the rear door. He made sure it too was locked. He then walked around to the front yard, crossed the street, and approached an older couple still hanging out in their front yard. When the couple saw Sam approaching they both stepped to meet him.

"Are you guys going to be okay?" Sam asked.

"John and I will be just fine," The woman replied. "We spoke to Millie last night before the power went out and she and Dave are headed over here right now, walking I suppose. We're just thankful our daughter was in town when this thing hit."

"Sarah is tough enough for all of us," John said. "Don't know what I'd do without her. We'll survive."

"John, you're a scientist, what happened?"

"I've been retired from NASA a long time," John replied.

"Still, except for Sarah here, you're the smartest person I know."

Sarah smiled.

John motioned with his arm toward the sky. "Well, as you know, our planet is constantly bombarded by electrically charged particles from the sun's coronal surface. The vast majority of these particles do not make it into our atmosphere because they are repelled by the earth's magnetic field, our magnetosphere. A few particles do make it into the atmosphere at the magnetosphere's weak points, the northern and southern poles. The northern and southern lights, the auroras, are generated by those charged particles striking the atmosphere."

"I saw the lights earlier this morning," Sam said.

"The fact that the lights were this far from the poles indicates this was a very strong storm, obviously strong enough to punch through our magnetosphere. We had a similar event in 1859. It has come to be called the Carrington Event. Charged particles entered our atmosphere causing electrical surges that were seen and felt in telegraph lines and even railroad tracks. Of course, back then the world's civilizations were not advanced to the point where electrical surges could cause much damage. That's not the case today."

"How long will this last?" Sam asked.

"The electromagnetic pulse or EMP dissipates quickly, but they will have to replace all the transformers and probably a lot of the wiring and relays. They'll need to rebuild most of the grid. That would be a tough job even with modern machinery, which we now do not have. The president was right last night. Getting power back up will take months, probably years."

"How serious will this get?" Sam asked.

"Hard to say," John replied. "I've read studies that projected losses in the ninety percent range with an event like this. That would be the extreme, I would think, over a multi-year period."

Sam dropped his chin to his chest and blinked his eyes several times as he considered what John just said. "I had no idea it could get that bad," Sam said, as he raised his head slowly and stared at John's eyes. He looked for any sign that John could be exaggerating but found none.

"Like I said, that's an extreme projection. But even fifty percent would be catastrophic."

Sam reached out with both hands and took John and Sarah's shoulders. "No matter what the percentage, things are going to get really bad around here. John, I know you have a gun, don't hesitate to use it if you feel threatened. Don't light any candles at night. Keep it dark. And only go out if you absolutely have to. There will be marauders around and they will take your stuff if they know you have anything."

John reached up and covered Sam's hand with his own. "We'll be okay, what about you?"

Sam dropped his hands and took a step back. "You know Chet, he's over here all the time—we're going to head out to the cabin. The buggy still works."

Sarah looked toward Sam's house. "Your buggy works?"

"Yep, no advanced circuits to burn out."

Sarah's expression drooped. "That's a long way, are you sure you want to do that?"

"Yeah, we'll be okay."

Sam reached into his pocket and came out with a key which he handed to John.

John took the key. "What's this?"

"The house. There's still some food in there. Take what you need. And there are tools in the garage if you need them."

Sarah reached out and took Sam's arm. "Are you sure? We have plenty."

"You'll need more, and I don't have room to carry it all."

"We'll keep an eye on the house best we can," John offered.

"Thanks. Look, I need to scoot. You guys take care and tell Millie what I said about staying low."

"We will. Be safe Sam Pratt."

Sam turned and headed back to his yard with one final wave. He entered the garage to find Chet organizing the provisions in the back of the buggy. "All set?"

"Ready."

Sam paused for a moment and stared at the buggy. His eyes wandered over to Chet. "Finally."

"Finally, what?" Chet asked.

"Finally, something important to do," Sam said. "I haven't been this energized since I left the military. Giving security seminars doesn't hack it."

"Important… driving to Tennessee?"

"Surviving. Activity worthy of the effort."

"I know just what you mean, brother," Chet said.

Sam went to the garage door, reached up, and pulled the red release cord. The lock clicked open. Sam reached low under one of the door's metal cross beams and lifted until the door was fully open. The door stayed up while he turned back to the buggy. He slid into the driver's seat and turned the key. The engine started immediately. Chet settled in for shotgun. Sam placed the shift in gear and backed out slowly. He stopped about five feet outside the door, got out of the buggy, and went in the garage. He closed the garage door from the inside and pushed up on the locking mechanism. There was an audible metal click as the release lock was reapplied. Sam looked around the garage to make sure he wasn't forgetting something. He noticed Chet's bike leaning against the far wall. Sam exited the side door, checked that it was locked, and returned to the buggy. He looked around the neighborhood one last time. All eyes were on him. More specifically, all eyes were on the buggy. Sam waved to John and Sarah as he and Chet sped away.

***

Sam and Chet received stares from everyone they passed as they cruised toward Ormond Beach. Sam noted that there weren't that many stalled cars on the road. *Logical*, he thought, *since the storm hit early in the morning*. Just as Chet indicated, there were a lot of people walking. Most walked with a purpose. Sam realized they were headed for the Publix grocery store and the Walmart at the major intersection ahead. Sam turned off before that and continued the short distance to Chet's house. The neighborhood was just like Sam's—people milled around and talked in small groups.

Sam turned into Chet's drive and switched off the engine. "I should probably wait here with the buggy."

Chet opened the door and slid out. "Good idea, I won't be long." He walked to his front door, inserted a key, and stepped in.

Several neighbors stared at Sam, obviously wondering about the buggy. A neighbor from directly across the street started walking toward Sam. Sam slipped out of the seat and was standing in the back of the buggy when the neighbor arrived.

"Howdy," the man offered, "still running I see— must be an old one."

"It is," Sam replied, "but it won't last long after the gas runs out."

"Yeah, but until then it will come in real handy if you can hang on to it."

"That's my plan—to hang on to it that is."

The man stuck out his hand. "I'm Fred, from across the way. Where are you guys headed?"

Sam shook his hand, "Not sure. Right now I'm just helping Chet with an errand."

"Always good to have friends," Fred said, with a little sarcasm. Fred peered into the buggy's bed. "Looks like you're planning to be gone a while."

"Nah, just moving stuff around. We'll be back here real soon. And we sure hope the house remains as it is."

"Yeah, me too," Fred replied. "Well, better head back to the missus, she'll be wondering where I got off to."

"It was nice to meet you, Fred. I'm sure we'll see you around."

Fred waved as he sauntered back to his yard. Sam reached into the back of the buggy and unzipped one of the front pouches on his pack. Inside were four automatic rifle magazines neatly attached with elastic bands. Sam took all four magazines, picked up one of the ammo cans, and got back into the driver's seat. He opened the can and proceeded to load the four magazines with M16—5.56mm—rounds.

***

The house front door opened and Chet stepped out wearing black tactical pants, a green and black Hawaiian shirt, and a cap sporting the 82nd Airborne logo. In one hand he held a large tactical looking backpack and two canvas bags. In the other hand, he held a green ammo can and two jugs of water. He carried the gear to the buggy and placed it in the back.

"One more trip," he said to Sam, as he headed back to the house.

He emerged a few minutes later carrying a medium nylon bag stuffed full in one hand and a cardboard box under the other arm. He placed both in the buggy's bed and turned back to the house. He reached in the front door and slid a box out to the porch. He then stood, locked the door, checked it, and then picked up the box. He approached the buggy. "Four gallons of water plus the other two. That's all I had on hand."

"Glad you had that. Otherwise, we would have had to stop soon and filter some water. I packed a Katadyn Mini. It's small and slow but better than nothing."

Chet placed the box in the back, came around to the passenger's side, opened the door, and immediately noticed Sam's Sig Sauer semi-automatic rifle with its red dot magnifying sight and a thirty round magazine. It was on the floor leaning against the seat.

"What's this?"

"Just keep it low but handy. I think things are going to get dicey pretty quick."

Chet slid the rifle over a bit, sat in the seat, and slammed the door. "We're off—a road trip," Chet cackled.

"I hope that's all it is," Sam said.

CHAPTER 3

Sam steered the buggy out of the community and back to the main road. There were more stalled cars and trucks along this section of road and more people, some walking in the middle of the road. Everyone stared at the buggy. Sam had to slow to maneuver around the vehicles and the people. At the Publix grocery store on the corner of the major intersection everyone was walking toward, a long line of people snaked through the parking lot toward the store's entrance. Several police officers managed the civil crowd. The Walmart parking lot on the other side of the highway also had a line of people, again managed by police officers.

Chet motioned with his chin. "I wonder how long order will last."

"Not long. Tonight will be the start of chaos I'll bet, if not earlier," Sam replied.

Sam steered around the stalled vehicles and people in the intersection and was about to turn left to head toward Ocala when he noticed a police officer in the Walmart parking lot motioning for him to come over.

Chet noticed the officer too. "They'll seize the buggy."

"Not today," Sam said, as he continued the turn and accelerated west.

Soon they were out of the congestion and were able to speed up. They passed several gas stations where a few people stood about and they passed two large churches, one on each side of the road. People filed through the doors of both churches.

Sam looked over at Chet. "Praying might not be a bad idea. By the time this is over a lot of these people won't be here."

Chet nodded. "Yep."

As they continued west, the number of homes and businesses became less and less with fewer and fewer people out and about. Pretty soon they entered the Ocala National Forest where there was only an occasional stalled car or truck, conveniently pulled off to the side leaving the center of the highway wide open.

"There are a couple of old maps, one for Florida and one for the southeastern United States," Sam said, as he pointed to the glove box.

Chet opened the box, pulled out both maps, and unfolded the one for Florida. "Back roads I presume."

"Actually, I was thinking the interstates might be better in the rural areas. We can take back roads around the larger cities."

Chet studied the map a couple of minutes and then placed his finger on a particular spot. "We can turn off on route 326 which goes around Ocala to the north and intersects I75."

"I like it," Sam responded.

Chet put the maps back in the glove box, reached in his pants leg pocket, and came out with two granola bars. He handed one to Sam.

***

About an hour later the sign for highway 326 came up, and Chet pointed to the turnoff. Sam slowed for the turn. They proceeded north on the road which soon curved around to the west. Soon, more and more cars littered the road. People were on foot, and Sam had to slow down. Both Sam and Chet kept their gaze moving from side to side on the lookout for anything not kosher, other than the apocalypse unfolding before them. About three hundred yards out from the intersection of route 326 and highway 301 they came upon a group of about fifteen people spread along the side of the road running away from the intersection.

A middle-aged man in the group yelled to Sam and Chet, "They've got guns up there and they've already shot two people, one was a deputy. I'd turn around."

Sam and Chet looked at the man and then at each other.

"What do you think?" Chet asked.

Sam looked to his left and right. "Can we go around?"

At just that moment there was a *bang* from up ahead and Sam heard the whoosh of a bullet as it flew past, just missing the windshield. Two hundred yards up in the middle of the intersection two men, each with a rifle pointed in the buggy's direction, stood behind a car. Sam heard another *bang* just as he jerked the wheel to the right and ripped across an open grassy field toward a line of trees. "They want the buggy—they'll aim to miss it!"

Chet grabbed hold of the dash with both hands. "They won't aim to miss us!"

Sam nodded. "Yeah, I know."

The buggy bounced over grass humps and sped forward until Sam slammed on the brakes inside the tree line. The buggy slid to a stop just short of a massive pine tree.

Chet grabbed the Sig rifle and thrust it toward Sam.

Sam took the rifle, took the keys from the ignition, and lunged out of the buggy. He ran around to the back, unzipped the front pouch of his pack, and snatched the three remaining rifle magazines, each full of 5.56 rounds. He shoved the magazines into various pockets of his tactical pants. "I'm going to head northwest through the trees, cross 301, and try to flank them from the rear!"

Chet nodded. "I'll try to move up on their front to keep them occupied."

"Okay," Sam said, "try to move in when you hear me blasting away. But stay low."

Chet nodded, and both men moved out at a low trot. Sam zipped through the trees until he emerged onto 301, about one hundred yards north of the intersection. He took a knee in the tall dogfennel lining his side of the road and spent a full minute checking in both directions. Sam saw two men in the intersection. Both stood behind a stalled car and both aimed a rifle in the general direction of where the buggy had left the road. They seemed to be arguing. One was motioning to the other, apparently trying to get him to leave his cover and check out the buggy. Sam also saw a woman with her hands behind her back sitting against the front wheel of a blue pickup to the right of the two men. She would be in the line of fire with a frontal assault. And two other people, also with their hands behind their backs, sat against a large bread truck directly behind the two shooters.

When Sam was fairly sure the two men were occupied more with each other than they were with their surroundings, he sprinted across 301 and dove to the ground as soon as he reached some high weeds. He then crawled the remaining thirty feet to the opposite tree line and got to his feet behind a large magnolia tree. He immediately checked the intersection. One of the men, the one that had done most of the motioning, still stood behind the car. But the other man was gone. Sam looked for movement and finally saw the second man dashing from vehicle to vehicle along the south side of highway 326. He was making his way toward Chet.

Sam was a good hundred yards off of the first man's left rear flank, all open space. The man was doing a good job of sweeping all areas to his front and sides. He even glanced to his rear occasionally. He would pick up Sam running across the open space in a matter of seconds. Too risky. Sam continued through the trees being careful not to step on any dead branches that might give away his position. He intended to come out on highway 326, west and well to the rear of the first man. He was fifty yards from the road when he heard the sharp report of three shots. They sounded like 9mm—probably Chet. A louder five shots answered. Probably the second man. Sam quickened his pace as shots continued.

A few seconds later he burst into the open alongside 326 and immediately dropped to the ground. There were several stalled cars that blocked his view of the intersection, including the bread truck he had seen before. He couldn't get eyes on the first man. Sam low trotted from vehicle to vehicle until he was behind a Mercedes at the northwest corner of the intersection. The bread truck completely blocked his view of where he had last seen the first man—standing behind a white Honda Civic.

Sam ran to the bread truck, dropped to the ground, and looked under the truck hoping to see the lower part of the man's two legs. He saw the backs of the two people reclined against the opposite side of the bread truck, but he didn't see anyone standing. He hopped back to his feet and made his way to the right, toward the back of the bread truck. He had his rifle shouldered and swept it from his center to his right as he stepped. At the back of the truck, he lowered the rifle and peered around the corner. Nothing—except an occasional exchange of rounds from Chet and the second man further up the highway.

Sam shouldered his rifle and inched forward around the back of the bread truck, between it and the blue pickup, being ever vigilant of his surroundings. He again lowered his rifle and peered to his left around the right rear corner of the bread truck and into the opening between the truck and the white Civic. The two people, a middle-aged man and woman, still sat against the truck with their hands tied and a gag in their mouth. Their eyes were wide open and darted back and forth. To his right sat the woman he saw earlier leaning back against the pickup's front wheel. She had not moved from that position. Even in this situation, Sam couldn't help but take a moment to admire her tan, muscular legs and short blond hair. Her hands were tied behind her back and she was gagged. Her eyes darted from side to side as she looked up at Sam.

Sam swept all directions including his rear and came up empty. He had just stepped into the opening between the truck and Civic when he heard a light crunch of boots on gravel to his right rear. Sam spun around, but not before he heard a sarcastic "dumbass" from a deep male voice and the sharp crack of a 5.56 round. The bullet split the air just an inch in front of Sam's nose. Sam dove for the asphalt, banged his knee in the process, and rolled onto his side. He saw a man in jeans, a T-shirt, and a 'CAT' ball cap approach fast along the side of the pickup. The man had his automatic rifle pointed straight at Sam's head.

At the last moment, the young woman with blond hair thrust her right foot forward in front of CAT man. He was so focused on Sam he did not see the foot until it was too late. He stumbled a bit and had to dance to keep his footing. More importantly, he lost his sighting on Sam's head for a split second. Sam rolled onto his back, raised his rifle, and fired three quick shots. Two caught CAT man mid-chest throwing him backward and to the ground. He immediately dropped his rifle and clutched his chest. Sam got to his feet keeping his rifle on target. With a slight limp, he approached the man until he stood directly over him.

"Asshole," Sam spat. A second later the light in the man's eyes went out. Sam reached down and untied the girl's gag, "Thanks, my name is Sam, Sam Pratt."

"Anytime, my name is Tiffany Conway, Tiff."

Sam reached inside his shirt flap on his left side and slid his Buck knife from its sheath. The woman rolled onto her side to expose the nylon zip tie around her wrists. Sam bent down and with a quick flip of his wrist cut the tie. The woman massaged her wrists as she got to her feet.

"Boy am I glad…"

Sam jerked his attention down highway 326, "Excuse me, one more to go."

Sam took off at a low trot, wincing each time he put weight on his banged knee. He found cover behind the same vehicles the second man had used to approach Chet's position. Chet and the second man still exchanged shots. Sam saw the second man crouched behind a green Lincoln a hundred yards down and almost directly across from a group of trees on the north side of the road. *Chet must be there*, Sam thought, *pinned down and out-gunned. He only had his Glock 17.*

Sam moved to the north side of the cars and low trotted down the highway. He kept his rifle shouldered and ready. He had gone about fifty yards when he stopped and inched around the back of a Buick. He took a quick peek down the south side of the cars. The second man stood crouched behind the same car. Sam slowly brought his rifle around the tail light and took careful aim on the second man who was in full view. The man rose up over the hood to take another shot at Chet when Sam pulled the trigger twice in quick succession. The man spun and went down.

Sam rose and walked slowly forward with his rifle pointed at the downed man. Sam glanced to his left at Chet leaving his cover and heading for the second man, his Glock at the ready. They arrived at the man's position at the same time. Blood oozed from the man's left shoulder and from his chest, just above the heart. He looked at Sam as though he wanted to say something. But the man's eyes went lifeless before he could utter a word. Sam picked up the man's automatic rifle and handed it to Chet.

"It appears this might come in handy."

Chet holstered his Glock, took the rifle, and turned it side to side inspecting the components. "Cheap but it'll go bang. We'll have to check around for more 5.56 ammo and magazines.

"There's another one back at the intersection," Sam offered. "Do you mind going for the buggy?" Sam asked as he threw the keys to Chet. "There're some people in the intersection that need to be untied."

"Gotcha," Chet replied, as he started walking toward where they left the buggy.

Sam jogged back to the intersection and saw that Tiff had already removed the gag and untied the couple. The three of them stopped talking and turned to Sam as he approached.

Sam looked at Tiff. "What happened here?"

Tiff took a step toward Sam. "They stopped me last night; I was out-gunned by the two ARs."

Tiff then walked down to CAT man, bent down, and removed her XDs 9 from the man's front waistband. "Asshole!" she said, as she kicked the man in the side. She then bent down, picked up the M16 style rifle next to his body, and examined the components as she returned to Sam and the couple.

"I'm Mildred; this is Ted," the middle-aged woman said, "same thing, they stopped us in the intersection last night. When we told them we lived nearby, they just zipped-tied our hands and made us sit down. That's about when this young lady arrived. I think they were interested in what we might have at the house. And they did not keep secret what they had in mind for her. That's all they talked about."

Ted pointed to the southwest corner of the intersection. "The deputy over there showed up just after that but he didn't have a chance. They gunned him down as soon as he stepped out of his car." Ted pointed to a red Mustang with a man, obviously dead, behind the wheel. "The other gentleman over there came up at about the same time. They opened up on him before the car even stopped."

Mildred continued, "A few minutes later we all saw the lights in the sky. The two men wanted to leave but none of the cars would start at that point. Without a working car, they couldn't figure out how to get everyone to my house. So we just sat and listened to them argue with each other. They got real excited when they heard your car coming."

"Speaking of working cars, I was hoping to get farther down the road in mine," Tiff said, as she patted the white Civic.

Everyone turned to the sound of Chet arriving in the buggy. He pulled up in front of the Civic, killed the engine, hopped out, and stepped up to the group. "I guess these guys were trying to get an early start on the festivities."

"Yeah, well, their party didn't end well, mostly because of this young lady," Sam said, as he pointed to Tiff. "This is Tiffany Conway. Thanks again Tiff for the footwork."

Tiff smiled. "You guys did all the heavy lifting. If you hadn't happened by, we three would have been goners."

Sam turned to Chet. "This is Chet Stevens. Chet, this is Mildred and Ted."

Chet nodded and then shuffled his feet. "Now what?"

Sam turned to Tiff. "Where were you headed?"

"My Mom and Dad are in Ohio, that's where I was headed. Looks like I'll be walking, but I planned for a long hike. I'll be fine."

Sam slowly rubbed his face, starting at his forehead and working down. "I guess, but still."

Tiff looked at Sam. "I can do it; I've done worse."

Mildred spoke up, "Honey, you're welcome to stay with us as long as you want."

"I appreciate the offer," Tiff replied, "but my parents will need my help."

Sam caught Chet's gaze and raised his chin, silently asking what Chet thought. Chet subtly nodded.

Sam caught Tiff's attention. "Look, we're headed for Tennessee; you're welcome to ride along if you want. It will be tight, but we'll make room."

"Thanks, but my Mom told me to avoid strange men," Tiff said with a smirk.

"Chet over there is the only strange one, but suit yourself," Sam said, as he turned toward CAT man. "Let's see if these guys had any extra magazines or ammo."

"I think that beat up old Ford over there was theirs," Ted said. He pointed at the southeast corner. "I guess Mildred and I will head for home. Thanks again to all of you."

Sam and Chet both nodded. "No problem," they said in unison, as Mildred and Ted turned and walked away. Ted paused and looked back. "I'll get a couple of neighbor friends to come back and help me bury these bodies."

"Thanks," Sam said, as Ted turned and caught up with Mildred.

Tiff opened the rear door of the Civic and started pulling out her gear which she laid on the asphalt next to the rear wheel. Chet set out for the Ford while Sam checked CAT man's pockets. Sam came up with one extra fully loaded magazine. He walked over and handed it to Tiff.

"You'll need this," he said, "and Chet might come up with more."

Tiff took the magazine and smiled. "Thanks," she said, as she turned back to her gear.

Sam watched as Chet opened the Ford's trunk. He reached in and shuffled some items around but came up with nothing. He then started opening the car doors.

A couple of minutes later he came back carrying two extra magazines and two boxes of 5.56 ammo, along with the rifle. "Every bit helps," he said. He carried the items to the buggy and placed all in the bed. He then walked over to where Tiff was sorting her gear.

Sam entered the back of the bread truck and found numerous cases of various kinds of bread. He grabbed six bags of bagels and then jumped from the back of the truck holding the bags up so Chet could see. "Like you said, every bit helps."

Chet smiled, nodded, and then turned back to what Tiff was doing.

"We should probably head out," Sam said.

"Agreed," Chet said, as he stood up.

He looked down at Tiff. "Do you have room for any rifle ammo? We have some extra."

Tiff surveyed her pack, two jugs of water, tent, sleeping bag, her first aid kit, food bag, the rifle—and then looked back to Chet and Sam. "Does that offer still stand?"

"It does," Sam responded, as he and Chet grabbed everything except the pack and started toward the buggy. Tiff followed carrying her pack.

"Okay then," she mumbled.

CHAPTER 4

Sam and Chet, with Tiff, stuffed in the back with all the equipment, some on her lap, cruised down 326 toward the interstate. They were passing a Home Depot on the right when Sam whipped the wheel for a last-second turn into the parking lot.

"I've got an idea," he said.

Chet looked over at Sam and then glanced back at Tiff to make sure she and the equipment were still there. Tiff was holding on to the roll bar with one hand and the pack sitting in her lap with the other.

Sam pulled to a stop at the far end of the parking lot as far from the store entrance as possible. Several people were entering and exiting the door.

Sam slid from the seat and slammed the door. "I think you two should stay with the buggy, I'll be right back."

"Gotcha," Chet replied, "we'll be here."

Sam hustled across the parking lot and entered the store. There were fewer people than Sam would have expected, but business was brisk and orderly. He made his way to the rope aisle where he picked up a large spool of parachute cord along with several high-tension bungee cords. He continued to the lumber aisle where he picked up four eight-foot two-by-fours. With all in hand, he headed straight to the checkout and found the shortest line. He noticed that the clerk was accepting cash from the people ahead of him.

Sam emerged from the store, in and out in only fifteen minutes, and started across the parking lot. He immediately noticed a group of eight or ten people surrounding the buggy. Chet and Tiff were standing in the middle of the group, Tiff being rather animated with her gestures, apparently arguing with someone.

As Sam got closer, he heard a male raised voice. "Like I said, sir, the Marion County Sheriff's Office is hereby confiscating this vehicle. It will be used for emergency service."

Chet stood his ground. "Don't think so, we're just passing through and we'll be out of here in a few minutes."

Sam walked up behind the group and heard several people siding with the deputy. The group was becoming agitated as Tiff argued with several people, especially a mouthy overweight woman.

"I can take this vehicle by force if necessary," the deputy said.

"Don't think so," Chet replied calmly.

Sam pushed his way through the crowd using the two-by-fours to clear a path. Everyone stopped talking and stared at Sam as he went to the side of the buggy and placed the two-by-fours length-wise on top, across the roll bars. He then dropped the bungees and cord in the bed, all without saying a word. He then motioned for Chet and Tiff to get in the buggy. The group and the deputy just stood staring, obviously not sure what to do.

The deputy continued, "Like I said, I'm confiscating this vehicle!"

Sam held the deputy's stare, inserted the key in the ignition, started the engine, and looked over at Chet. "Hold on to the two-by-fours."

Chet and Tiff grabbed hold of the boards and Sam pulled slowly away from the crowd. All the people just stared without saying a word.

Sam exited the parking lot and turned back onto 326 heading west. He went about two blocks and then stopped at the back of a closed gas station. No people were in sight.

"Let's lash these boards down to the roll bars," Sam said, as he opened the door and jumped out.

Chet and Tiff jumped out and then lined the boards up a few inches apart so they stretched across the roll bars covering most of the buggy's width.

"Let's put most of the overhang in the back so Tiff will have some shade," Chet said. He grabbed the spool of cord, slid the boards more to the rear, and began lashing them tight to the bars.

Tiff held the board steady. "I like that idea."

Sam walked to the rear of the buggy and dropped the tailgate. He hooked the chains so the gate would ride parallel to the road. He then pulled the two five-gallon gas cans from inside the bed and placed them on the tailgate behind the bench seat. He used several bungee cords to affix them tightly to the back of the seat and the side of the bed. Chet and Tiff finished lashing the boards about the same time Sam finished with the gas cans.

"Let's put the backpacks up top," Sam said, as he grabbed his pack and placed it on top of the boards which now formed a solid platform.

"Another good idea," Tiff said, as she grabbed her pack and placed it on top.

They proceeded to tie all three packs to the boards. When finished, they stood back to admired their work. The three packs, which made up the bulk of their gear, were on top of the buggy and the gas cans were behind the bench seat leaving plenty of room for Tiff, the food bags, rifles, and ammo in the bed, either on the floor or on the seat beside where Tiff would sit.

"I like it," Chet said. He brushed his hands together removing imaginary dirt.

Sam stepped forward, rummaged through the food bag from his house, and came out with three granola bars and three bottles of water. He handed out the food and water and everyone piled back into the buggy.

Sam pulled out from behind the building and turned right on 326 as he took a bite of the granola bar. The interstate was in sight and he headed for the on-ramp that would take them north. Sam had to slow at the ramp because of several stalled cars stopped in the middle of the road. The buggy had no trouble pulling through the soft sand on both shoulders. Once on the interstate, Sam was able to accelerate some despite the numerous stalled vehicles.

"With all these cars, gas shouldn't be a problem," Chet said.

Sam nodded and remained focused on maneuvering around abandoned vehicles. Tiff was busy in the back topping off 5.56 magazines.

"Should we stop at night or drive through?" Chet asked.

Sam glanced over. "I'd love to just drive through, but in the dark we wouldn't have a lot of heads up on what's ahead. We could find ourselves up against a roadblock, maybe even an ambush."

Chet reached into the glove box and came out with the Florida map. "You're probably right, better safe than sorry." Chet unfolded the map and scrutinized the squiggly lines. After a few minutes, he said, "Most of seventy-five runs through open country well into Georgia, we could stop anywhere." Chet continued looking at the map.

Sam glanced in the rearview mirror at Tiff. "Tiff, I meant to ask you, military?"

Tiff looked up. "Marines. Two years of college out of high school and then six years in the corps. That was three years ago. I intended to make it a career, but men are pigs."

"I'll go along with that," Sam agreed.

"What about you two?"

"Retired army airborne for me," Chet replied, looking up from the map. "Sam here is also retired, from the air force. He went to fancy lad school a few years after he joined—came out an officer."

Sam smiled.

Tiff focused on Sam. "Pilot?"

"I get that question a lot, no, OSI investigator—like NCIS in the Navy. I started out enlisted as a combat controller which is the nearest thing to a grunt in the air force. That's why I'm able to communicate with Chet. I went to school at night, then to officers' training, and then transferred into the investigator field which is what I did for the last fifteen years of my military career."

"What do you do now?"

"Security consulting. Mostly seminars to corporations on how to avoid internal theft and embezzlement. Started right after I retired about ten years ago. Chet joined me after he retired."

"We tag team; makes it more fun," Chet said. "We were supposed to be in Dallas today for a two-day seminar. I guess the sun had other ideas about what we should be doing today."

Sam pointed ahead. "Could be trouble."

Chet and Tiff looked where Sam pointed.

Half a mile up, four men were going from vehicle to vehicle, breaking windows, and opening doors.

"Shitheads are looting already," Tiff said.

Tiff handed one of the cheap rifles to Chet. Chet took it and eased the charging handle back a smidge to see if the chamber was loaded. It was. Tiff also handed Sam's Sig rifle to Chet to hold for Sam. Chet checked the Sig's chamber and then placed the rifle on the floor, barrel down, next to him so it would be easy for Sam to grab.

Sam came to a stop behind a large van about two hundred yards from the men who were now looking intently in the buggy's direction. Sam, Chet, and Tiff jumped out, brought their rifles immediately to bear, and spread out. All three started moving forward using stalled vehicles for cover as much as possible.

The three had gone fifty yards when all four men ahead ran down the embankment to the east, hopped the fence, and ran into the tree line.

Sam stopped, "Anybody see weapons?"

"Two had side arms, not sure about the other two," Chet replied.

"That's all I saw," Tiff said.

Sam lowered his rifle and turned around. "Let's go back."

All three jogged back to the buggy and got in. Sam glanced at Chet and Tiff. "We'd be sitting ducks driving by those dick heads. I don't like it."

"How about if we cross over to the southbound lanes and punch it," Chet offered.

"That I like," Sam replied, "but keep low until we are well past."

"Count on it," Tiff said.

Sam started the engine, wrenched the wheel hard left, and shot straight across the lanes, through the wide grass median, onto the southbound lanes, and headed north. He kept to the far left and whipped around cars, pickups, and semis as fast as safely possible. Chet and Tiff kept their eyes in the direction of where they had seen the four men and looked for any movement.

Eight minutes later and two miles down the road Sam glanced back. "I think we're good."

Tiff motioned with her rifle barrel. "No sign of the dick heads."

"I'll second that," Chet said.

Sam slowed, made his way back across the median, and back onto the northbound lanes. He proceeded north at a good pace dodging stalled vehicles where necessary. Sam took the rifle from his lap and handed it back to Tiff. She leaned it against the seat.

"I'll hang onto mine," Chet said, as he pointed the barrel to the floor between his legs.

***

They had driven about an hour when Sam brought Chet and Tiff out of their reveries. He pointed ahead to a heavy bank of dark clouds hanging low over the highway. "We're about to get wet."

"Must be four o'clock in Florida," Chet said. "Rains the same time every day."

Tiff tapped Sam and Chet on the shoulder and pointed up. "You two have a rain resistant roof, I don't."

Chet glanced at Tiff and smiled. "Hey, she's right."

"There's an exit up ahead," Sam said, motioning with his hand. "Maybe we'll get lucky."

"Sign says highway 234 to Micanopy." Chet said the name slowly, rolling the syllables off his tongue.

Sam glanced over. "Most people get that wrong."

"I taught Native American history at Yale," Chet said with a smirk.

"Uh-huh. Was that before or after you served in the Senate?" Sam countered.

"I'm not sure I can make it to Tennessee with you two," Tiff said, shaking her head.

Sam took the off ramp and came to a full stop at the intersection. The area seemed deserted, but they were not able to see far because of the overpass on the left and trees on the right.

Chet looked left and then right. "All the people must be in Micanopy." He rolled the syllables again.

Sam looked left and then right. "Uh-huh, which way?"

"Left," Tiff spoke up.

"Left it is," Sam said, as he stepped on the gas and turned the wheel to the left.

A Shell gas station was on the right just past the overpass. It looked newer than the few other buildings around but like every other place, there was no activity.

"This must be a really small exit," Tiff offered.

On the left stood a much older and smaller building that had fallen into disrepair. The metal roof over the pump island gave it away as what used to be a gas station. The next building down, also on the left, was surrounded by a chain-link fence with a *For Sale* sign in front. The building also was formerly a gas station. This one was a little bigger and even had two service bays, both with an overhead door closing off the entrances.

"Looks promising," Sam mumbled, as he pulled to a stop in front of the chain link gate.

Everyone hopped out and approached the gate only to find it secured with a chain and padlock.

"Let's see if there's a key around here," Chet said, as he walked off to the right toward the ditch.

"I'll check over here," Tiff muttered, as she stepped off to the left.

Twenty seconds later Chet returned with a rock about the size of a softball. He approached the gate and slammed the rock against the padlock. It took several strikes but finally, the lock broke open. He removed the chain and opened the gate wide enough for the buggy to enter. Sam returned to the buggy, started the engine, and drove through the gate as Chet walked toward the service bay doors. He reached down to the metal handle on the left door and lifted. It didn't budge. He stepped over to the right door and lifted. The door rolled up with almost no effort and, even better, the bay was completely empty.

Sam drove the buggy into the bay, turned off the engine, and hopped out. Tiff closed the chain link gate and repositioned the chain with the broken lock, making the gate appear secure. She then walked into the bay, turned, and closed the overhead door.

Sam, Chet, and Tiff explored the rest of the station. The main customer area and the parts room were completely empty. Tiff unlocked the front door from the inside and walked around the building out of sight. She returned a few seconds later.

"Both bathrooms locked tight," she said. "No water anyhow. Looks like our only bathroom is in the trees out back, mind if I go first?"

Sam looked through the window at the dark sky outside. "Looks like you have about three minutes. Chet and I are going to top off the tank and try to refill the cans."

Tiff nodded and then exited through the front door and disappeared around the corner of the building.

Sam unhooked the bungees on one of the gas cans, sat it below the gas cap on the side of the buggy, and then retrieved a funnel from under the front seat. He opened the gas cap and inserted the funnel while Chet lifted the can and poured slowly until the can was empty. Chet set the can on the concrete and grabbed the second can, unscrewed the cap, and poured slowly until it too was empty.

"Ten gallons should just about fill the tank," Sam said, as he removed the funnel. He replaced the gas cap and returned the funnel back under the seat.

"That Shell station had a car in the drive," Chet said. He picked up both empty cans. "I think we have time before the rain."

Sam reached back under the front seat and produced a short plastic hose with an accordion pump toward one end. He took one of the cans from Chet's hand and they both exited through the station's front door. At the gate, Sam removed the chain, opened the gate, and followed Chet through the opening. Sam closed the gate, and they both walked the short distance to the Shell station.

"Maybe we'll get lucky again," Sam said, as he pulled on the driver's side door handle. The door opened and Sam reached in and pulled up on the gas release. The little door popped open. Chet removed the cap. Sam inserted the plastic hose and began squeezing the accordion pump. Gas flowed into the gas can.

They had just finished filling the second can when suddenly there was a bright flash and a loud clap of thunder. They hustled back down the road, crossed over, went back through the gate, and secured it as before. They had just stepped into the station when fat raindrops began pummeling the area. Lightning flashed and thunder clapped again. They found Tiff sitting in the buggy's driver's seat.

"Lucky we found this station," Chet said, as he sat his gas can on the buggy's tailgate. "Everything would have been soaked through in this downpour."

Tiff jumped out of the buggy and helped Chet fasten the bungee cords while Sam did the same with his gas can.

Sam turned to Chet and Tiff. "Sleeping arrangements?"

Chet and Tiff looked at each other and then back to Sam. "What did you have in mind?" Chet asked.

Tiff zeroed in on Sam. Her eyes narrowed. "Yeah, what did you have in mind?"

Sam shook his head with mild annoyance. "What I meant was, it's only been one day since the blackout. I think we should keep watch through the night, one up while the other two sleep. And no lights."

Chet glanced at Tiff as she visibly exhaled with relief and then back to Sam with a smirk. "I don't have any lights."

Sam turned to the buggy. "And we should also start thinking about dinner."

"I can take care of that," Tiff said, as she joined Sam at the buggy. She jerked her nylon food bag from the bench seat. "Black beans and rice with sardines sound okay."

"It does," Sam said, as he began untying the backpacks on the roof. "I have a stove; we can crack the overhead door and set up over there."

***

An hour later, with fading light, Tiff was out front using the deluge pouring from the roof to wash the aluminum dishes and pots from dinner. She returned inside with clean dishes to find Sam laying out his sleeping bag on the concrete floor next to the buggy.

Tiff approached Sam. "Where's Chet?"

"Setting up in the parts room," Sam replied, as he stood up. "He snores."

Tiff reached for her sleeping bag from the back of the buggy and pointed to the far wall. "I guess I'll set up over there."

Sam nodded. "I'm going to turn in so I can take the last watch. If you can take the first watch, wake Chet in four hours or so."

"Will do," Tiff said, as she turned toward the far wall, walked over, and rolled out her sleeping bag.

As the last bit of light disappeared from the overcast sky, Tiff walked into the customer area of the station and took a position on the floor up against the back counter. With no lights of any kind and no moon, she was soon immersed in total blackness. This meant there was nothing she could really do except sit there, thinking and listening.

Her mind wandered as she thought about her parents and how they were doing, to the life she left behind in Orlando, and to her two traveling companions. Sam and Chet seemed decent enough, unlike other men in her life. But it was probably too early to form that kind of conclusion. All the men in her life pretty much turned out to be assholes, eventually. Lately, she had started thinking maybe it was her. Maybe in each of her relationships, she did something to bring out their faults. All the men she had known started out nice, almost overly accommodating. But as soon as the relationship moved to the sexual stage, they changed. They became possessive, clingy, and had to know Tiff's every move. When she resisted, things got ugly and then she left.

Because the scenario had repeated so many times she decided to take a break. That's where she had been for the last six months or so, on a break from men. That's why lately she spent her nights alone. She didn't have to worry about Sam and Chet in that regard. While they were both handsome enough, physically in good shape, and had many of the qualities Tiff admired, they were both too old. So far they had treated her with respect, as an equal, and had done nothing to make her think they were assholes in disguise. If they remained as they seemed, they could be friends, close friends, brothers in arms. She hoped they were as they appeared because she could use some close friends on this trip.

It was still early evening when she first heard the voices, two male voices. They came from the street in front of the station. She could not understand what they were saying, but they were getting closer. Tiff got up, walked to the front, and cracked the door just a hair so she could hear better.

"Anything is better than being out in this rain," Tiff heard one voice say.

The other man responded with a younger voice, "The gate is right over here."

Tiff was thinking late forties and maybe early twenties when she heard the rattle of the chain and the chain link gate.

"This thing is not even locked," the younger man said.

Tiff heard the sound of chain sliding against metal and then heard the gate swing open. Being as quiet as possible she closed the front door and made her way toward Sam. She was able to find him in the dark by following the soft snoring coming from that side of the service bay. She gently poked his shoulder. Tiff heard the rustle of the sleeping bag as he moved. "There are two men outside," she said, barely audible.

"Where?" Sam whispered as he rolled to his hands and knees and then got to his feet.

"They are through the gate probably heading for the front door."

Sam took two steps in that direction and froze at the sound of the door opening.

"This place is wide open," the younger man said.

"There could be people in here," the older man said in a lower voice.

Tiff heard the distinctive sound made when a pistol leaves a Kydex holster followed by two pairs of footsteps heading in Sam and Tiff's direction. She also heard the soft rustle of wet clothes. Tiff felt Sam's fingers on her side and then on her shoulder. He gently pressed down as he crouched beside her. Tiff lowered to one knee beside him keeping one hand on her holstered pistol.

"Can't see shit in here," the older man said.

"At least it's not wet," the younger man responded.

"Yeah, but I don't want to sit in a puddle of grease."

"Good point, the parts room should be cleaner."

Tiff heard both men pivot and then footsteps moved away.

"Freeze," Sam yelled, as he stood up.

Tiff leaped with a startle at the sudden noise, glad the pitch blackness hid her reaction. She sensed that Sam had quietly drawn his weapon and had it pointed at the sound of the men's voices.

Almost instantly the deafening roar of a round going off broke the silence. A bright orange flash in front of the two men lit them up for a split second. Just as Tiff thought, one of them was older and the other was younger.

Not wanting to be where the two men last saw them with the flash, Tiff immediately jumped to her right. Tiff heard Sam do the same to his left.

"Cease firing," Sam yelled, "we're in here to get out of the rain, just like you."

"We won't fire if you don't," the older man said.

"Deal," Sam replied.

At that moment a flame pierced the darkness and Tiff saw Chet with a lighter in one hand and his Glock in the other standing behind the men. He pointed the Glock at their backs. The older man glanced over his shoulder and then lowered his pistol, a small revolver. Sam rushed forward and took the man's revolver from his hand while Tiff hung back with her XDs pointed in their direction.

Sam shook the revolver in the older man's face. "What the hell, man!"

"You scared the shit out of me," the man said. "The gun went off by accident."

Chet pushed both men forward with the barrel of his Glock, "Anybody ever teach you to keep your finger off the trigger."

"Yeah, but—" the man started.

"But nothing," Chet cut him off. Chet kept the lighter going so they could see.

"Okay, okay, nobody was hurt," Sam said, looking back toward Tiff, "Tiff, you okay?

Tiff stepped closer to the group while keeping her 9mm pointed at the men. "I'm fine."

With the barrel of his Glock, Chet pushed the older man again. "Start talking."

The older man glanced back at Chet and then faced Sam and Tiff. "I'm Frank Simmons; this is my son, Tim. We live about three miles down the road."

Chet lowered his pistol. "So why are you here?"

"The power was out this morning at the house and not even the cars would work. So we walked into town. That's when we found out about the solar storm. The mayor had a meeting, and we stayed for that. We started walking back home a while ago when the rain stopped, but then it started again. So we ducked in here. This property is owned by Ed Jenkins, a friend of mine."

Tiff saw Sam look at Chet and nod. Chet holstered his Glock and stepped in front of the men and faced Sam. "Now what?"

Tiff stepped up to the group. "Yeah, now what? It's still raining."

Sam glanced out a window then faced Frank. "You guys are already wet. If you keep walking, you'll be home in forty-five minutes."

Tim spoke up, "Sounds like a good idea Dad."

"I'll need my gun back," Frank said, looking at Sam.

Sam released the revolver's cylinder, dumped the six rounds in his hand, and handed the revolver, cylinder open, to Frank.

Frank took the gun. "Ammo is going to be hard to come by around here."

Sam looked at the six rounds and then handed them to Frank.

"Keep the gun unloaded until you're down the road," Chet said.

Frank and Tim turned toward the door and took a step.

In the dim light of the lighter, Sam pointed in the direction of town. "What's it like in town, how are the people reacting?"

Frank and Tim stopped and turned. "The mayor and Chief Michaels are trying to hold it together, but the people are worried, real worried. Micanopy is a small town, everybody knows everybody. For now, we're working together, but I expect that to change when the food runs out."

Chet holstered his Glock. "Does anyone have a working vehicle?"

Frank turned to face Chet. "The Chief has an old Ford pickup that still runs."

"Any word on what's happening in Gainesville, especially on the west side out by the interstate?" Tiff asked.

"That's a good fifteen miles up," Frank said, as he turned to Tiff, "nobody has come through from there."

Sam stuck out his hand and approached Frank. "Sorry for the rough greeting, but we have to be careful."

Frank shook his hand. "We all do; no harm done."

Sam shook Tim's hand and then Frank and Tim walked out of the station with a final wave.

As they passed through the gate and closed it behind them, Sam turned to Tiff. "Nice heads up, thanks."

"Just doing my job."

Sam nodded to Chet, "Thought you were a heavy sleeper."

Chet clicked the lighter off. "Not when a cannon goes off."

Sam turned and headed toward his sleeping bag. "We might as well resume our positions."

Chet headed back to the parts room.

Tiff stepped back into the customer area and returned to her spot against the counter. She was glad it wasn't her turn to sleep. Adrenalin still pumped. She thought back to the sequence of events and realized things could have gone much differently. She liked the way Sam and Chet handled the situation. Most would have returned fire, simply blasted away in the dark. That would have resulted in at least two innocent deaths in this case. Tiff was all about surviving and defending one's self, but, like Sam and Chet apparently, preferred to take the easy way out when possible. Sam and Chet were growing on her, and she was beginning to feel more and more comfortable in their presence.

***

Tiff awoke at daybreak, heard shuffling, and slowly opened her eyes. She focused on Sam over by the buggy tying his backpack to the two-by-four top. He was dressed in the same clothes as the day before. She didn't make a move to get up. "Did anyone bring coffee?"

Sam glanced over at Tiff. "Not me, I don't drink the stuff. Chet might have brought some."

Chet suddenly appeared in the service bay doorway. "Sorry, I didn't want to take up space with non-essentials," he quipped.

Tiff grumbled as she rolled to her feet still dressed in her shorts, sports top, and button-down shirt from the day before, including boots. "Fine, no coffee then," she said, as she headed for the station front door, "I'll be in the trees out back for a bit, don't leave without me."

"Wouldn't think of it," Chet said.

"I have breakfast bars and water when you return; we should probably head out as soon as possible," Sam said, as he moved around to the back of the buggy.

Tiff walked out of the station, around back, and into the tree line. She found a bush that provided adequate concealment, unbuttoned her shorts, pulled them down, and squatted. She shook her head as she thought about where she was. No bathroom, no shower, no warm bed, no real cooking, and none of the organic food she preferred. To make matters worse, the world in the best of times had plenty of shitheads, but now, in this apocalypse, even otherwise normal people had an opportunity, an excuse, to act out their true nature. She contemplated how a simple cruise up the interstate with maybe a night in a nice hotel had become a battle for survival every inch of the way. She thought about whether she could have actually hiked all the way to Ohio dodging the dregs of society every step. And she thought about how life works in mysterious ways, how Sam and Chet happened by at the right time for her. Too late to save the deputy and the man in the Mustang back in Ocala, but just in time to save her from a terrible ordeal. Tiff glanced at the cloudless sky. She thought about what this day would bring.

CHAPTER 5

Chet stood outside by the open service bay overhead door as Sam backed the buggy through the opening with Tiff sitting in the back.

Sam stopped the buggy about five feet back and looked down at the dash gauges. *Gas topped off, good night's sleep, for the most part, nice dinner—they're prepared*, Sam thought. With any luck, they'll be in Tennessee in short order. At the moment, Sam had the most control possible over his little world, a world that included two other people. Sam was a *what-if* kind of guy. He constantly ran scenarios through his mind and came up with solutions to problems yet to surface—that might never surface. This little exercise of his was likely the consequences of a lifetime of dealing with security issues. The *what ifs* of every situation. What if the buggy gets a flat tire? What if someone is able to take the buggy? What if one of them gets seriously hurt? What if Tiff turns out to be a serial killer? The scenarios ran the gamut from plausible to ridiculous. Sam's mind, which never really stopped until he fell asleep, tried to consider all the possibilities. Unless he was focused on a particular task, it was a game he played with himself. Consider the possibilities. That's what he was doing when the overhead bay door slammed shut with a *bang* jolting him back to the there and then.

Chet walked past the buggy and back to the gate. He opened it wide and waited for Sam to back out.

Sam backed the buggy through the gate and onto the paved road. He shifted gears and waited for Chet.

Chet closed the gate, reposition the chain and lock, and then jumped in the passenger seat.

Sam let out on the clutch, accelerated through the underpass, and turned left onto the northbound ramp. Sam maneuvered around the one stalled car on the ramp and then sped up onto the interstate. Cars stalled in the middle of the highway were sparse; most were pulled over to the side. Sam kept the speedometer on fifty and cruised.

"Once we get through Gainesville, it should be smooth sailing up to Lake City and then on to Valdosta," Sam said.

Tiff slid forward on her seat and placed her arms on the back of Sam and Chet's seats. "Do you think people are starting to wake up to reality?"

"If not today then certainly by tomorrow," Chet replied. "The store shelves should be empty by today and some people will be without food and water."

Sam glanced back at Tiff. "There's probably been looting already, existing gangs are getting organized, and new gangs are forming. People alone won't have much of a chance for long."

Chet glanced back. "Yeah, and unfortunately we have to get through Atlanta right when people will be starting to realize the seriousness of their situation. This buggy will be considered prime real estate, more by the police than by the people."

Tiff looked at Sam. "Roadblocks?"

"If I were the police chief of any of these towns, that's what I would do," Sam replied. "They know older vehicles will still run, they'll want them, need them."

Tiff repositioned the rifle leaning against her leg and the seat. "We'll need to find a less urban route around Atlanta for sure."

"That's a fact jack," Chet cracked, as he winked at Tiff.

***

Just past a rest area and a sign that read *Gainesville next five exits*, Sam slowed and pointed. "Speaking of roadblocks."

Chet and Tiff jerked their heads forward.

About a mile or so down the road, at the top of an overpass with concrete guard rails, stood five men behind stalled vehicles that had been lined up to block the roadway. The same was true of the southbound side. There were ten men in total. Unfortunately, the crossroad did not have an exit or entrance onto the interstate.

"Shit," Chet spat, "can we go around?"

Sam stepped on the gas and jerked the wheel to the right. "We sure as hell are not going through them," he yelled.

The buggy crossed the shoulder at high speed and continued into the grassy verge running alongside the interstate. Within seconds the buggy crashed through the chain link fence with ease and entered the tree line about fifty yards from the road. Sam immediately stomped the brake pedal, and the buggy slid to an almost complete stop. Sam glanced in the rearview mirror and saw Tiff grab the roll bar as the gear in the bed shifted hard. It was a miracle nothing spilled out. Sam stepped on the gas and whipped the wheel from side to side as he navigated around trees and palmetto bushes. Sam checked the mirror again. Tiff had both hands on the roll bar, her eyes wide, and her teeth clenched.

Chet had one hand on his rifle and one on the roll bar. "Do you know where you're going?"

"Nope, but I plan to get there as fast as possible."

After only a few seconds in the brush, the buggy bolted from the trees and roared up an embankment onto a two-lane tree-lined road that paralleled the interstate. Sam whipped the wheel to the left and punched the gas. The tires screeched as they caught traction on the asphalt. Luckily there were no stalled vehicles on this road and Sam was able to accelerate to full speed. The buggy shot down the road passing a large parking lot and the Florida Farm Bureau building on the left. The intersection of the road leading to the overpass came up quickly. Sam glanced to his left, through a gas station on the corner, and saw five men, one wearing a uniform, running toward the intersection with rifles leveled at the buggy. Sam zigged around two stalled cars in the intersection as shots rang out. Sam heard the loud ping of a bullet hitting the roll bar next to his head. Another bullet buzzed invisibly through the cockpit in front of Sam and Chet. Sam stomped the gas pedal to the floor and steered the buggy straight through the intersection. The single lane became three lanes after the intersection. A sign read *121 North*.

Sam looked side-to-side trying to get his bearings. "Anyone know where this road goes?"

Chet looked back at the sun. "I think we're headed due north which would be veering away from the interstate and straight into west Gainesville."

Tiff slid to the edge of her seat and stuck her head between Sam and Chet. "Not good, gentlemen, not good." Her voice was even but tense.

Sam checked his rearview mirror. "Jalopy coming up fast."

Tiff and Chet looked back to see an old Chevy about two blocks back but closing.

Chet brought his rifle up from the floor, swiveled in his seat, and pointed the barrel toward the Chevy.

Tiff pushed the barrel up with two fingers until it pointed at the two-by-four roof. "In the interest of preserving my hearing, let me take care of this."

Tiff brought her rifle up, swiveled in her seat, and took aim at the approaching car.

In the mirror, Sam could see the man in the Chevy's passenger seat leaning out of the window and pointing a rifle.

"Anytime!" Chet said.

Tiff squeezed off five rounds in rapid succession. Sam had one eye on the mirror and one on the road ahead. Two of Tiff's rounds hit in the middle of the Chevy's windshield. The car kept coming. The passenger, still hanging out of the window, fired multiple rounds as fast as he could pull the trigger. None hit the buggy. Tiff fired three more shots.

Sam saw the passenger take one in the right shoulder. He dropped the rifle and fell back into the seat. The rifle bounced twice and ended up in the gutter next to where a man and woman on the sidewalk dove for cover. The Chevy slowed and fell back as Sam raced on.

Chet yelled over the sound of the engine and the wind, "Let's try a left at the next major intersection; maybe it will take us back to the interstate."

"You read my mind," Sam yelled back.

Tiff spun back around to face forward but kept her rifle at the ready. People up and down the sidewalk fixated on the buggy as it sped by.

"Intersection coming up," Chet shouted.

Sam slowed a bit.

As they entered the intersection Tiff scooted forward in her seat. "The sign says Archer. I think it's a main drag through town." She glanced back. "And as a side note, the Chevy is still behind us—but hanging back."

At the highest speed possible, Sam swerved around several stalled cars, yanked the wheel to the left, and accelerated through the turn.

Chet looked back. "What are we going to do about the guys back there?"

Sam glanced in the mirror. "They're apparently not giving up and we can't outrun them." He glanced to the right and jerked the wheel sending the buggy in that direction. Sam sped through a Taco Bell parking lot and screeched to a stop behind the building. Sam was surprised there were no people around.

Sam, Chet, and Tiff leaped out of the buggy, rifles in hand, and ran to the back corner of the building. Sam carefully peered around the edge, making sure not to expose his body. Within a couple of seconds, he heard the Chevy's engine approach the intersection and saw the car make the left turn. As the car sped by, Sam saw the four men inside. The passenger was pressing a rag to his right shoulder and his face was ashen. The driver had a determined expression on his face, apparently, hell-bent on catching the buggy. The two men in the back each held a semi-automatic rifle.

"They just went by. Two ARs in the back seat. The front passenger is wounded."

Sam, followed by Chet and Tiff, ran back to the buggy and hopped in. Sam eased the buggy around the building and back on to Archer heading west behind the Chevy.

Chet glanced at Sam. "Looks like I'm up."

"You are," Sam replied.

The Chevy was a block up maneuvering around stalled vehicles. Sam was able to close the gap quickly as Chet leaned out his window and aimed his rifle. When the buggy was within two hundred feet of the Chevy, Chet let loose with ten quick rounds. Hot brass spewed from the ejection port. The jacketed hollow points peppered the rear window of the Chevy. Everyone in the car ducked except the guy in the right rear seat. His head, lifeless, drooped to the side and rested against the door frame. The Chevy suddenly veered sharply left and smashed into a stalled Prius.

The driver and left rear passenger bailed out just as the buggy screeched to a stop fifty feet short. Sam, Chet, and Tiff leaped out, rifles in hand, and took up positions behind stalled cars. All three opened up on the two men before they could find cover. They went down. Sam, Chet, and Tiff ceased firing. Sam and Chet, with rifles shouldered and on target, stepped from their cover and moved forward. Sam glanced back to see Tiff facing to their rear, sweeping her rifle side to side in a wide arc, covering their rear and flanks. The few people on the sidewalks ducked into storefronts.

The two men, both in their 20s and covered with tattoos, were sprawled on the asphalt, lifeless. Blood began to pool beside their bodies. The right front passenger, still in his seat and still holding his shoulder, just stared with dark eyes. Pain etched his face.

While covering the passenger, Sam moved around to the right side of the car and opened the front passenger door. Sam grabbed the man—also in his twenties and covered with tattoos—by his right injured arm and dragged him from the car. The man screamed in agony. Sam kicked the man's legs from under him causing him to crumple to the asphalt. Sam planted his foot on the man's chest and pointed the rifle at his head.

"You're dead," the man hissed.

Sam looked around, then at his rifle, and then back to the man on the ground. "Do you see something I don't?"

Chet joined Sam and pointed his rifle at the man on the ground. "Yeah, do you see something we don't?"

Sam stepped to the Chevy and opened the right rear passenger door. The man in the seat had a large exit wound in his throat. Sam then walked back around the Chevy to the front and pumped three shots into the grill. Water began pouring from underneath. He then joined Chet on the right side of the car and bent down to check inside the front passenger area. He stepped back to the rear door, looked inside again, reached over the dead man, and stood up holding a green ammo can in his left hand. He set the can on the asphalt and flipped open the lid.

"Five-five-six, we can use it."

While keeping his rifle on the man, Chet stepped backward and glanced at the ammo. Sam kept one eye on the man on the ground while he watched Chet pick up and examine each of the rifles used by the tattooed men.

"We already have better," Chet mumbled, as he tossed each of the rifles onto the top of a nearby building.

Sam nodded and motioned with the barrel of his rifle toward the man on the ground. "What about this guy?"

Chet glanced over at the man. "He's not going anywhere, at least not in this car."

Sam kicked the man's foot. "Your lucky day."

The man glared without saying a word as Sam and Chet backed away. They turned and joined Tiff who was still sweeping their rear.

"Time to leave," Sam said in a calm voice.

All three hopped back in the buggy. Sam placed his rifle on the floor next to Chet's leg and started the engine. He shifted the lever to first gear, gave it some gas, and pulled away. The one tattooed man remaining alive was on his feet and spit on the asphalt as the buggy passed by.

The overpass for the interstate was in sight about a mile down the road. Sam weaved around the few stalled cars on the roadway and was able to keep up a moderate speed. Stores and businesses of all kinds lined both sides of the street. Looting was evident. The whole area was alive with people who all stared as the buggy passed. Sam glanced at Chet and smiled as they passed a group of people hauling TVs and other electronics from a Best Buy store.

"Dumbasses don't have a clue," Chet said.

Tiff stuck her head between Sam and Chet. "I actually feel sorry for these people."

"I guess," Sam said, as he glanced at Tiff. "In a few days this place will look like a hurricane tore through—and then it will be a ghost town when all the food is gone."

Tiff dropped her head a bit. "I'm getting really worried about my parents."

Sam twisted the wheel for the on-ramp without slowing and then accelerated when he merged with the right lane of the interstate. "Where exactly are they in Ohio?"

"Lebanon, about fifteen miles northeast of Cincinnati—it's a small town, but people from the city will be heading out and Lebanon is directly in the path."

"House or apartment," Chet chimed in.

"Small house. It's just the two of them. Before the storm hit and we still had power that night, I told them to go get as much food and water as possible. It was late but Walmart was open."

"Any other family up there?" Sam asked.

"No, I have aunts, uncles, and cousins, but they're all out west, mostly in Colorado. Mom and Dad never wanted to move. I actually grew up in that house."

Sam was able to cruise up the interstate, slowing only occasionally to navigate stalled cars in the middle of the road.

Chet glanced at Tiff, "You seem like the lucky type, I'm sure they are too. Surviving this thing for any length of time will take a lot of luck."

"I'm not sure that makes me feel any better but thanks."

"As long as they hunker down they'll be fine," Sam added.

Chet turned in his seat. "What do you plan to do when you get there?"

"Whatever I need to—beyond that I don't really have a plan. What about you guy, any family?"

Sam spoke up first. "I have a brother. He lives in an apartment in St. Louis. I have no doubt he will be trying to make his way over to our cabin outside of Knoxville at some point. That's where we're headed. My parents are dead and I've lost touch with cousins and such."

"Other than his brother I'm pretty much his family," Chet interjected. "We actually grew up together in Orlando. As for my family, parents died years ago, no brothers or sisters, and I've lost touch with everyone else."

Tiff laughed. "And you guys just plan to hole up in your cabin and wait this thing out?

"That's pretty much the plan," Sam replied. "We have plenty of water, food can be had from the land, and the place is well built and defendable."

"How big is your cabin?"

"Two bedrooms, one bath, kitchen, small family room, separate garage. I already have it stocked pretty well, assuming no one squats on the property before we get there."

"I've been there several times with Sam," Chet added. "It's isolated. Nearest neighbor is half a mile away. And it's hard to find if you don't know where you're going."

"Sounds perfect, can't wait to see it," Tiff offered.

"Me too," Sam said.

Chet pointed with his thumb into the bed, "If you'll hand me the food bag I brought we can have lunch."

Tiff moved a couple of items to get to the bag and then handed it to Chet. He pulled out a block of sharp cheddar cheese, a log of salami, a box of crackers, and a small aluminum camp plate. He reached to his side and produced a Bark River Mini Kephart fixed blade knife, began slicing the cheese and salami, and placed the pieces on the plate. When finished, he moved the plate, piled high with cheese and salami, to the buggy's center console. Tiff handed a bottle of water to each of the men. Chet opened the box of crackers, took one, placed a piece of cheese and a piece of salami on top, and popped the whole thing in his mouth.

"Dig in," he mumbled with his mouth full.

CHAPTER 6

"Any chance for a potty break," Tiff asked.

"Why not," Sam said. He slowed the buggy and pulled to a stop in the shade of an underpass. "We're about thirty miles from Lake City."

Tiff jumped out, walked forward and around the abutment, through the grassy verge, hopped the fence with one hand, and disappeared into the trees.

After a couple of minutes, Chet opened his door and slid out. "Might as well take advantage of the stop."

Sam nodded and relaxed in his seat as Chet walked a few feet behind the buggy. Sam heard him unzip his pants and begin to pee. Sam closed his eyes and shook his head. When he opened his eyes a few seconds later he saw Tiff come around the corner of the abutment. She stopped, stared at Chet, and placed her hands on her hips.

"Really! At least I had the courtesy to go in the trees," Tiff said. She then continued to the buggy and leaned against the rear on Sam's side, with her back to Chet. "I'm beginning to wonder about the company you keep," she said to Sam.

Sam glanced in the mirror and saw that Chet did not skip a beat. He continued peeing. Eyes closed. Smirk on his face.

"Uh-huh, but he can be entertaining," Sam said, as he opened his door and slid out. "Might as well make it a hat-trick." He started walking away toward the rear. Sam shook his head in mock disgust as he passed Chet.

Just before Sam went around the abutment he heard Tiff say, "See, not that hard to be a gentleman."

"Sam's an officer and a gentleman, I'm just a lowly old grunt, can't be helped. So don't think you need to go in the trees for my sake."

As Sam jumped the fence he heard Tiff say, "I'll try to use the word *gentleman* sparingly around you."

Sam lost their conversation as he stepped into the trees.

***

Tiff jumped in the bed of the buggy while Chet opened the door and slid into the driver's seat. "Might as well give Sam a break from driving."

They sat without making a sound. Chet had his eyes closed apparently enjoying the light breeze blowing through the underpass. A couple of minutes had passed when Tiff heard a soft scuff on the asphalt behind her. Thinking it was Sam returning, she didn't turn around to look—until she realized the sound was from the left rear instead of the right rear. She jerked her head around but too late to prevent a large man with a beard from grabbing her from behind in a bear hug. She screamed as the man lifted her out of the buggy with her arms pinned to her sides. She looked to Chet for help.

Chet whipped his head around, but only to face a second middle-aged man wearing one earring who raced up pointing a large nineteen-eleven style pistol at his head. Chet faced front and slowly raised his hands. "Like they say in the movies, let us go on our way and I won't kill you," he said softly.

The man let out a laugh and moved to the driver's door. "Yeah, like they say in the movies, kill me! I'm the one with the gun, remember." He then jammed the end of the barrel against Chet's head. "Ooh, sorry, that might leave a mark."

"What do you want?" Chet asked, obviously trying to remain calm.

The gunman laughed again. "We want it all of course, especially the girl. You, we can do without." The man motioned with his gun for Chet to get out of the buggy. Chet kept his left hand in the air, opened the door with his right, stepped out, and then raised his right hand again.

Tiff struggled with the bearded man who still had her in a bear hug. She was immediately struck with two impressions: he was strong and he stunk. The man switched to a one arm hold while he removed her XDs from its holster and placed the gun on the floor in the back of the buggy. He then resumed a two-arm hold around her body with her feet off the ground. Tiff violently jerked her head back trying to catch the man's nose, but she only caught the empty air behind her. The man had his head to one side. Tiff adjusted her aim and tried again but he was able to move his head before Tiff could connect.

Tiff saw the gunman motion for Chet to turn around. The man took Chet's Glock from its holster and his knife from its sheath. Tiff saw the man draw back with his pistol and clunk Chet in the back of the head. Chet crumpled to the ground.

The man then turned to the bearded man and Tiff. Tiff struggled harder. "Get control of that bitch!"

"Bitch is right, she's already tried to crack me in the face with her head twice," the bearded man responded.

At that moment Tiff caught some motion in the corner of her eye and turned her head to see. Sam walked around the corner of the abutment—with his hands in the air. A third man, wearing a red ball cap, walked behind holding a revolver pointed at Sam's back. Sam's M&P and his fixed blade knife were stuck in the man's waistband.

"I caught this one with his dick in his hand." Ball Cap said.

Sam walked to the back of the buggy, stopped, and turned to face Tiff, still in the man's arms. "Chet?"

"Dip shit over there conked him in the back of the head," Tiff said with a sneer.

Sam faced Ball Cap. "Mind if I check on him?"

"I do mind—stay right where you're standing." The man's voice was even and direct, as though he was used to people doing what he said.

"Okay, you seem to be in charge here, now what?" Sam asked.

"Now you do exactly what I tell you," Ball Cap replied. "Start by getting some cord or rope from your jeep."

Sam rummaged in the back of the buggy and came up with the parachute cord.

Ball Cap took the roll and handed it to the earring man, "Tie all three up real good."

The earring man took the roll, stuck his pistol in a holster on his side, and walked back to Chet. He rolled Chet on his stomach and tied his hands behind his back, feet together, and then pulled his hands and feet together in a hogtie.

Ball Cap motioned his revolver at Sam. "On the ground and on your stomach."

Sam did as he was told. The earring man tied Sam the same way he tied Chet.

Ball Cap then motioned to Tiff. "Tie her hands behind her back and put her in the jeep."

The earring man did as he was told with a little help from the bearded man.

Once she was tied, the two men lifted her into the back of the buggy. The bearded man jumped in with her. Ball Cap slid into the driver's seat while the earring got in the passenger's seat.

Tiff wiggled in the back trying to free her hands but the cord was too tight. There was nothing she could do except look back at Sam and Chet as the buggy pulled away.

The buggy immediately swung left, crossed the northbound lanes, the median, the southbound lanes, and entered the trees on the other side of the interstate through an opening in the fence.

Tiff felt the cord constrict around her wrists and her hands going numb. She began to feel pinpricks in her fingertips as they starved for blood. She glanced at her XDs, still on the floor, but there was nothing she could do to get it. She glanced at the bearded man to her left and the two up front. She thought about how these three were at the opposite ends of the universe compared to Sam and Chet. There must have been some inbreeding involved when these guys were conceived. And for them, it all went downhill from there. Despite her determination and her years of marine training, the way out of this predicament wasn't immediately apparent. As she bounced along on the rutted path through the trees, a wave of dread, mixed with intense anxiety, washed through her mind. She took deep breaths to get control and keep her mind focused.

Tiff knew what these guys intended. Although never raped, she had come close once—by someone she knew and thought she cared about. It wasn't until she and the man started an actual relationship that his true colors showed. She knew he was the jealous type but didn't know how deeply insecure he really was until one night she came in late from being out with a couple of girlfriends. The guy flew into a rage. Accused her of having an affair. Tiff recalled the man's veins in his neck popping and his face a deep red as he screamed in her face. When he ripped her blouse open and pushed her to the sofa, Tiff fought back. He was stronger and larger, but Tiff got lucky with a knee to his groin. That gave her the time she needed to get away. She joined the marines within a week and was gone a short time later. She often counted her blessings that she never married the guy.

She had been able to put that out of her mind and move on even though the guy lived in her hometown and she would occasionally run into him when she returned home on leave. But she never let herself be alone with him again. And she became a pretty good judge of character. She could spot the telltale signs of trouble in a person fairly quickly. When she saw those signs, she would back off and steer clear. Plenty of men came on to her in the marines, and she had been harassed more times than she could count, but she had always been able to keep things from going too far. She joked and cussed with the best of them, all the time keeping a wary eye.

But nothing in her past compared to this situation. All she could do was be ready to strike when the opportunity presented itself. What was that saying? Luck is when preparation meets opportunity. She was definitely prepared; she just needed the opportunity.

CHAPTER 7

The man with the ball cap wheeled the buggy along the sandy firebreak through the trees. Earring sat in the passenger seat focused on the trail ahead. Tiff, with her hands behind her back, sat on the rear bench seat next to the bearded man.

Tiff wrinkled her nose. "When was the last time you guys took a bath?"

"As a matter of fact, I'll be taking one tonight — with you," Ball Cap answered.

Tiff turned her head to the side, away from the bearded man, as the three men chuckled.

"I'm after you," said the earring. Another round of chuckles.

Ball Cap looked over to Earring. "We need to make a quick stop at the house and then we'll head out to Jimmy's."

"Food and water?"

Ball Cap nodded. "Yeah, plus there's gas in the truck. We can top off this tank at least. And I want to get the trailer."

Earring picked up Sam's rifle and examined it closely. "This is mine."

Ball Cap smiled at Earring. "Whatever floats your boat rat brain."

Earring frowned. "Don't call me that," he said, with a voice in a higher octave. "You might be the oldest brother but it ain't right."

"Okay, okay, don't get your panties in a wad," Ball Cap said.

Earring went back to examining the rifle and held it up to show the bearded man.

The beard smiled but didn't say anything.

Tiff shook her head trying to comprehend her twilight zone situation. On the one hand, it was comical watching these three. But on the other hand, it was deadly serious. She would likely end up raped multiple times and then dead. And setting aside for a moment her dire state of affairs, what about Sam and Chet? They now had no vehicle, no food, water, or weapons. Not even a knife. Tiff shook her head again and clenched her jaw.

***

Birds. Chet heard birds chirping as the fog lifted in his brain and he regained consciousness. And then he sensed a pounding headache. Opening his eyes just added to his pain and confusion. He was face down on asphalt and unable to move. He then realized his hands and feet were tied together. And then he remembered the two men that had accosted him and Tiff. Tiff? What happened to Tiff?

Chet began to struggle against his bindings and then heard Sam's voice.

"I was starting to worry about you."

"What the hell happened? Where's Tiff?"

Sam shifted in his own bindings, "They took her, along with the buggy, food, water, and all our gear."

Chet was able to roll to his side so he could face Sam. "How long was I out?"

Sam was on his side. "Half hour or so."

Chet saw that Sam was rubbing his hands against the asphalt trying to abrade the parachute cord. "How long have you been at that?"

"Twenty-nine minutes or so—hopefully it's working."

Just then Sam's hands popped free. Sam rolled onto his back and sat up. He reached into his pocket and came out with a Victorinox pocket knife. He opened the knife and sliced through the cord around his feet. He then hopped up and did the same to Chet's bindings. Chet got to his feet with Sam's help.

"How are you feeling?" Sam asked.

"Wobbly, but I'll live."

Chet walked over and leaned against the abutment. "Which way did they go?"

Sam pointed to the opening in the fence on the other side of the interstate. "That way."

Chet winced when he rubbed the knot on the back of his head.

"Turn around and let me see," Sam said.

Chet turned around. "I'll be okay."

Sam ran a finger over the knot. "You'll probably have a headache for a while."

Chet leaned back against the abutment and rubbed his neck.

"As soon as you're up to it we'll head out," Sam said.

Chet pushed away from the wall and gained his balance. "I'm up to it, let's go."

Actually, he wasn't up to it at all. He probably needed a hospital. He felt wobbly and nauseated. He had the worst headache of his life. His neck was stiff and his legs were like noodles. Pain meds, a soft bed, and the tender touch of a Charlize Theron look-a-like nurse were what he needed. But all of that was secondary to his primary sensations—the need for payback and the need to save Tiff. So he jogged on, putting one foot in front of the other, despite the pain.

***

Ball Cap punched the buggy from the trees and into a clearing. Everything appeared to be the same as they left it. Their non-running pickup was still in front of the cabin. The barn off to the side looked undisturbed. *Everything was as it should be*, Ball Cap thought. Even better—they now had a running vehicle, more food and water, weapons, and best of all, a good looking girl that would keep him satisfied until he got tired of her, which would likely not be for a long time.

Ball Cap brought the buggy to a stop in front of the barn and next to an open-air trailer. He hopped out and turned to the beard. "Lift her out of there."

The beard did as he was told and set her on the ground behind the tailgate.

Ball Cap tossed earring the keys. "Top off the tank and hook up the trailer."

Ball Cap then walked over and grabbed hold of the girl's arm. *Firm*, he thought, *not too soft, just right*. This was going to be fun. He spun her around to check out her ass. Nice curves.

Ball Cap glanced at the beard. "Load everything of value into the trailer. That means hand tools from the barn and the food and water from the house. I'll be inside with fancy pants here."

Beard nodded and turned toward the barn.

Ball Cap dragged the girl toward the cabin as Earring stood watching. Ball Cap threw a hard stare at

Earring. "I said, top off the gas," he said in a slightly raised voice. "Then help your dumb shit brother."

Earring turned toward the barn as Ball Cap continued to drag the girl, struggling, to the cabin. Ball Cap opened the front door, pushed the girl inside, and followed her in. He shut the front door and then dragged her to his bedroom, connected to the main room. Ball Cap pushed her onto the dirty-sheet covered bed in the corner and stepped forward.

With her hands still tied, she spun around to her back, lifted her feet, and started kicking.

A fighter, he thought. He liked that. He just hoped she didn't give up too easily. Ball Cap pinned her legs and flipped her to her stomach.

The girl squirmed. "You're going to die a painful and slow death you inbred son-of-a-bitch," she screamed.

"Someday maybe," Ball Cap said with a laugh.

The girl continued to spew obscenities as Ball Cap grabbed her by her belt and waistband, drug her back to the edge of the bed, and then pinned her with his body as he reached around and undid her belt and waistband button. He stood up and jerked her shorts and panties down to her ankles. She continued to wiggle, squirm, and scream a string of obscenities a sailor would be proud of.

"Keep it up, it makes it more exciting," Ball Cap said. He planted one hand between her shoulder blades to hold her down on the bed and used the other hand to undo his belt and unzip his pants.

Just as he started to lower himself, there was a knock on the door.

He paused and stood up. "This better be good," he yelled.

Earring yelled through the door. "Duncan, the coupler on the trailer is too small for the ball on the jeep."

"Danny, you dumb son-of-a-bitch, do I have to do everything around here," Duncan screamed, as he adjusted himself and zipped his pants up.

"Sorry Duncan, me and Dale couldn't figure a way around it," Danny said through the closed door.

"I'll be out there in a minute," Duncan screeched. Duncan started toward the door. He stopped halfway and looked back at the girl still bent over the edge of the bed. "I'll be right back," Duncan said in a soft voice. "Nice ass by the way."

He watched the girl slide off the bed and sit on the floor, naked from the waist down. Tears ran down her cheeks. Duncan took a final peek, smiled, and then closed the door behind him. He took some keys from his pocket, locked the door, and then turned to head outside. The image of the girl's naked ass burned in his mind. The only thing he wanted was to get back as soon as possible.

***

Sam and Chet, with sweat dripping down their face and their shirts soaked, jogged down the middle of the firebreak. Sam kept his eyes on the buggy's wheel tracks which were easily discernible in the soft sand. The firebreak weaved back and forth to avoid major tree trunks but generally continued in one direction—west.

Sam heard a distant metal clang coming from the direction they were going. He stopped and cocked his ear. Chet stopped next to him.

"Did you hear that?" Sam asked.

"I did," Chet replied, breathing hard.

They took off at an even faster pace.

Five minutes later Sam heard another clang. They were getting closer.

They jogged a hundred yard farther along the firebreak and came to an abrupt stop. Sam could see a clearing through the trees, a compound with a cabin, barn, truck—and the buggy. Sam stepped carefully as he approached the tree line. Chet followed close behind.

Sam could see the three shitheads through the trees. Two were trying to attach a trailer to the buggy; the third was walking from the cabin toward the other two. All three were focused on the task and were not paying any attention to the tree line.

"They obviously didn't expect us to get loose this quick," Chet whispered.

Sam nodded as he and Chet moved forward slowly, ducking from tree to tree.

Finally, Sam stopped behind a large trunk at the very edge of the tree line. Chet pulled up behind him.

"I don't see Tiff," Chet said with barely a whisper.

Sam nodded, looked around on the ground, and picked up a thick dead limb about four feet long. He placed one end on the ground and pushed softly in the middle with his other hand to test for strength. Satisfied, he looked at Chet and then pointed to the right. "I'm going to make my way around and come in from behind the barn." He whispered. "Work your way to the left and approach from behind the truck. We need to take them out fast before they know what's happening."

Chet nodded, and they moved off in their respective directions. Sam placed each foot with care.

***

Danny and Dale were bent over fiddling with the trailer hitch when Duncan, revolver tucked in his waistband, walked up. "That won't work, you pea brains. You can't chain a trailer to a jeep like that. Just use the ball from the truck!"

Danny stood up. "We thought of that; it's rusted tight."

"Danny, get me the two biggest wrenches we have and some WD-40," Duncan said, as he stomped off toward the pickup truck. "Dale, get that chain off of there!"

"Will do Duncan," Dale said, as he bent down and started removing the chain.

Danny ran off while Duncan examined the ball on the truck. A couple of minutes later Danny returned from the barn and dropped two large wrenches and a can of WD-40 on the ground next to Duncan.

Duncan picked up the can of spray. "The mount is welded but maybe we can get the ball off," he said, as he bent down and sprayed the ball. With the nut underneath the mount dripping with the oil, Duncan applied the largest wrench and began heaving.

***

Tiff scrambled to her feet with her shorts and panties still around her ankles. She hopped over to a dresser on the opposite side of the room. Porno magazines littered the top along with some loose change, an ashtray with cigarette butts, a greasy comb, and a lighter. Tiff turned her back to the top left drawer and pulled the handle. She turned around to check the contents and saw only socks. She turned back around and pulled open the top right drawer. "Thank you, God," she said, as she peered into the drawer.

Inside was an old Kabar pocket knife among other miscellaneous junk. With her hands still tied behind her, she reached in and retrieved the knife. Careful not to drop it, she pried open the small blade with her thumbnail and then fingered the knife until the blade was against the cords. She sawed as best she could given her awkward hold on the knife. The blade was dull, but even so, after a couple of minutes, she felt the cords loosen. She continued sawing back and forth until finally, her hands were free.

She immediately pulled up her panties and shorts and fastened her belt. She massaged her wrists as she ran to the door and tried the knob. Locked. She then bent down and tried to jiggle the doorknob lock with the knife blade. After thirty seconds she realized that would not work, so she inserted the knife blade between the door and door jamb and tried to pry back the latch bolt.

***

Sam peered around the corner of the barn and saw Dale, the man with a beard, trying to unhook a chain from the front of the trailer. The other two were bent down behind the pickup engaged in something that occupied their full attention.

Sam eased around the corner and made his way along the side of the barn. Dale, with his back to Sam, worked on the chain as Sam silently stepped up behind him. Sam glanced over at Duncan and Danny, still occupied with their task and saw Chet crouched in front of the pickup. His hands gripped a tree limb.

Sam swung his limb in a wide arc and connected with the side of Dale's head with a loud *whack*. Dale fell over the trailer hitch out cold. Sam then raced toward Duncan and Danny who had jerked their heads in Sam's direction. Danny stepped from behind the truck and met with a loud *whack* on the side of his head from Chet's tree limb. Danny's body bounced against the tailgate of the truck and sank to the ground out cold.

Duncan, facing both Sam and Chet with tree limbs drawn back ready to swing, backed away from the truck and pulled the revolver from his waistband. "I can see I should have left you two dead." He raised the revolver.

Sam and Chet stopped their advance and were about to dive to the side of the truck when suddenly Duncan stiffened. His arm holding the revolver fell to his side and then he fell, face first, into the dirt. A kitchen butcher knife protruded from the base of his skull.

With Duncan out of the way, Tiff became visible, standing rigid, behind where Duncan previously stood. "Sorry you couldn't die slowly like I promised," she said. "You inbred piece of shit."

Sam and Chet stood frozen, staring at the scene, eyes moving from Duncan to Tiff and back again. Finally, Sam marched over to Duncan, knelt, and placed two fingers on his neck.

Sam looked up to Tiff with the two fingers still on Duncan's neck. "He's dead alright." Sam then stood facing Tiff. "I'm wondering how many times you're going to save my life on this trip."

"I'm wondering how much of this shit we'll have to wade through on this trip."

Sam raised his chin in agreement.

Chet motioned toward Danny and Dale. "What about them?"

Sam started toward the buggy. "I say we tie them up while they're out and get the hell out of here. They won't know what happened."

Sam stopped short and looked back at Tiff. "Are you okay?"

Tiff glanced at Sam and then returned her gaze to Duncan. "I will be."

Chet looked at Tiff. "Did they — "

Tiff cut him off. "Shithead here came close but was interrupted before he could do any real harm. Like I said, I'll be okay."

Chet joined Sam at the buggy, grabbed some cord from the back, and proceeded to tie up Danny and Dale who were still out cold.

"Think they will live?" Chet asked.

"Don't care," Sam said, as he continued tying Dale.

Sam, Chet, and Tiff met at the buggy and visually checked their gear.

Chet picked up Sam's rifle. "It all seems to be here, even your rifle."

"I think so," Sam agreed, as he picked up his M&P, Tiff's XDs, and Chet's Glock from the floor of the buggy's bed and handed their respective weapons to Chet and Tiff. He then found his knife and Chet's Kephart in the buggy's center console and handed Chet his knife. All three checked their gun's chamber to ensure they were still loaded.

"Let's get out of here," Sam said, as he slid into the driver's seat.

Chet took his usual seat while Tiff jumped in the back. Sam glanced back at Tiff to make sure she was settled, started the buggy, and pulled away in the direction of the firebreak.

CHAPTER 8

Tiff reclined on the bench seat as much as physically possible. With the small amount of space, it wasn't easy. Her butt on the seat, her feet wedged against the side of the buggy, knees up, and head and shoulders against the pile of gear, her mind wandered as she relished the sun on her face and the wind in her hair. She thought about the life she left behind in Orlando. She thought about her friend, Megan, and what she was doing right then. She thought about the report she left half finished at work. She thought about what she would do when she reached Ohio and how her Mom and Dad were doing. She tried to think of anything other than Duncan. It didn't work. His scraggly face, his stench, and his hands kept coming back into focus.

She thought about what Chet had said earlier about luck—about how Tiff seemed like the lucky type. Maybe so, with Duncan at least. She shivered with revulsion when she thought about how close he had come to getting what he wanted. But for whatever reason, luck or not, it didn't happen.

Sam and Chet remained quiet as the buggy raced north. Tiff appreciated the lack of conversation. She glanced up occasionally and saw that Sam was able to keep the speedometer at around fifty. He pretty much maintained that speed even when he swerved around the occasional car or truck stalled in the roadway. Most were pulled off to the side and abandoned. Except for an infrequent walker, the road was deserted.

After nearly an hour of no talking, Tiff saw Chet glance back at her and then looked over at Sam. "How far have we gone?"

Sam looked down at the speedometer. "About forty miles. In another twenty miles, we'll be in Georgia."

"Maybe we should look for a place to stop?"

Sam pointed ahead. "Remember that time we hiked the Florida trail?"

Tiff knew of the Florida trail—Okeechobee to Pensacola. Tiff had wanted to do the whole thing but never got around to it. The whole idea of hiking, especially to Ohio, made her appreciate the buggy and the hard crowded space she occupied in its bed as they cruised down the road. Most of all she appreciated Sam and Chet.

"That was years ago," Chet said.

"Yeah, but remember when the trail crossed 75 along the Suwannee River?"

"I do. I remember thinking we should stop along there to camp," Chet said.

"That spot is up the road from here, not far. What do you say we camp there for tonight?"

Tiff saw Chet glance back at her. "Feel like stopping for the night, Tiff?"

Tiff raised her head and looked toward the sinking sun. "Yeah, sounds good."

***

Sam steered the buggy across the bridge for the Suwannee River and then continued another hundred yards in order to get past the steel barrier on the side of the road. He slowed and turned off at the end of the barrier, made a U-turn to the right, and drove back to the bride along the grassy verge. Tiff sat up in her seat and faced forward.

For her benefit, Sam pointed ahead. "The trail runs along the river and passes under the bridge right at water's edge. Actually under the bridge might be a good place to camp."

Tiff shifted forward. "If people come along and need to stop for the night that's where they would go."

Sam glanced at her. "Good thinking. I know of another spot."

Sam turned under the bridge, half expecting to see people there. The spot was vacant. He drove on, creeping along at barely an idle, passing under the north and southbound lanes and into trees and thick brush on the west side of the interstate. About two hundred yards up, where the river made a bend to the right, Sam pulled to a stop in a clearing along the river. There was even a small beach of white sand that contrasted sharply with the dark water.

"We're home," Sam said with a smile, as he opened the door and stepped out. "We have plenty of room for the tents and we're out of sight from the bridge."

Chet and Tiff hopped out and immediately walked up to the water's edge.

"The first thing I need is a bath," Tiff announced.

"I think we could all use a bath," Chet added.

Sam joined them at the water. "Watch out for wildlife—there are plenty of snakes and alligators around here."

"And the sooner the better," Chet said, as he turned back to the buggy. "Mosquitoes will be out early along this water. And if you go into the thick of it, the bushes are loaded with ticks."

All three began untying their packs and sifting through gear.

"Tiff, let me have your tent and I'll set it up while you wash up," Sam suggested.

Tiff handed Sam the nylon bag and then opened her pack.

Sam took the bag and walked to the other side of the buggy, away from the water. He opened the bag and pulled out the contents.

Chet joined him with a similar bag and began setting up a second tent. "This will be plenty big enough for the both of us," Chet said, as he unfolded his tent.

Sam nodded as he continued with Tiff's tent. He could see Tiff rummaging through her gear near the water and saw her pull a change of clothes from her pack along with a small nylon bag, a camp pot, and a small piece of canvas. The last two items piqued his interest, but he turned his focus to setting up the tent.

"I decided to avoid the ticks so I'll be right here," Tiff said, loud enough for Sam and Chet to hear.

Sam and Chet both paused, looked at Tiff to see her beginning to strip, glanced at each other, and then resumed their work without saying a word. *Ah hell,* Sam thought, *he might be an officer and a gentleman, but he wasn't immune to the fact that Tiff had a body that would stop a truck.* So he couldn't help but glance in Tiff's direction every few seconds.

Tiff stripped naked and carried her shorts, panties, and sports top into thigh-deep water. She began sloshing the clothes back and forth, washing them the best possible given the circumstances. After a few minutes of this, she wrung as much water out of the clothes as possible, walked back to the beach, and hung them on a dry branch at water's edge. She then unfolded the canvas, which turned out to be about four square feet, and laid it on the sand, several feet from the water. She then obtained a bar of soap from her nylon bag, picked up the cook pot and waded calf-deep into the river. She filled the pot and poured the water over her head several times. She then filled the pot again and walked back up to the beach away from the water, put the pot on the ground, and began soaping up. Once well lathered, including her hair, she poured the pot of water slowly over her head to rinse. She walked to the river, filled the pot, and returned to her spot to continue rinsing. She did this several times until all the soap was rinsed from her body and hair. She then made a final trip to fill the pot and walked to the canvas where she rinsed the sand from her feet. Sam chuckled when he realized this was the slowest he and Chet had ever set up a tent—easily triple the time it would take if a naked woman wasn't bathing in front of them.

Sam and Chet were about to slide the last tent pole into place when Tiff walked up wearing long tactical pants, fashionably tight, a dark green sports top, and her holstered XDs.

Chet greeted Tiff with a smile. "What was all the back and forth down by the water?"

Tiff smiled. "Something my Dad taught me. He believed it was bad for the environment to bathe with soap directly in a body of water. He taught me to soap up and rinse out of the water. The fish appreciate it."

Chet glanced back at the river. "Never thought about it, but I guess you're right."

"Let me finish up here while you guys wash up," Tiff said, as she reached for the tent pole.

"Deal," Sam said. And both he and Chet turned toward the river.

They stripped naked and went through pretty much the same process as Tiff, including washing the clothes they had been wearing for the last two days.

Cleaned, dressed, and sporting their side arms they returned to the tents to find that Tiff had a pot of chili boiling over the fire.

Sam sniffed the air. "Smells good."

"Hope you don't mind, I went through both your food bags and found two cans of chili. Thought we could have that and the bagels you found."

"Perfect," Chet said, as he turned back to the buggy. He returned a second later with camp plates and three bottles of water.

"I thought a fire would be nice, plus it saves the gas for our stoves," Tiff said. "And it will help keep the mosquitoes at bay."

"The fire is a nice touch, thank you," Sam said.

Tiff took the plates from Chet. "I normally try to eat organic, heavy on fruits and vegetables, but this is better than starving."

While Tiff dished out the chili Sam brought out a 5X8 foot piece of tarp and spread it on the ground in front of the tents. They sat on the tarp to eat.

Sam took a couple of bites and paused. "About today—"

Tiff cut him off. "No need to talk about it. It happened, shithead got what he deserved, and that's that. I'm ready to move on. Duncan was not able to do to me what he had in mind. I'm fine."

Sam continued, "What I was going to say—you saved our bacon today. Had you not been there, Duncan would have shot us," nodding at Chet, "and our time here would have come to an end. Thank you."

Chet, with his mouth full, nodded. "Ditto."

Tiff put her spoon down. "Actually, you guys did the saving. If you had not come for me my life would have been worse than death."

Chet spoke up, "It's just a good thing they stopped for the trailer. This is what I meant by luck. Survival is at least fifty percent luck."

"Yeah, three gun battles in two days with no serious injuries—I'll take luck over talent any day," Tiff said. "By the way, where did you guys serve?"

Sam put his empty plate down next to his leg. "We both joined the military out of high school. I picked the air force, Chet here wanted to slosh through the mud. We caught the Gulf War, Afghanistan, and Iraq, but in radically different roles as you can imagine. What about you?"

"Afghanistan and Iraq. A tour each. That was enough for me." Tiff looked at Chet. "I was lucky to survive. What about wives?

"Guilty," Sam said. "Twice actually. Divorced the first one. Lost the second one ten years ago. Cancer."

Chet slapped his neck. "Mosquitoes are out."

"What about you?" Tiff asked Chet.

"Yeah, I was married once. Didn't take. I guess I was gone too much. I heard she married an accountant."

"Kids?"

"Nada," Sam said, "Same with Chet. You?"

"Engaged once. Couple of boyfriends. Nothing serious. No kids."

Chet slapped at another mosquito. "Engaged sounds kind of serious."

"He showed his true nature just before we were to be married. I called it off."

Sam got to his feet and picked up everyone's plate and the empty chili pot. "I'll wash these in the river and put the fire out before I turn in. I think we should be safe without a watch for tonight."

Chet got to his feet and headed for the trees. "Little boy's room."

Tiff slid inside her tent and zipped the netting closed.

Sam scrubbed the pot, plates, and utensils with sand from the beach. He thought about Tiff's reaction to the ordeal—actually, two ordeals. Kidnapped and on her way to being raped and probably killed twice in two days. She was either putting on a strong front or she really was a tough little cookie despite the nice packaging. Hopefully, things would level off and the rest of the trip would cruise along without further incident.

***

Shortly after daybreak Tiff awoke to the aroma of food cooking. She unzipped her tent, crawled out, and saw Chet hunched over a small frying pan and a camp stove. "What smells so good?"

Chet looked up while continuing to stir the contents of the pan. "Powdered eggs, the cheese left over from yesterday, and bagels. Egg and cheese sandwiches."

Tiff heard the other tent being unzipped and saw Sam crawl out. "Smells good," he said. "I'll start tearing down these tents."

Sam and Tiff had barely started on the tents when Chet called them to breakfast. All three sat on the tarp and ate.

"What's the plan?" Chet asked, looking at Sam.

"Pack up, get back on the highway, and get through Valdosta as quickly as possible."

Tiff emptied the last of a water bottle into her mouth. "How are we on water?"

Chet got up, started toward the river with the frying pan in hand, and peeked in the back of the buggy. "We still have four jugs of water plus whatever's in your personal water bottles."

Sam stood up. "I think we're good for now. Filtering would take too long; I'd rather get on the road."

Tiff nodded and then rolled up the tarp while Sam finished taking down and packing the tents. Chet returned from the river with a clean pan and packed it along with the stove. The three of them retrieved their now dry clothes and stuffed them in their respective packs which they reattached to the top of the buggy.

Chet stuck out his hand to Sam. "I'll drive."

Sam tossed the keys to Chet and then slid into the passenger's seat. Tiff took her position in the back while Chet made a final scan of the camp area to ensure nothing was left behind. He then jumped into the buggy, started the engine, and pulled away.

Chet steered the buggy back through the trees, under the bridge, and made the left turn in the grass to parallel the bridge back to the northbound lanes. He accelerated when he reached the asphalt and fell into a steady pace at fifty miles per hour. A few miles up, stalled vehicles completely blocked the northbound lanes and Chet had to veer into the wide median. Except for an occasional lone walker, they passed no one.

"Welcome to Georgia!" Sam said, as they passed the state line.

Chet smiled. "The peach state is on my mind," he added.

Tiff perked up. "Glad it's not a rainy night."

Sam and Chet did a slow look back at Tiff and frowned without a word.

Soon the Valdosta city limits sign came into view. "I was stationed here, twice, at Moody," Sam said. "I enjoyed the small town atmosphere back then."

Tiff shifted forward in her seat. "I've driven by a few times but never stopped.

Chet glanced back. "Add another drive-by; we're not stopping."

The number of stalled vehicles increased when they passed the Madison Highway exit, but there were no people around. The same was true for the airport exit. But as they approached the route 231 exit, a line of military Humvee's and trucks, including a military ambulance, came into view. They were parked alongside the road just past the northbound ramp. Some were painted desert tan, and some were dark green.

Chet let off the gas a bit. "What do you think?"

Sam leaned forward in his seat. "I think we have come upon a military presence."

Three men in desert uniforms stepped onto the roadway and motioned for the buggy to pull over. All three wore side arms and one carried a rifle.

Sam glanced at Chet. "Better do what they say."

CHAPTER 9

Chet came to a stop ten feet short of the three men. Sam opened his door and stepped out as two of the men walked up. The one with the rifle hung back. Chet and Tiff remained seated.

In an authoritative voice, one of the men said, "I'm Lieutenant Jensen. This is Sergeant Thompson, army guard. Need to see some ID."

The lieutenant's tone brought back memories of a time Sam missed. He cherished the time he spent in the air force and often wished he was still a member. Wearing the uniform meant being part of something big and important. Decisions could mean the difference between life and death. There was nothing like it on the outside.

Sam put his hands up to chin level, palms facing out. "We're just passing through."

"ID, sir," Jensen said, with even more authority.

Sam dropped his hands and pulled out his wallet. From the wallet, he produced his military retired ID card and handed it to Jensen.

Jensen inspected the card and then looked up at Sam. "Major, US air force?"

"Retired," Sam replied.

Jensen handed the card back to Sam. "Sorry, sir. Just being careful."

"No harm done."

Jensen looked at the buggy. "Who are your friends?"

"The driver is Sergeant Major Chet Stevens, army retired. In the back is Tiffany Conway, former US marine corps."

Jensen nodded to Chet and Tiff and then looked back at Sam. "Where you headed?"

"Tennessee. I have a cabin up there. Plan to wait out this situation in the cabin."

"Probably a smart move," Jensen said.

Sam pointed to the convoy. "Where are you guys headed?"

Jensen jabbed his thumb back over his shoulder. "Be glad to let you speak to the captain."

"I'd like that."

"This way," Jensen said, as he and Thompson turned to leave.

Sam motioned to Chet. "I'll be right back."

Chet nodded.

The soldier with the rifle stayed put.

Jensen and Thompson led Sam to the lead Hummer where a group of men in uniform stood. When Sam got closer, he could see that some were army, and some were air force. As he reached the group, three of the men standing with an army captain saluted, turned and walked away, leaving just the captain and an air force lieutenant. The captain was a little shorter than Sam; the lieutenant a hair taller. Both were in excellent physical shape with flat stomachs and broad shoulders.

Jensen saluted. "Sir, this is retired Major Sam Pratt, US air force. He's traveling with two other former military on their way to Tennessee. Major Pratt here wanted to speak with you."

"Thank you, lieutenant."

Jensen and Thompson saluted again and then walked away.

The captain turned his attention to Sam, "I'm Captain Frank Jeffries, army guard. This is Lieutenant Tom Harvey, US air force. What can I do for you major?"

"I was hoping for an update on the situation. We'll be driving around Atlanta on our way to the Knoxville area. Any word on what we can expect?"

"Well, what the president said has come to pass. Except for most military and some government facilities, the country is without power. And it's expected to be that way for a couple of years at least. That's a conservative estimate."

Sam glanced at the line of Hummers. "The military?"

"Police action. My guard unit has joined up with some security forces from Moody Air Force Base and we're headed to Atlanta. As you can imagine, gangs have taken the opportunity to wreak havoc, especially in the large metropolitan areas. Local police have either deserted or they're overwhelmed. The Bloods and Crips were a problem before. Now they're growing exponentially and spreading out. The Aryan brothers are coming out of the woodwork. Even LGF is on the rise again."

Lieutenant Harvey spoke up. "We'll be joining other military units and local LE's once we reach Atlanta."

"LGF?" Sam asked.

"La Gran Familia, the Hispanic gang from the nineties," Harvey said. "They're back at it."

Jeffries pointed to the buggy. "Looks like you found one that runs."

Sam glanced back. "It's mine. Built it myself."

"Do you have what you need?" Jeffries asked.

"For the most part. We're a little short on food and water, but we can make do."

Jeffries turned to Harvey. "Load these guys up with a couple of cases of MRE's and a bottle of water."

"Will do, sir," Harvey said, as he turned and marched away.

"This convoy includes two hundred troops, forty vehicles including three trucks with provisions, and the ambulance. My orders are to help restore order in Atlanta and help anyone in need as best we can."

"I appreciate the food and water, captain. One other thing—mind if we tag along behind for the trip to Atlanta?

Jeffries scratched his neck. "No, I don't see a problem with that. I'm sure we'll need to stop to move vehicles out of the way some but I expect to make good time."

"Thank you. We'll be bringing up the rear then."

"Fine. If you'll excuse me I need to get this wagon train on the road. Be safe."

"Will do; you too."

The two men shook hands and parted. Sam walked back to the buggy where Chet and Tiff leaned against the grille.

"Well?" Chet asked.

"They're headed for Atlanta. Gangs are out of control and they'll be joining other units to help restore order. A Captain Jeffries is in charge and he gave the okay for us to tag along."

Lieutenant Harvey and an airman approached carrying two cases of MRE's and a large water cooler type bottle of water. "Here you go," Harvey said, as he and the airman placed the items in the back of the buggy.

Sam, Chet, and Tiff joined them at the rear and shook hands. Harvey patted one of the boxes.

"Spaghetti is the best."

"I always preferred the barbeque," Chet said.

Tiff lifted the edge of one of the boxes to read the print. "Any chance they're making it organic these days?"

"I wish," Harvey replied. "You guys take care."

"Will do," Sam said. "Thanks again."

Sam, Chet, and Tiff piled into the buggy with Chet behind the wheel and waited for the convoy of forty vehicles to pull out. Finally, Jeffries, standing at the lead Hummer, circled his arm in the air, yelled mount up, and did just that.

Chet waited for each of the vehicles to pull out before he started the engine. He then took up a position about fifty yards behind the last Hummer. Soon the entire convoy reached a cruising speed of fifty.

Sam reached into the glove box and pulled out the eastern United States map. He unfolded the map and studied the area around Atlanta.

"Are we driving through Atlanta?" Tiff asked.

"That would be the fastest, but probably not the safest," Sam said, without looking up.

"How do we know what's the safest?" Chet asked. "The military may be pushing the gangs to the suburbs."

Sam looked up. "True."

Tiff scrunched forward. "Maybe we should hang with the convoy as long as possible."

Sam glanced back. "That might get us into town; getting out of town might be a different story."

"I say we hang with the convoy as long as possible and then play it by ear," Chet said.

Sam looked at Tiff. She nodded.

"Atlanta it is," Sam said.

***

Forty-five minutes later they reached Tifton, and the convoy ran into its first obstacle. Sam could not see what was happening at the front of the line but when all the vehicles stopped, he knew something was up. Chet came to a complete stop directly behind the last Hummer and shut the engine off. Sam, Chet, and Tiff exited the buggy and stepped into the middle lane. It was nearly half a mile to the front of the spread out convoy but Sam could make out a barrier of vehicles across all lanes manned by a group of men.

"I think there's a uniform behind the barrier," Tiff said.

Chet stretched his neck as if it would get him a better look. "Must be a police barrier; otherwise, there would probably be shooting by now."

Sam walked to the back of the buggy. "I say we take this opportunity to top off the tank and refill the cans."

"Good idea," Chet said.

They removed the gas cans from the tailgate and poured the first one into the buggy. Sam immediately took the empty can over to a stalled car and began siphoning gas. Before he was finished, Tiff brought the second can over.

Chet came over and picked up the first can which was now full. "Keep going, I'm going to fill up the buggy with this can."

"Gotcha," Sam replied.

Sam had to move to another stalled car to fill the second can and then topped off the first can when Chet brought it back over. When they were finished, the buggy and both gas cans were full. They reattached the gas cans to the tailgate and wiped their hands with a rag. Sam then walked up to the last Hummer in line.

"I presume your radios work. Any word on what's happening up there?"

The driver, an air force staff sergeant, stepped from the Hummer with a cigarette in his hand. "Police barricade. They're probably getting the skinny on Tifton while they move the cars out of the way. We should be moving soon."

"Thanks," Sam said. He turned and walked back to join Chet and Tiff.

"Police barricade."

"Yeah, we heard," Chet said. "Anyone want a bagel?"

Tiff moved with Chet to the back of the buggy. "I'll take one."

Sam joined them. "Me too."

Sam, Chet, and Tiff were munching bagels and washing them down with water when engines began starting. The three piled in and Chet pulled out, keeping their position immediately behind the last Hummer. When they arrived at the barricade, several police officers stared as the buggy passed by.

"We're with them," Chet said, as he smiled and waved.

The convoy snaked around stalled vehicles until they were leaving Tifton and then were able to pick their speed back up to fifty.

Chet glanced over at Sam. "It will be getting late when we arrive in Atlanta. Any thoughts on where we might spend the night?"

"Been thinking about that. Why don't we try bivouacking with the guard?"

Tiff spoke up. "Men are pigs, remember?"

Sam glanced back at Tiff. "That was the corps. This is the army and air force."

"Big difference," Chet added.

Tiff slid back in her seat. "Ha-ha."

Other than stopping occasionally to move stalled vehicles out of the way, the convoy was able to cruise. Sam noted that people leaving the moderately sized towns, like Tifton, and heading for the countryside, were becoming more evident. Even families, kids in tow, were on the move with what they could carry. Even the smaller towns were apparently becoming more dangerous. Large cities, like Atlanta, were probably war zones at this point.

Sam understood that not even the entire military, much less this convoy, could solve the food and water problems the masses were only beginning to experience. It would only get worse. Much worse. The strong would take from the weak. Marauding armed gangs would sack homes and individuals at will. Places and persons with anything of value would be a target. High on the list would be food, water, tools, guns and ammo, and any sort of transportation from horses and bikes to vehicles still running. Without legal constraints, people would act on a whim. Rape and death for anyone caught in the wrong place at the wrong time by the wrong people would be all too frequent. Surviving in a gang would be perilous. Surviving outside of a gang would depend on cunning, preparation, perseverance, and luck. Chances are, either way; life for most people would be tragic and short.

Sam also realized that soon, government officials, and even the military, would put themselves and their families first. And then, any semblance of order would cease. Where once there was calm there would be total chaos. Dystopia was not far off. Hell, it was already here.

Sam was jolted from his reverie by brake lights, Chet's sudden deceleration, and the stop.

"We're coming up on Macon," Chet said. "It's probably just another blockade."

Sam nodded but then stepped out and over to the center lane. "Much bigger barricade than Tifton. There seems to be some arguing going on up there."

Sam walked over to the staff sergeant in the last Hummer. "What's happening?"

"Apparently, a bunch of rednecks with guns want some kind of tribute to let us through."

Chet walked up and joined the conversation. "Do they know you guys have bigger guns?"

"You would think," the staff sergeant said.

Just as Sam glanced up to the barricade again, small arms fire erupted from behind the cars pulled across the lanes. Sam saw someone in uniform go down. And then came several bursts from the unmistakable Hummer mounted Browning fifty caliber M2 machine gun. Sam and Chet ducked behind the Hummer. And then it was quiet.

A few minutes later an engine revved from up front. Sam stepped out for a peek and saw a Hummer racing to the rear of the stopped convoy. The Hummer screeched to a stop next to the ambulance which was three vehicles in front of the buggy. Two guardsmen leaped from the vehicle, grabbed a third man from the back, obviously wounded, and hauled him to the back of the ambulance.

Sam and Chet, now joined by Tiff, started walking toward the ambulance. As they got closer Sam recognized the face of the injured man—Jeffries. The two guardsmen lifted the semi-conscious Jeffries onto a stretcher.

"Shit!" Sam said. He continued forward and came up next to one of the men who had carried Jeffries to the ambulance. "How bad?"

"Hit in the shoulder and losing a lot of blood."

As two combat medics lifted the stretcher and slid Jeffries into the ambulance, another Hummer screeched to a stop. Lieutenant Harvey jumped out and raced to the back of the ambulance.

"Son-of-a-bitch," Harvey yelled, as he stared at the two medics working on Jeffries.

One of the medics looked up from his work. "I'll let you know as soon as I can. Better if you back off for now."

Harvey turned away and came face to face with Sam. "Those stupid rednecks," Harvey said.

"What happened?" Sam asked.

"They wanted food and water—they wanted one of our three trucks. The captain said no."

"And the rednecks just opened up when he said no?" Sam asked.

"That's right. The captain was hit immediately and went down. The fifty did all the talking after that. The rednecks are dead."

"I'm sorry. I'm sure the captain will be okay."

"I hope," he said.

Harvey paced back and forth behind the ambulance.

"Lieutenant Harvey," Sam said. "This puts you in charge. You can't leave the convoy exposed like this. Those rednecks might have friends."

Harvey stared into Sam's eyes for a moment and then nodded. He turned back to the medics in the ambulance.

"Can we move without making it worse?"

The same medic raised his head while continuing to work. "We have the bleeding stopped. But keep it slow." The medic returned his focus to his work.

Harvey addressed everyone standing around. "Let's load up." Harvey glanced at the medic. "Let me know if anything changes."

The medic nodded without looking up.

Harvey got in his Hummer. Before pulling away he stuck his head out the window. "Sam, it's still okay for your group to tag along—if you want to."

"Where are we headed exactly?"

"The Atlanta airport. We'll be rendezvousing with other units at the hotels on the north side of the runways. There will be a field hospital set up there as well."

"That's on our way to Tennessee. We'll be bringing up the rear."

Harvey put the truck in gear and drove off, heading back to the front of the line. Sam saw him stop at the front and speak to Lieutenant Jensen and Sergeant Thompson for a few moments. Sam could see Thompson directing men to push the barricade cars out of the way. Within a few minutes, everyone was loaded and moving, including the ambulance. When the buggy reached the barricade, it was obvious that little attention had been paid to the dead rednecks. Seven men were sprawled about, each lying in a pool of blood from massive wounds inflicted by the fifty caliber rounds.

Chet glanced at the bodies. "Desperate people doing desperate things. This trip is starting to get real."

"The last three days haven't been real enough for you?" Tiff asked.

"It's getting more real," Chet said, without taking his eyes off the road.

The convoy motored along the 475 beltway around Macon, keeping a pace of about forty, except when they had to snake around vehicles in the middle of the road. They had just passed the route 74 exit at West Oak when Chet looked in the mirror.

"There's a pickup approaching fast—still a couple of miles back."

Tiff and Sam looked to the rear. Sam saw three men in the front seat and four men standing in the bed of an old Chevy. The men in the bed held rifles. *Seven men in a pickup attacking a forty vehicle convoy*, Sam thought. What are these people smoking around here?

"Isn't there a song about redneck friends?" Sam asked. "Flash your lights at the tail Hummer to let him know something's up."

Chet flashed the lights and blew the horn as Sam, rifle in hand, crawled in the back with Tiff.

"Sorry for the close quarters," Sam said to Tiff.

"Apology accepted," she said. They both rested their rifles on the back of the seat.

The last two Hummers slowed; one had a mounted M2. The rest of the convoy, including the ambulance and a trailing Hummer, continued on. The pickup was within less than a mile when the men with rifles opened up. The four men in the back, along with one hanging out the passenger window, were able to send a heavy volley at the buggy and the two Hummers. Rounds began pinging off metal. One splintered the end of the two-by-four above Sam's head. Sam and Tiff returned fire. Due to their more stable firing platform and Sam's magnified sight, they were able to land several rounds on the truck. But it kept coming, and the men kept firing. Rounds whizzed by as Sam and Tiff returned fire.

Sam had just emptied his first magazine when he heard a pop. The buggy immediately veered to the right and onto the shoulder. Sam instantly knew that the buggy's right rear tire had taken a round. As Chet maneuvered the buggy to a complete stop, the gun-mounted Hummer peeled off, made a U-turn in the middle of the highway, and raced back toward the approaching pickup. A second Hummer, a transport, peeled off, made a U-turn, and pulled up next to the buggy.

Sam slammed a second magazine into his rifle, charged the chamber, and took advantage of the now non-moving seat to take careful aim. He fired three quick rounds and then another three. Two rounds hit the pickup's windshield. One of the men standing in the truck's bed fell backward and didn't get up.

At that moment, the gunner on the M2 mounted Hummer opened up with two short bursts. All landed wide to the pickup's right as the truck veered sharply left, into the median, and then accelerated back the other way. The gunner sent a third burst intentionally wide, probably to ensure they got the message, and then turned back. The mounted Hummer pulled up next to the buggy and the transport Hummer as Sam, Chet, and Tiff exited the buggy.

Sam went to meet the troops stepping from the Hummers as Chet and Tiff walked around to examine the buggy.

An air force security forces technical sergeant, along with an airman from the transport Hummer, approached Sam. "Everyone okay?" the tech sergeant asked.

"We are but I think the buggy's wounded," Sam said.

The three of them walked over to join Chet and Tiff.

"This tire is literally shot," Chet said, as he bent down and stuck his finger into a gaping hole.

"Do you have a spare?" the tech sergeant asked.

Sam kicked the tire. "Afraid not. And there's no way this thing can be patched."

Tiff looked back down the roadway. "The shitheads will be back for sure."

The tech sergeant stuck his hand out and shook hands with Sam. "I'm Sergeant Forsyth, forty-seventh security forces, Moody Air Force Base."

"Sam Pratt. This is Sergeant Major Chet Stevens, army retired, and Tiffany Conway, former marine corps."

Forsyth shook hands with Chet and Tiff and then looked back to Sam. "You're the retired major?"

"Guilty," Sam replied.

"Can't leave you guys to the mercy of redneck justice. Let's load your gear into my Hummer. It's just me and Airman Davis here; we have plenty of room."

"Are you sure?" Sam asked.

"Absolutely, major," Forsyth said. "Your buggy isn't going anywhere."

"We were headed for Tennessee," Chet said. "This puts a serious dent in our plans."

Forsyth grabbed two bundles of gear from the buggy and headed toward his Hummer. "For now, it doesn't appear you have an option."

Sam kicked the buggy and then did a slow hand rub of his entire face. "Dammit to hell and back!"

Tiff began untying the backpacks from the top. "My sentiments exactly."

Sam, Chet, Tiff, Forsyth, and Davis transferred the gear from the buggy to the back of the Hummer, including the two gas cans, while the men from the machine gun mounted Hummer kept watch. When all was loaded Sam did a final exam of the buggy to ensure nothing of value was left behind. He then removed the keys from the ignition and stuck them in his pocket.

Chet walked up. "Memento?"

"Yeah," Sam replied. "I hate leaving her behind. A lot of work went into building this thing."

Forsyth joined them. "Gentlemen, we need to scoot."

Sam admired the buggy for a second more and then turned toward the Hummer.

Chet put his arm around Sam's shoulders. "You can build a better one," he said with a repressed chuckle.

"Not funny."

Chet removed his arm. "Okay, okay." They piled into the Hummer where Tiff was already waiting.

"Finished with your goodbyes?" Tiff asked.

"He'll be okay," Chet said with a smirk and a raised eyebrow.

Sam was quiet as he looked back at the buggy one more time.

"Everything loaded?" Forsyth asked, as he slid into the driver's seat.

"We're set," Tiff responded.

Forsyth started the Hummer, put it in gear, and pulled out. The mounted Hummer fell in behind and they accelerated to fifty to catch up with the convoy. They had gone about five miles when they came up to the convoy pulled over to the side. Forsyth pulled up and stopped next to Lieutenants Harvey and Jensen standing behind the open ambulance.

Everyone piled out of Forsyth's Hummer and approached.

"Is the captain okay?" Sam asked.

"I'm fine," Jeffries said in a weak voice from the back of the ambulance.

Sam walked over and peered inside. Jeffries was still on the stretcher. His shoulder was bandaged, his arm was in a sling, and his face was ashen. Jeffries tried to raise his head but then put it back down.

"Probably better not to move too much," Sam said. "How are you feeling?"

"Like shit but better than before."

"I understand there's a field hospital set up at the airport," Sam said.

"Yeah, that's where I'll be for a couple of days," Jeffries replied. "How did you make out back there? Where's your buggy?"

"Shot to hell. Sergeant Forsyth here took pity and offered us a ride."

"Looks like you're going with us to Atlanta then," Jeffries said.

"Looks like. Seriously, we really appreciate the ride."

Jeffries tried to raise his head again. "Don't mention it."

The medic sitting next to Jeffries' stretcher looked at Sam. "He needs to rest easy."

"I actually don't feel that bad," Jeffries said.

"That's the drugs, sir. You don't want that shoulder to open up. You need to lie still."

Sam tapped Jeffries's foot. "I'll check on you at the hospital. It looks like we'll be hanging around a bit longer than expected."

"The more the merrier, major," Jeffries said with a weakening voice.

Sam turned to Harvey and Jensen. "Okay with you guys if we tag along, at least to Atlanta?"

"No problem, major," Harvey said. "We'll be moving out as soon as Lieutenant Jensen and I get back to the front. You guys can stay with Sergeant Forsyth in his ride."

"Thank you, lieutenant. We'll try to stay out of your way."

Harvey nodded. He and Jensen returned to their Hummer, got in, and sped off.

Forsyth, Davis, and Tiff hopped in the Hummer. Chet hung back with Sam.

"I don't relish the thought of walking to Tennessee," Chet said. "We need to find another vehicle."

"I don't think I *could* walk to Tennessee. We definitely need to find another vehicle."

Sam and Chet took their seats in the back of the Hummer and waited for the convoy to start moving. Sam watched as Harvey's Hummer pulled into the front of the line.

Forsyth broke the silence. "I've worked with Lieutenant Harvey for a couple of years. He's a good man."

"I think you're right, sergeant," Sam replied.

The radio in the Hummer squawked with Harvey's voice. "Oscar mike."

Engines along the line came to life, and the vehicles pulled out, one after another. Soon the convoy was up to their forty cruising speed with Sam, Chet, and Tiff in the second to the last vehicle. The mounted Hummer brought up the rear.

Sam looked over at Chet. "Is one of those ammo boxes handy?

Chet reached behind the seat and produced a box of 5.56.

Sam flipped open the lid and began refilling his two magazines.

Tiff popped the clip out of her rifle and started doing the same.

Soon, the convoy was back on Interstate 75 and moving north. Two hours later they crossed the 285 beltway exchange and then exited onto North Central heading west. Sam saw plenty of people heading out of the prior towns, walking along the roadsides carrying what they could, but none of that compared to what he saw now. The number of people leaving Atlanta all at once was unimaginable. Sam was reminded of the ants that suddenly appeared after he stepped on an ant bed when he was a child. Except, in this case, all the ants were traveling in the same direction.

"Where are all these people headed," Tiff asked.

"Anywhere out of Atlanta," Forsyth answered. "It's like this with all the large cities."

"Fear to chaos to pandemonium," Chet said.

"The only difference between them and us is we have a plan," Sam said.

Everyone was silent.

Finally, Sam cleared his throat. "Has anyone been to this part of town?"

"Not the streets," Tiff replied, "but I've flown into the airport numerous times."

"Somebody knows where they're going," Chet said.

Sam made a mental note of the turns. North Central to Atlanta Avenue, then Airport Loop, a left on Taffy Terrace, and then into the Fast Jet terminal area.

Sam leaned forward to get Forsyth's attention. "Fast Jet?"

Forsyth glanced back. "Yeah, all units are rendezvousing at this terminal. There's plenty of space in the building and on the pad, it's fenced, and there are several hotels across the street."

Chet leaned forward. "Power and water?"

Airman Davis turned to face Chet. "Nope. Not in the hotels. We have shielded generators for essentials, like the field hospital, but nothing else."

"Who's in charge?" Sam asked.

Forsyth glanced back again. "Last I heard it was Lieutenant Colonel Matthew Byers. He's active duty army out of Fort McPherson."

Chet leaned forward. "Why not just rendezvous at Fort McPherson?"

"Not enough room. Plus, they wanted the security forces closer to the southeast counties. Most of the gang activity emanates from there."

Forsyth followed the convoy around the right side of the large Fast Jet hangar and came to a stop on the pad between the building and a smaller hangar across the pad opposite Fast Jet. A group of men in uniform walked out of the large open hangar and met Lieutenants Harvey and Jensen as they stepped from their Hummer. The Lieutenants saluted the man leading the pack. They spoke for a few minutes and then started walking toward the end of the convoy.

Sam, Chet, and Tiff exited the Hummer along with Forsyth and Davis.

Chet looked around the area. "Now what?"

"Good question," Sam said, as he started walking to meet the group approaching the ambulance. "Looks like we're about to meet Colonel Byers."

Chet and Tiff accompanied Sam. Everyone met at the rear of the ambulance as the rear doors opened. The two combat medics lifted and carried Jeffries, still on a stretcher, and set him on the tarmac in front of Byers.

"How are you feeling, Frank?" Byers asked.

"Better. I should be ready for duty in a day or two."

Byers looked up at the medics. "How's he doing?"

The ranking medic pointed to his own right shoulder. "The round went through the shoulder. I couldn't detect any broken bones. We stopped the bleeding and put him on antibiotics to prevent infection. And he's on pain meds. If no complications develop, he should be mobile in a couple of days. Of course, the doc needs to take a look."

Byers looked down at Jeffries. "Frank, we're going to get you over to the field hospital so the doc can make sure all is okay."

Jeffries nodded. "Sorry about this sir."

"Not your fault. Just get better soon."

The two medics picked up the stretcher and headed toward a large enclosed trailer with a red cross on the side parked at the edge of the tarmac. Jeffries nodded at Sam as the medics carried him by.

Byers approached Sam. "Who might you be?"

Before Sam could answer, Harvey spoke up. "Sir, this is retired air force Major Sam Pratt. He and his friends were traveling in a working vehicle to Tennessee when they happened upon the convoy in Valdosta. They lost the vehicle when we came under fire by some rednecks. I saw no harm in giving them a ride."

Byers looked at Sam without offering a handshake. "Sorry about your vehicle, but we won't be able to host civilians at this facility."

Sam glanced at Chet, who was beginning to develop a perturbed expression, and then back to Byers. "We understand colonel. We'll be out of your hair as soon as we can get our gear together."

"Fine, major." Byers immediately turned to Lieutenant Harvey. "Lieutenant, you'll be in command of your force until Captain Jeffries can return to duty. That includes the army guard. Any problems with that?"

"No sir." Harvey saluted as Byers and his entourage turned and walked away.

Sam stepped closer to Harvey. "Sorry if we got you jammed up."

A smile returned to Harvey's face. "Not a problem, major. You being here didn't change anything. The word is he's mighty pissed. Some troops, mostly guard but some active, have already deserted. His command is dwindling."

"Just the same, we should probably get out of your hair," Sam said, as he turned to Chet and Tiff. "We need to unload our gear."

Sam, Chet, and Tiff started toward the Hummer.

Harvey stepped toward the Hummer as well. "Hold up. The colonel said he couldn't host you guys. He didn't say I couldn't help."

"It's okay, we'll find some wheels and be on our way," Sam said.

Harvey went over to Forsyth and Davis who were still standing beside their Hummer and motioned for Sam, Chet, and Tiff to jump in. Harvey stuck out his hand to Forsyth. "I'll drive."

Forsyth handed Harvey the key and then he and Davis got in the back with Chet and Tiff. Sam took the passenger seat next to Harvey. "What did you have in mind, lieutenant?"

Harvey started the vehicle, made a U-turn, and started back the way they had come. "You need a place for tonight. Most of our guys will be in the Vacation Suites and the Royal across the street. There're a couple of other hotels with room."

"Are these hotels occupied?" Chet asked.

Harvey glanced back. "The patrons left when the food and water ran out. Only took a day. The hotels around here are pretty much empty except for us."

Tiff slid forward in her seat. "What about gang activity?"

"Fairly quiet around here," Harvey answered. "The center of town is a war zone but they are spreading out as food becomes scarce?"

"How did you get all this information?" Chet asked.

"Updates over the radio as we drove up," Davis replied.

Harvey made a left on Taffy, drove over Airport Loop, and a left on Virginia. He then made an immediate turn into the parking lot for the Huddle Hotel.

"You seem to know your way around," Tiff said.

Harvey stopped near the hotel's front entrance. "I lived near here for five years when I was younger."

Everyone piled out of the Hummer and entered the hotel lobby. There were several people in uniform in the lobby but no one behind the desk.

Harvey stopped an air force staff sergeant walking by. "Sergeant, what's the story with this hotel."

"The remaining guests left yesterday, along with management and the employees. No food or water. Some security forces have taken rooms on the first floor."

"Thank you, sergeant," Harvey said, as he turned to Sam. "This should be okay for tonight. To maintain a low profile you may want to bunch up in one room."

Tiff peered out a lobby window. "We're right across the street from the Fast Jet facility."

Harvey motioned to Forsyth and Davis. "I think we'll stay here as well. I'll walk back over to the pad and help get the convoy situated. We have patrols going out tonight. You guys can find a room and get settled."

Sam shook hands with Harvey. "Thanks again for all your help. We recognize the limb you're standing on."

"I'll be fine," Harvey said, as he headed for the door.

Chet motioned with his arms. "Let's get situated."

CHAPTER 10

"This is never going to work," Chet said, as he sat on a sofa trying to organize the gear in his pack.

Sam stood looking out the second-floor window at the Fast Jet compound across the street. Men in uniform were scurrying about, fueling Hummers, and loading equipment. Sam mopped his forehead with a towel. "It must be a hundred degrees in here." He continued gazing out the window. "Looks like they're sending everybody out tonight on patrol."

Tiff sat on one of two double beds, also organizing her pack.

Chet looked up at Sam. "You're blocking the breeze from that window."

"There is no breeze from this window," Sam said, as he continued gazing out. He finally turned from the window and walked over to his own gear. He stood for a moment looking down and then kicked his pack. "We need wheels."

Tiff dumped everything from her backpack onto the floor. "Everything moving around here has US government property written on it."

Chet paused. "Do you think they would miss one?"

"Martial law, remember," Sam said. "They could shoot us for that."

"Maybe we should go out tonight and look for an old car," Tiff said.

Sam rested his forehead in one hand. "Anything that runs is either way out of town or in the hands of the gangs."

Tiff nodded and went back to work.

Sam bent down and dumped the contents of his pack on the floor. "Looks like we'll be walking tomorrow," he said, as he began selecting items to go back in the pack. "Lighten the load. Take only what we absolutely need. We can get by with one tent."

"Oh, joy," Tiff said.

"Ditto," Chet said.

Sam stuffed most items back into his pack and then pushed everything into a corner. "I say we eat, get some rest, and figure this out tomorrow."

Chet dropped what he was doing and leaned back against the sofa. "When did we last eat?"

Tiff lay back on the bed. "I don't know, but I don't feel like cooking."

Sam walked over and picked up one of the boxes of MREs. "Almost no cooking necessary."

***

Tiff gathered the empty containers from her MRE and tossed them in a garbage can near the window. Sam and Chet continued eating.

Tiff walked back over to the sofa. "I guess I'll sleep here tonight."

"You can have the bed if you'd rather," Sam said. "I don't mind the sofa." Actually, he wanted the bed and hoped she would decline. Sam didn't think he could actually fit on the sofa.

Tiff opened the closet next to the bathroom and retrieved a blanket from the top shelf. She then spread the blanket over the sofa and added a pillow from one of the beds. "I'll be fine here. You boys need your beauty sleep."

Chet looked at Sam. "She must be talking about you."

"Suit yourself," Sam said, as he tossed his trash in the garbage can and peered out the window. "The patrols are about ready to move out."

The sound of engines starting drifted up from the Fast Jet compound. Sam glanced at his arm where his watch used to be and realized he didn't have a watch. "The sun is setting. It must be around eight-thirty."

Chet joined Sam at the window. "Night patrols— makes sense."

Sam moved closer to the window to get a better angle. "Yeah. The colonel isn't leaving many men behind to protect the compound."

Chet returned to his bed and lay down. "I'm sure he didn't get to lieutenant colonel by being stupid."

"It's been a while since you were active duty, hasn't it," Tiff said.

Sam looked down at the parking lot and the two Porta-Potties along the back fence. "Think I'll hit the head and then turn in."

Chet stood up, followed by Tiff. "Right behind you," Chet said.

***

Sam preferred to sleep on his side, which was the position he was in on top of the bed when he heard the voices. He had just entered that dreamy state before actual sleep, and before Chet started snoring. Sam came fully awake and listened for a few moments. Nope, wasn't his imagination. There were definitely voices. Sam slipped from the bed and padded over to the window. There was just enough moonlight for Sam to see the silhouette of men, lots of men, lined up outside the chain-link fence that wrapped around the Fast Jet compound.

Sam crept over to Chet's bed and poked him softly on the shoulder. Chet's eyes blinked open.

"Problem outside," Sam whispered. He looked over at Tiff and found she was already sitting up on the sofa.

They all three padded over to the window. Sam counted the silhouettes—thirty-three, all in single file. Four or five men were bunched at the head of the line.

"What are they waiting for?" Chet whispered.

Tiff cocked her ear. "They're cutting the fence."

"Who would expect a bunch of thugs to attack home base using guerrilla tactics while the main force is away?" Chet asked sarcastically.

"I feel like I owe Jeffries," Sam said. "You guys don't have to come."

"Uh-huh, fat chance," Chet replied.

Tiff turned toward the sofa. "Ditto."

They all three pulled their boots on, laced them in the dark, and grabbed their rifles.

"What's the plan?" Chet asked, as Tiff opened the door and stepped into the hallway.

"Surprise the hell out of them," Sam replied.

In pitch dark, Sam, Chet, and Tiff hustled to the end of the hall, down the stairs, and out the front entrance. In stealth mode, they scurried around to the rear of the building and then dashed across the grass to a tall hedge and a six-foot concrete block wall that stood between the hedge and the road. Chet slipped into the hedge, leaned his rifle against the wall, and got down on all fours. Sam motioned to Tiff who then stepped up on Chet's back so she could see over the wall. Almost immediately she stepped back down and Chet got to his feet.

"The last of them just poured through a hole in the fence," Tiff whispered. "One lookout left behind, about fifty yards down."

Sam leaned toward Chet. "Give me a hand over the wall and then help Tiff up so she can give me cover. I'll try to take him out quietly."

Chet nodded and then clasped his hands together to form a step. Sam stepped up, took a look over, and then hopped on top of the wall. The lookout was barely visible standing against the chain link fence, as Tiff said, about fifty yards up the road. Since the hedge behind Sam was taller than the wall, Sam was able to remain in shadow. Sam quietly lowered himself to the ground and then crouched while he swept the area with his rifle for more lookouts. Tiff popped up with just her head and shoulders above the wall and brought her rifle to bear. The sole lookout was peering through the hole in the fence with his back to Sam.

Sam ran across the pavement to the lookout's side of the road and then inched along the fence without making a sound. Sam made it to within fifteen feet of the lookout when suddenly the man spun around. Sam found himself nose-to-nose with a large caliber automatic pistol. In that same instant, a single gunshot boomed from behind and the impact of a round to the man's chest tumbled him backward and to the ground. The man dropped his pistol, grabbed his chest, and tried to stem the flow of blood.

The man, covered in tattoos, locked eyes with Sam. "You a dead man!" he moaned.

Sam stepped closer. "You first." Sam heard footsteps and turned to see Tiff running up. "I've lost count, is that three or four?" Sam asked.

"Three or four what?" Tiff replied.

"Times you've saved my life."

"It is becoming a bit of a habit."

More footsteps and Sam and Tiff turned to look. Chet came running up. He immediately kicked the pistol away from the lookout who was still moaning in pain with both hands over the wound in his chest. At that moment, a fury of sustained gunfire blasted from the compound. Sam, Chet, and Tiff peeked through the hole in the fence and then dashed through, taking cover behind a Hummer. When the firing stopped Sam raised from his crouched position just enough to see through the Hummer windows. He did not expect what he saw.

All the men who previously rushed through the hole in the fence were sprawled on the tarmac either dead or dying. At least thirty guardsmen, all with shouldered weapons, stepped from various spots around the scene. It was obvious that the men who Sam now assumed were gang members had been caught in a classic pincer. Sam then saw Lieutenant Colonel Byers and some other men leave their cover and walk toward the scene. At that same moment, Sam heard movement behind him and turned to see Lieutenant Harvey and three other men, all with shouldered weapons, step through the hole in the fence.

Sam slowly raised his hands, still holding his rifle. "It's Sam Pratt."

Harvey lowered his rifle. "What are you guys doing here?"

"We heard activity from our window and saw the gangbangers about to attack."

"So you came down to help," Harvey said.

Chet stepped closer. "It was the least we could do."

"You could have gotten yourselves killed."

"We had no way of knowing you were expecting the attack," Tiff said.

"We have a metro gang squad detective with us. He knows the gangs and figured they might attack the compound when we sent out our patrols."

"How did you know they would attack here?" Sam asked.

"It's the weakest spot," Harvey replied. "But we could actually have responded no matter where they entered."

"You must have been watching us," Tiff said.

"Night-vision. We were down the road about a hundred yards. We didn't know who you were but when you took the lookout down, we figured you were friendly."

Sam turned to the sound of men approaching and saw Byers and a civilian—middle to late thirties, dark hair, good shape, dressed in tactical gear—marching over. Based on the colonel's stride he didn't seem happy.

"What's going on here lieutenant?" Byers asked.

"Sir, Major Pratt and his two friends spotted the commotion and thought it might be a sneak attack," Harvey replied. "They came to help."

Byers turned to Sam. "Major, I appreciate the thought, but you people could have screwed up our plans."

"Sorry, colonel. We thought we were helping."

The civilian stepped over to the hole in the fence, peered out, and then walked back to the group. "Looks like they did help some. The lookout is down." The civilian turned to Sam and stuck out his hand. "Detective Paul Elliot."

Sam caught a whiff of eucalyptus from the detective as he stuck out his hand to shake. Sam took his hand in a firm grasp. "Sam Pratt. This is Sergeant-Major Chet Stevens, army retired, and Tiffany Conway, former marine corps. Tiff took out the lookout." Elliot shook hands with Chet and Tiff.

"I've read a couple of books on security by a Sam Pratt, is that you?"

"It is."

"Good stuff," Elliot said. He turned to Tiff. "Good work Ms. Conway."

"Thank you," she replied, keeping her gaze locked on Elliot's face a beat too long.

Even in the dark Sam noticed the obvious attraction.

Byers cleared his throat. "Lieutenant, we have work to do here. Please see to these people."

"Will do, sir."

Byers turned and marched off. Elliot lingered a bit.

"Coming detective?"

Elliot looked at Sam and then Chet. "Nice to meet you all." He then turned his gaze to Tiff and held it a few beats longer. "I hope to see you again."

Tiff nodded with a slight smile as Detective Elliot turned and hurried to catch Byers.

Sam glimpsed at Tiff. "Interesting man."

"Isn't he though," Chet said. "Even with the eucalyptus."

"Eucalyptus?" Tiff asked.

"A natural bug repellant," Chet said. "I use it sometimes when mosquitoes are bad. No bad chemicals, but it is pungent."

"You guys should probably head back to the hotel," Harvey said.

Sam nodded. "Sorry about the mix-up."

"Not a problem," Harvey said.

Sam, Chet, and Tiff stepped back to the fence, slipped through the hole, and began walking back to the hotel, taking the long route around to the front.

***

The magnified image of the two men and one woman walking in the distance was replaced with the lookout lying on the sidewalk. The man removed the binoculars from his eyes and stared into the distance. He stood with three other young men on top of the ten-story Vacation Suites building on the north side of Interstate 85. All four men were covered in tattoos and they each wore at least one red article of clothing. The man with the binoculars wore a red handkerchief tied around his neck. From this vantage point, the men were able to see everything that had transpired, including when the woman shot the lookout.

One of the men stepped closer to the edge of the roof and then glanced back at the man with the binoculars. "Toothpick, they iced Gizzy."

Toothpick gritted his teeth and flexed his jaw muscles. "My brother knew the risks." He then motioned to the three walking down the sidewalk. "Just the same, those three are done," he said calmly.

"What about the soldiers?" one of the men asked.

"Them too," Toothpick grunted. He then pointed to the two men and one woman in the distance. "They're probably in the Huddle. Put some people on them. If you get the chance, take them alive."

CHAPTER 11

Just after sunrise the next morning, pounding on the door brought Sam out of a deep sleep. Chet and Tiff bolted upright as well. Chet laid his head back on the pillow and rolled to his side while Tiff got up and ambled to the door rubbing her eye. She checked the peephole.

Tiff opened the door. "Detective."

Sam joined Tiff at the door. "What's up?"

Elliot and Tiff exchanged gazes as he stepped inside and then faced Sam. "There's a place downtown that houses classic cars. Thought we might find you guys some transportation."

Tiff closed the door. "Lieutenant Harvey told you about Tennessee and our dilemma."

"Correct," Elliot said. "We'll be lucky if any are left, but it's worth a try."

Chet rose up, swiveled, and put his feet on the floor. "What about breakfast?"

"Wheels or breakfast," Elliot said. "Your choice."

Sam, Chet, and Tiff, dressed in the same t-shirts and tactical pants as the day before, put their boots on, holstered their side arms, and picked up their rifles.

"Ready," Sam said.

They all strode out the door and down the hall.

"You got a ride?" Chet asked, as they were going down the stairs.

"Lieutenant Harvey was nice enough to loan me a Hummer."

Tiff glanced at Elliot. "Does the colonel know?"

"I'm out collecting Intel," Elliot replied.

Sam and Chet squeezed into the back of the Hummer parked out front leaving only the front passenger seat available for Tiff. She shook her head and then slipped into the seat while Elliot got behind the wheel. He started the engine and pulled away.

"Where is this place?" Sam asked.

"Up eighty-five to five points. The place is aptly named classic cars."

"Why would we expect any cars to be there?" Chet asked.

"They're in a warehouse not that well marked. Maybe no one has thought of it yet."

"Maybe," Chet mumbled.

"We *really* appreciate your effort," Tiff said.

Elliot smiled at Tiff and then turned to focus on driving. Sam looked out the windows mesmerized by what was happening. Looting was rampant. Broken windows and doors lined the street. People ran about with arms full of merchandise. There was even an occasional gunshot and a couple of vehicles were on fire. Hardship these days seemed to bring out the worst in way too many people. Sam was amazed how a person could be a fine upstanding individual one day and a raving lunatic the next, having reverted to the dark side in a matter of hours.

"This place is out of control," Sam commented. "There's no way the guard will be able to reign in this chaos."

Elliot glanced back at Sam. "We know. We knew it pretty much day one but last night confirmed our fears. People have gone crazy."

"Are you getting a lot of desertions from the force?" Chet asked.

"Yes. In droves. And much earlier than any of the brass expected. Even the guard and regular army are feeling the pinch. People on both sides are scared."

"What about the gangs?" Sam asked.

"Rampant. Drugs were their merchandise of choice before the lights went out. Now it's drugs, food, and water. To some degree, gangs that would never have cooperated before are now joining forces to control what food is left. Primarily, it's the grocery store distribution centers they want. That's why Byers is here."

"Is it safe driving through here?" Tiff asked.

Elliot smiled at her. "The distribution centers are on the outskirts. That's where the gangs are most active. But to answer your question, I would not be venturing out alone tonight. I wouldn't go out with a squad of navy seals come tomorrow. Right now, people are focused on looting. By tomorrow they'll be turning on each other."

Sam peered out the window and noted that as they got closer to the center of town, the number of looters grew fewer. "I suppose even the little people are beginning to realize that only food and water really matter at this point," Sam said.

Elliot looked to his right and left. "Yeah, less food sources in the center of town. We should be okay down here at least long enough to check on the cars."

Elliot slowed to weave through some stalled vehicles, driving up on the sidewalk when necessary. He pointed ahead. "The place is right up here on the right."

Tiff put her hand on her rifle and scrunched forward in her seat as Elliot turned into a small parking lot in the rear of a large two-story building. A regular door and a metal roll-up door faced the parking lot. There were no people around.

"Were these cars for sale?" Tiff asked.

"It's grown into more of a museum. Started out as a private collection with just a few cars. The original owner died years ago with no known heirs, so the city took possession until an heir could be found. Enthusiasts donated money to help maintain the collection. They even donated more cars. Over time it grew into the modest display that it is today. The city moved it to this location a few years ago."

"Will any of them still run," Chet asked.

Elliot pulled to a stop and opened his door. "That's what we're here to find out."

Tiff stepped out followed by Sam and Chet.

"Rifles?" Chet asked.

Elliot glanced around and then back to Chet. "No one around. I'm okay with just my Glock."

Sam glanced at Chet and shrugged his shoulders.

Chet left his rifle in the Hummer and slammed the door.

Everyone moved to the rear door.

Sam knocked on the door. "Metal. Won't be busting through this anytime soon."

Chet tried lifting the roll-up door but it would not budge.

Tiff headed for the corner of the building. "What about windows?"

"Just those thick glass blocks on the sides," Elliot replied. "Probably tougher than the doors. The front has glass windows and a glass door, but I'd prefer to keep this low key."

Chet kicked the roll-up door. "A cop, a marine, a grunt, a flyboy and we can't even open the door."

Sam kneeled in front of the door and examined the knob and lock. He then produced a small classic Victorinox pocket knife and opened the nail file. "I need a piece of wire, like a paper clip."

Tiff returned to the Hummer and searched throughout, including under the seats. Finally, she stood up with something silver in her fingers. "How about a paperclip?"

Sam smirked as Tiff walked over and handed it to him. He straightened a two-inch length and added a tiny bend at the end. Sam used the very tip of the fingernail file stuck in the bottom of the keyhole to provide tension while he manipulated the pins with the paperclip. Everyone watched as he worked. A few minutes later there was an audible click. Sam used the fingernail file to turn the lock tumbler which also turned the knob. The door popped open.

"One of my many skills," Sam said, as he smiled and stood up.

Elliot moved to the open door. "So you're a cat burglar."

"Today I am," Sam said, as everyone stepped through the door.

Inside, light from the side glass-block windows was enough to illuminate everything.

"Wow!" Chet said, and then he whistled.

"Wow is right," Sam echoed.

Sam scanned the large room. Scattered around the open floor were classic cars of nearly every era, size, color, and shape. Each was polished to a high gloss. And each included a placard on a stand displaying the make, model, and year.

"There must be fifty cars in here," Tiff said, as she started walking among them. She let her fingers glide over the shiny paint. "When did they start putting computers in cars?"

"Anything prior to the early seventies should run," Sam responded, as he too started walking among the cars. "Cars prior to that didn't have circuits susceptible to an EMP."

Chet remained by the door. "Maybe one of us should wait outside by the Hummer."

Elliot started toward the door. "I can do that."

Chet opened the door. "That's okay, allow me."

Chet stepped outside and closed the door. Elliot walked over and accompanied Tiff as she examined the various cars.

"Chevy, Ford, Dodge, Buick… they're all represented," Sam said. "Even Hudson and Studebaker." Sam saw Tiff examining a bright red Cadillac convertible. "Nothing too flashy."

Tiff turned her attention to a black and white 1956 Chevy Bel Air. "What about this?"

"Nice car, but we'd have to move twenty cars to get it out of here," Elliot said.

Sam, Tiff, and Elliot then converged on the cars nearest the roll-up door and gravitated to a dark green 1963 Ford Galaxie 500.

Sam walked slowly around the car. He paused at the double headlights and the large round tail lights. He stuck his head in the open driver's window and the stepped back and opened the door. "Keys?"

Elliot looked around the area. "They probably keep them all in one place. Maybe a lockbox on the wall."

They all spread out and searched the area.

Tiff headed up some stairs. "I'll look up here."

Elliot hustled over. "Mind some company?"

"Nope, don't mind at all," Tiff replied, as they both disappeared up the stairs.

Sam continued searching the first floor. He checked all the walls and then moved to the front of the building where he found a lobby, a counter, and three offices, all well lit by the large glass windows. Sam ducked behind the counter when he saw three men crossing the street in front of the building. They stepped up on the sidewalk but kept walking until they were no longer in view.

Sam popped up and continued searching. He searched the first two offices and found nothing. When he entered the third office he immediately saw a large box hanging on the side wall. He opened the box and set his eyes on hundreds of keys, all on rings. Some rings had two and three keys. Every key ring included a tag neatly printed with a car's description. It took several minutes to find the one for the Galaxie.

Sam snatched the key ring, returned to the main display room, and slid behind the wheel of the Galaxie. He inserted the key in the ignition and twisted. The engine turned over for several seconds before it finally coughed to life and settled into a purr. Sam noticed that the gas gauge needle was almost on empty.

He switched the engine off and stepped out just as Elliot and Tiff emerged from the upstairs.

"Nothing up there of importance," Tiff said, as she and Elliot walked over to the Galaxie.

"Uh-huh," Sam said, as he rolled his eyes. "Let's see if we can get this door open. And we need gas."

"There's an extra can on the Hummer along with a siphon hose," Elliot said.

Sam checked the roll-up door. "No key lock, just this," he said, as he pulled up on a handle. The door clicked loose.

At that moment the other door swung open and Chet stuck his head in. He had his rifle in his hand. "Possible shithead alert. We have six or seven guys approaching. Some have guns."

Sam, Elliot, and Tiff joined Chet outside. Elliot pulled the Glock from his holster under his shirt. Sam and Tiff retrieved their rifles from the Hummer, spread out, and took cover behind stalled cars in the street. Elliot took cover next to Tiff.

Sam saw Chet take off running through the parking lot that ended at a parallel street. He stopped, scanned in all directions, and then disappeared around the corner. Sam had never known of Chet to run from the action in his life, so Sam knew he must have something in mind. Sam turned his attention back to the approaching gang members.

***

In the open, six men and one woman stopped about ten yards away from where Sam, Tiff, and Elliot were crouched behind stalled cars. The man in the lead, flamed out with a blue bandana wrapped around his waist, pointed. "Better check your six, man."

Sam and Tiff both looked over their shoulder and saw four additional men walking up from behind. They were still a half block back.

"We have more guests coming," Tiff said to Elliot.

Elliot glanced back and then pointed his Glock over the hood of his car, taking aim on the bandana man's head. "You'll be the first one down, man."

"Nobody has to die, we just want the Hummer," the bandana man said.

The woman in the group stepped forward and raised a pistol, pointing it at Elliot. "If Turtle goes down, you'll be next."

Turtle placed his hand over the woman's gun and slowly pushed it down. "Easy Rose. These people look like the reasonable type. I'm sure they can be persuaded."

Elliot maintained his position. "Turn and walk away. Do it now!"

Turtle's group began spreading out.

Keeping her rifle shouldered, Tiff turned to face the group approaching from the rear. She moved to a different stalled car for better cover.

Suddenly, gunfire erupted from behind Turtle's group. Two men went down immediately as Chet came into view. Sam fired multiple shots at Turtle but hit Rose instead when Turtle leaped to the side. Rose fell to the ground bleeding from her neck. Elliot opened up with his Glock and hit one additional man. That left Turtle and two men crouched behind the same stalled car.

Sam could see Chet closing behind Turtle, taking cover as much as possible. Turtle and his two remaining men began firing. Bullets pinged into the metal of the cars surrounding Sam and Elliot. Sam glanced back to make sure Tiff was okay.

The men approaching Tiff from behind quickened their pace without taking advantage of the available cover. Tiff began firing in two and three round bursts. One of the men fell to the ground, grabbing his stomach. The other three jumped for cover.

Sam and Elliot fired a few more rounds at Turtle but then stopped firing for fear of hitting Chet who was still moving up on Turtle's rear. One of Turtle's men kept popping his head up to look over the hood of the car they were behind. Sam took careful aim with his magnified sight and tried to time the pop-ups. Sam pulled the trigger before he actually saw the man's head. A cloud of red from the man's head splattered the car behind him. Chet took the opportunity to rush forward before Turtle knew what was happening. Sam fired a few shots high to keep his attention forward while Chet got closer.

Finally, Chet lunged from behind a panel truck giving him a clear shot on Turtle's flank. Chet let loose a hail of gunfire which lasted only a couple of seconds. After the firing stopped, Sam saw Chet move in on Turtle's position, duck down, and then stand back up. He then joined Sam and Elliot who had turned to face the threat from the rear with Tiff. All four fired a short burst at the three remaining men. Rounds peppered the car they were standing behind. When Sam, Chet, Elliot, and Tiff stopped firing, the three men made a hasty retreat and were soon out of sight.

Tiff stood up and turned to Elliot. Seeing a stream of blood running down his face, she immediately ran to his side. "Are you hit?"

Elliot holstered his Glock and leaned back against a car. "Just a crease. Another millimeter and it would have been serious."

"Let's get you over to the Hummer," Tiff said, as she took hold under Elliot's arm and led him away. Sam and Chet followed. At the Hummer, she grabbed the first aid kit from the back and retrieved some gauze. She held the gauze against the small wound.

Sam and Chet watched as Tiff rummaged in the kit for some tape.

"Think he'll live?" Chet asked.

"I don't know," Sam replied. "Looks serious."

Tiff faced Elliot, noses only an inch apart. "They're being assholes, ignore them."

Elliot kept his gaze into Tiff's eyes. "Consider them officially ignored."

Chet turned serious. "We need to skedaddle before the shitheads return with friends."

Sam motioned, led Chet back to the car museum, and opened the roll-up door. Ten feet inside sat the Galaxie. "Our new ride," he said, as he walked over and slipped into the driver's seat. He started the engine and backed the car through the door and into the parking lot. "She needs gas."

Tiff and Elliot walked up. "The siphon hose is in the back of the Hummer," Elliot said.

Chet went to the Hummer and returned with the siphon hose and a five-gallon can. He siphoned from nearby cars and emptied the can of gas into the Galaxie. He then refilled the can and drained the second five gallons into the car.

Chet returned the can and siphon hose to the Hummer. "I think we're ready."

"I'll ride with Elliot," Tiff said, as they both moved off toward the Hummer.

Sam and Chet hopped in the car, started the engine, and pulled out behind Elliot and Tiff.

CHAPTER 12

Elliot had only driven a few blocks when he pulled to the side, jumped out, and ran back to the Galaxie. "The compound is under attack!"

"By whom?" Sam asked.

"Gangs. Apparently, the major gangs have come together against a common enemy."

Chet leaned over toward Sam's window. "How can we help?"

"Lieutenant Harvey says there are two main forces. The largest moved in from the actual airport. The second is keeping up steady fire from the Taffy and Virginia area."

"Perhaps we can do some damage there," Chet said.

"If they're smart, they'll have a rear guard," Sam said.

"I suggest we enter the area via Hartsfield and then go on foot from the La Quinta," Elliot said.

"Sounds like a plan," Sam said. "We'll follow you."

Elliot returned to the Hummer and pulled away from the curb. Sam followed as Elliot returned to the Interstate and then took the Hartsfield off-ramp. As they were approaching the Virginia intersection, Sam saw three men run toward the highway from a wooded area and take cover behind the center support for the Virginia overpass. Three additional men were visible on top of the overpass. They all started laying down fire from semi-automatic rifles when the two vehicles got within a hundred yards. Several rounds pinged against the Hummer and then rounds started peppering the Galaxie. The Hummer suddenly accelerated and Sam lost what little cover he had. Sam and Chet ducked as gunfire raked the windshield, the hood, and Sam's side of the car. Sam stomped on the gas pedal as he peeked above the dashboard. The car lurched and began gaining on the Hummer but then coughed and slowed as steam poured from under the hood. As they passed under the overpass, three men behind the center support fired point blank. Both tires on Sam's side of the car exploded causing the car to jerk to the left. Sam wrenched the steering wheel to the right which overcompensated. The car spun around, slid, and finally came to rest halfway up an embankment with the front of the car facing back toward the gangbangers.

Sam looked over his shoulder and saw that the La Quinta was in sight but the Hummer was not. Sam and Chet slung their doors open, leaped out with their rifles in hand, ran to the back of the car, and took cover behind the trunk. The gang members at the center support and on top of the overpass concentrated a steady stream of fire on the Galaxie. Sam and Chet returned fire as best they could while keeping themselves low.

Suddenly, gunfire erupted from the top of the embankment which was behind Sam and Chet. Sam braced for the lead that would surely rip through his body. But none came. He glanced around and saw Elliot and Tiff, both lying prone on top of the embankment, firing at the gang members. Sam and Chet increased their rate of fire, emptying all four magazines for their two rifles. They then pulled their side arms and continued firing.

Two of the three men on top of the overpass were hit. One fell over the side rail and hit the pavement below. The third man began running east on Virginia, away from the firing. One of the three men below was hit in the back before he could dash behind the center support. His two friends continued firing but Sam could tell their enthusiasm was waning. Soon they stopped firing altogether and run back up Hartsfield.

Sam and Chet took the opportunity to race up the embankment where they joined Elliot and Tiff at the top.

"I'm out of ammo," Chet grunted as he plopped down next to Tiff.

"Me too," Sam said.

Elliot rose to his feet and started walking backward while still pointing his Glock toward the overpass. "There's ammo in the Hummer,"

Sam and Chet rose to their feet while Tiff remained prone on the ground.

"You guys load up," Tiff said. "I'll keep watch in case they decide to return."

Sam and Chet jumped up and ran back to the Hummer parked below the crest of the embankment. Sam rummaged in the back, flipped open an ammo can, and began filling his 5.56 magazines. Chet did the same. And they both placed extra rounds in their pockets.

"What about 9mm? Sam asked.

"Sorry, fresh out of nine," Elliot responded, as he holstered his Glock and picked up an automatic rifle from the rear of the Hummer.

Sam looked to the west. "I can see the Huddle from here."

Elliot yelled for Tiff as he, Sam, and Chet got in the Hummer. Tiff came running, hopped in, and Elliot jammed the fuel pedal. Tiff reloaded her magazines and stuffed extra rounds in her pockets.

Sam pointed to the top of the Huddle Hotel. "Shit! Gang members are firing on the compound from the top of the building."

"They'll be firing on us any minute," Chet said.

Elliot whipped the wheel to the right and headed off toward a Ruby Tuesday's restaurant which was basically on the La Quinta property. "We'll ditch the Hummer and head in on foot."

As they approached the restaurant, Sam lost sight of the gang members firing from the south side of the Huddle roof because of the angle, but he could still hear the firing. "If we can't see them, they can't see us."

Elliott slid to a stop against the east wall of Ruby Tuesday's and everyone piled out.

"This way," Elliot said, as he took off around the north side of the restaurant. "Keep your eyes open."

As they were running, Sam noticed blood on Chet left arm. "Are you hit?" he asked Chet.

"Just grazed, I'll be fine."

The bleeding didn't seem bad, so Sam turned his attention back to his surroundings.

Elliot left the cover of the Ruby Tuesday's building and ran to another small restaurant building, a steakhouse, on the other side of Taffy Terrace, the last building between them and the Huddle. Sam, Chet, and Tiff followed one at a time. They each plastered themselves against the east wall of the steakhouse and began inching along the wall in single file. Elliot peeked around the northeast corner, and then continued around the corner, and on along the wall. Sam, Chet, and Tiff followed close behind. At the northwest corner, Elliot stopped. He turned his body so his stomach would be against the wall and then eased one eye around the corner. After a few seconds, he moved slightly back and turned his head to face Sam.

"Nothing between here and the Huddle's side entrance. Hopefully, the door is unlocked."

Sam nodded. Elliot took off running. He covered the two hundred feet of open territory in a few seconds and slammed to a stop against the Huddle's east wall, next to the side entrance. He peeked in the entrance and then motioned for the others to follow. Sam, Chet, and Tiff hustled across the open area and bunched up next to Elliot.

"No one in sight down the hall to the lobby," Elliot said, as he pulled on the door handle. "Locked," he whispered.

Elliot eased down the wall to the southeast corner of the building, followed by Sam, Chet, and Tiff. Elliot peeked around the edge and then pulled his head back. "I count six out front. No telling how many are in the lobby. Any thoughts?"

Chet wiggled closer. "Two of us work our way around the north and west side of the building. If either of those doors is open, we'll go in. If not, we'll continue to the southwest corner and have the main entrance in a crossfire."

"I like it," Sam said. "I'll go with Chet."

Elliot and Tiff nodded.

Sam and Chet hustled down the east side of the building, rounded the northeast corner, and dashed to the center set of double doors. Sam stopped at the edge of the doorway and took a quick look. Sam brought his right hand up with his thumb and index finger together so Chet could see, indicating no people in sight. Sam stepped quickly to the doors and pulled on both handles. Locked. He continued down the north wall followed closely by Chet and stopped at the north-west corner long enough to check around the edge. Sam then continued to the west side entrance where he pulled on the door handle. Locked.

Sam and Chet moved to the southwest corner. Sam carefully peeked around the edge and saw the six men Elliot had seen.

Sam pulled back from the corner. "How do you want to play this?"

Chet inched up to the corner, looked around, and then backed up. "You go high, I'll go low. Elliot and Tiff will start firing when we do. Watch the collateral damage; we don't want to hit them and vice versa."

Sam nodded and moved up to the corner. Chet did the same but kneeled next to Sam's legs. They both eased the barrel of their rifles around the corner and took careful aim. Sam and Chet both fired within a second of each other and kept firing. Two of the six fell to the ground immediately. Another grabbed his shoulder and got behind a car parked near the entrance.

Elliot and Tiff opened up before the other two gang members had a chance to move. They both went down. A final shot took out the wounded man from behind. All six were down.

Sam and Chet rushed forward and converged with Elliot and Tiff at the main entrance. Sam slung the door open, and all four stepped inside with weapons shouldered. The lobby was empty.

"Stairs at both ends," Elliot whispered. "I say we go straight to the roof." He motioned for Sam and Chet to go west down the hallway. Elliot and Tiff headed east.

Sam opened the stairwell door at the west end, did a quick sweep with his rifle, and then stepped in, followed by Chet.

"You think they heard the firing down here?" Chet asked in a whisper.

"No doubt. They'll be expecting something."

With extreme vigilance, Sam and Chet made their way up the seven flights of stairs until they were standing at the door to the roof.

"They'll be covering the doors," Chet whispered.

Sam nodded and then paused a few seconds thinking. "I say we go prone and reach up to turn the knob.

"Might work," Chet said, as he squatted and then went prone facing the door.

Sam did the same. They both had their rifles pulled back along their sides, fingers on the triggers, ready to thrust the barrels forward as the door opened. Chet reached up with his left arm, turned the knob—

"Wait!" Sam said. "This is too cumbersome. I'd rather be on my feet."

Chet took his hand off the knob and was about to rise up when gunfire erupted and rounds blasted through the door, about mid-level. After a few seconds the firing stopped and suddenly the door jerked open. Two gang members on the roof fired again through the open doorway before they realized Sam and Chet were lying prone. They stopped firing for a split second to adjust their aim. That was all the time Sam and Chet needed. They both twisted slightly, which brought their barrels up, and opened fire. The two gang members were cut down instantly.

Sam and Chet then jumped to their feet, scrambled through the doorway, and took cover behind a large air conditioning unit. Six more air conditioning units occupied the center of the roof along the entire length of the building, leaving the outer edges open. While Chet kept watch, Sam took the opportunity to switch magazines and top off so he had a full thirty rounds in each mag. Then Sam kept watch while Chet did the same.

Fully loaded, they were about to inch around the unit when gunfire opened up from the north side of the roof and rounds started pinging against the air conditioner. Some rounds passed through the unit above Sam and Chet's head. They ducked lower. Then more gunfire opened up from the south edge of the roof. Sam and Chet were pinned. The gunfire was so fierce there was no way they could get any shots off.

"This is not how I imagined this going," Chet yelled over the gunfire.

Sam glanced back. The door to the roof was still standing open. "Let's slide back through that door. The concrete door frame will give us better cover."

Chet motioned for Sam to go first.

Sam wiggled himself backward, staying as low as possible, and used the two dead gang members as cover. Once he was back inside, he jumped to his feet and was able to dart his head back and forth to get a better idea of from where the gunfire was coming. He brought his rifle up and started returning fire.

Chet slid himself backward through the doorway and stood up against the opposite frame which meant he'd have to shoot left handed to keep from exposing his body. He switched the rifle to his left hand, brought the barrel up, and started firing.

There appeared to be two gang members on the north edge and two more on the south edge. All four were behind air conditioning units and all four were aiming at Sam and Chet.

Suddenly, Sam saw Tiff crawl out to the far north edge of the roof. She had no cover. But she did have an excellent firing angle on two of the gang members. Sam stopped firing. An instant later, Tiff began blasting away until both gang members were down. Sam heard several more bursts of gunfire from the south edge. And then all firing stopped.

Sam and Chet eased forward, rifles shouldered. Sam went left; Chet went right. They each met Tiff and Elliot in the middle. The roof was clear.

"Anybody hurt?" Elliot asked.

Sam looked at Chet. He wasn't bleeding any more than he was before. "We're okay."

"I suggest two of us watch the doors for any unwelcomed company," Elliot said.

Chet and Tiff each moved back to their respective doors. Sam joined Elliot on the south side of the roof edge and looked out on the compound. A contingent of about eight gang members had made their way into the north side of the compound and had taken cover behind various items of equipment. They were firing on the guardsmen who were barricaded inside the open hangar. A larger contingent of gang members was advancing from the runway side of the compound toward the hangar. The guard was reduced to using small arms since they were cut off from the fifty caliber mounted Hummers parked on the tarmac.

Elliot pointed to the south contingent of gang members. "I say we take out those guys from behind and then commandeer one of the mounted Hummers."

Sam looked at Elliot. "Is that the best you got?"

Elliot perused the landscape for a few seconds before answering. "Yep."

"We better get moving then. Chet and I will meet you in the lobby."

Elliot nodded and dashed toward the east stairwell. Sam joined Chet and filled him in on the plan as they carefully made their way down the west stairs. Sam and Chet stopped at their room and grabbed several boxes of 9mm and then continued to the lobby. Elliot and Tiff were waiting. They all four took a few minutes to load up their sidearm magazines with 9mm and top off their rifle magazines. They then stepped through the front doors after checking the outside.

There was no opposition as they made their way through the hotel parking lot, out the main drive, and onto Airport Loop Road. They spread out in single file as they hurried down the road toward the hole in the fence.

"So, we just pour through the fence?" Chet asked Sam in a whisper. "We'll be sitting ducks."

"From what we saw from the hotel roof, they are mostly bunched up behind some barriers at the north edge of the tarmac about fifty yards west of the hole. If we can make it through the fence, we should have a good firing angle on their position."

"I say two of us continue down the road and come in from the west," Chet said.

Elliot and Tiff were stopped at the hole when Sam and Chet jogged up.

"How about if you two hold up here for a couple of minutes," Sam whispered to Elliot and Tiff. "Chet and I will climb the fence further down and we'll have them in a crossfire."

Elliot and Tiff nodded. Elliot held up two fingers and then pointed for Sam and Chet to proceed. Sam and Chet took off at a low trot being ever vigilant for stray gangbangers.

On the west end of the tarmac, directly across from the guard hangar, stood a parking lot and a smaller hangar. The parking lot contained several abandoned vehicles. A fence continued down the west side of the tarmac in front of the smaller hanger and the parking lot. Climbing the fence at the corner of the road and the parking lot would leave Sam and Chet exposed at the top of the fence, but only for a second. They could quickly drop down and take cover behind the equipment and supply containers stored in that corner.

Just as Sam and Chet reached the corner and were trying to decide how best to climb the fence, gunfire erupted from Elliot and Tiff's position. The two minutes were apparently up. Sam and Chet took advantage of the distraction to scamper over the fence and work their way through the equipment to a forward firing position.

When they made it to the final piece of equipment, an aircraft dolly, Sam had a clear view of the entire battle scene. The gang members at the north and south ends of the tarmac had the guard pinned down inside the hangar. Numerous guard soldiers were sprawled on the tarmac in front of their hangar.

"They must have caught them by surprise," Sam whispered to Chet.

"Payback for their last encounter."

Sam also saw that the field hospital building was riddled with bullet holes. The building was constructed of thin plywood so the rounds would have gone straight through. Sam thought about Jeffries.

The smaller group of gang members had turned their full focus to Elliot and Tiff when they started firing. The backs of the gang were to Sam and Chet but they were mostly protected by concrete barriers and a few pieces of equipment. Sam and Chet did not have a clear shot.

"Elliot and Tiff's ammo won't last forever," Chet said. "We need to move."

By moving, Chet meant running across a fifty-yard area of the tarmac that would leave them completely exposed should the gang notice their approach. They would also be seen by the gang members on the south side of the tarmac. The range would be well over two hundred yards but easily doable with rifles.

Sam thought about how Chet, being an army grunt, was apparently more comfortable rushing machine gun positions. Sam, not so much.

Chet pointed to the fence running along the north end of the tarmac. "Stay to the fence so we avoid Elliot and Tiff's fire. Move fast and stay low."

Sam just nodded.

"Got to go now," Chet said, as he turned and took off across the tarmac with his rifle shouldered.

Sam was right on his heels. Elliot and Tiff obviously saw Chet and Sam rushing forward because they paused their firing for a few seconds, long enough for Chet and Sam to cover the distance. They quickly ran up on the gang members who still had their backs turned to Chet and Sam. At point blank range, Sam and Chet opened fire and caught the gang members completely by surprise. All eight of them were down and out in a matter of seconds.

Elliot and Tiff took off running to join them and slid to a stop as rounds from the south gang members pinged off the equipment.

Tiff got to a crouch behind one of the concrete barriers within shouting distance of Sam and Chet. "We can occupy two Hummers," Tiff said, as she pointed to Sam. "You and Elliot drive. Chet and I can shoot."

Sam and Chet nodded and then Sam looked at the Hummers parked fifty yards away. They would be completely exposed to gunfire, but given the distance, it would take a lucky shot to do any damage. Elliot motioned, and all four took off running for the nearest mounted Hummer. Sam could hear rounds buzz by. Several hit the surrounding tarmac. Finally, all four slammed into the side of a Hummer.

Chet slung the door open and checked the turret. "This one's loaded," he said as he crawled in.

Elliot and Tiff ran to the next Hummer and crawled in. Elliot slid behind the wheel while Tiff scrunched up into the turret and loaded the fifty. "Loaded!" she yelled.

Chet did the same with his fifty as Sam started the vehicle.

"Ready?" Sam yelled.

"Go!" Chet replied.

Sam put the truck into gear and stomped on the fuel pedal. The Hummer lurched and then sped away heading directly for the gang members on the south side. Rounds from the gang started pinging off the truck but Sam kept barreling forward. Sam glanced to the side and saw that Elliot and Tiff's truck was keeping pace.

Suddenly, both fifty caliber machine guns opened up—loud and continuous. Most of the hot brass spewed far out to the right of the Hummer but a few rained down and bounced around the cockpit near Sam. He drove straight for the gang.

Sam saw sparks and splatters of red as fifty caliber rounds shredded equipment and the bodies taking cover behind it. Gang members dropped. Some tried to run. Against the far superior firepower, they didn't have a chance. Tiff and Chet picked them off one by one until none of them were left standing. Then the machine guns ceased firing.

***

As before, Toothpick caught the entire scene from the top of the Vacation Suites. He lowered his binoculars and dropped his chin to his chest. "The same three," he said. He looked at the man standing next to him. "Not possible." Toothpick returned his gaze to the scene below. "Topper, how is this possible?" he yelled. "Three men and a woman scatter our people guarding the rear, take out our people on the Huddle, and then save the day at the compound. Four people." Toothpick shook his head back and forth as he dropped his chin to his chest.

Topper stood speechless.

"Take them all out!" Toothpick grabbed Topper by his lapels. "I want it done tonight."

Toothpick released Topper's lapel and then turned back to the scene. Topper motioned for three men standing nearby to follow him. The four of them marched away.

***

Sam and Chet stepped from the Hummer as Byers, Harvey, and two other men approached. Other guardsmen spread out to attend to the wounded.

Harvey shook hands with Sam. "Talk about the cavalry. Thanks." Harvey then shook hands with Chet.

Sam turned to Byers. "Hope we didn't screw up your plan, colonel."

Byers' jaw tightened and then relaxed. "Not this time, major."

The other two guardsmen stepped forward and shook hands with Sam and Chet. "I think we are all glad you showed up when you did," one of them said,

Tiff and Elliot joined the group. Elliot scanned the remaining guard troops.

"I count maybe fifty guardsmen," Elliot said. "Where is everybody?

"Out of over two hundred, this is it," Lieutenant Harvey said. "Most never came back from patrol. We figure they deserted. They went home to their families when they realized they couldn't make a dent in what's going on here."

"We're pulling back tomorrow," Byers said. "Atlanta is lost."

Harvey motioned to the guardsmen sprawled on the tarmac. "We were in the process of packing up when the attack came. We'll be taking our dead back home to be buried."

Sam glanced at Chet and Tiff. "We'll be heading out tomorrow."

Chet and Tiff nodded and then Tiff looked at Elliot. Elliot let out a slow breath but didn't say anything.

"I guess we'll head back to the room and start packing," Sam said, as he took a step.

Byers turned to Sam. "Major—" Sam stopped. "Colonel."

"We have more Hummers than we have drivers. Take one of the transport models. We'll load you up with fuel and provisions."

"Thank you, colonel. We appreciate that." He shook hands with Byers who then turned and walked off. Sam turned to Harvey. "By the way, how's Captain Jeffries?"

"Still in bed. Infection. I believe he's doing better today."

"Thanks. We'll stop by and say hello."

"I'll be heading back to Valdosta in the morning if anyone wants to tag along," Harvey said.

"Thanks, but we're headed in the other direction," Sam said, as he nodded and stepped off with Chet, Tiff, and Elliot toward the hospital. "We'll see you in the morning," Sam said, as he glanced over his shoulder back at Harvey.

Chet pointed to the holes in the wall as they approached the door. "This place was shot to hell."

Sam opened the door, and they all stepped in. They immediately notice the debris scattered everywhere, obviously from the bullets flying through the building. They found Jeffries sitting up in bed.

"How did you survive this?" Sam asked, as he approached Jeffries' bedside.

"On the floor," Jeffries said, as he recognized Sam. "How are you guys doing?"

"Having our share of fun," Chet answered.

"You're bleeding," Jeffries said.

"Just a scratch."

"Yeah, my scratch turned into an infection," Jeffries countered. "Let's have the doc take a look."

Jeffries yelled for the doctor.

A major wearing a white coat walked over. "Yes, captain. What now?"

"My friend here is bleeding; please take a look and get him fixed up."

"Let's have a look," the doctor said, as he took Chet by the arm and marched him into another curtained off area.

Tiff stepped forward to Jeffries. "I hear you're heading home tomorrow."

"That's what they tell me," Jeffries said. He pointed to Elliot. "Who's your friend?"

Elliot stepped up. "Detective Paul Elliot, Metro PD. I've been advising the colonel."

"Gangs?" Jeffries asked.

"Right. Haven't been much good though. They've still managed to take over most of the city."

They chatted a few minutes more and then Sam looked around the room. "We need to scoot, where's Chet?" Sam said. "We'll be heading out in the morning as well."

"Right here," Chet said, as he stepped out of the curtained area. His arm was bandaged, and he carried a bottle of pills.

Jeffries looked at Sam. "Transportation?"

"The colonel was kind enough to give us a Hummer," Sam replied. "He has more of them than he has drivers."

"You guys take care," Jeffries said.

"You too," Sam replied, as he, Chet, Tiff, and Elliot stepped out of the hospital and began walking toward the Huddle.

"I'll get the Hummer from Ruby Tuesday's," Elliot said.

Tiff touched his shoulder. "Mind if I tag along."

"Not at all."

At the driveway for the Huddle, Sam and Chet peeled off while Tiff and Elliot continued walking down the road.

"I'll catch up with you guys shortly," Tiff said.

Sam waved while he and Chet continued across the Huddle parking lot toward the building.

"What do you think?" Chet asked.

"I think we pack up, eat something, and be ready to move out at first light," Sam replied.

At the front doors to the Huddle, Sam raised his rifle to his shoulder as he stepped over the dead gang member bodies. "There could be more shitheads around."

Chet raised his rifle and followed Sam into the lobby.

Sam swept his rifle in a wide arc. "Seems clear," he said, and then lowered his rifle. They proceeded up the stairs.

CHAPTER 13

Tiff and Elliot crossed over Taffy Terrace and then entered the La Quinta property. They walked through the parking lot and into the grassy area on the west side of Ruby Tuesday's, where they left the Hummer. Tiff saw that the Hummer was right where they left it. As they walked through the grass, Tiff swiveled her head side to side but saw nothing that raised an alarm.

"I say we head back to the Huddle and eat something," Tiff said, as they approached the Hummer.

Elliot reached for the driver's door handle. "Okay," Elliot said, as he smiled. "And maybe afterward we can go somewhere."

"One of these hotel swimming pools would be nice," Tiff responded. "I could use a bath."

With Tiff standing beside him, Elliot opened the driver's door. Tiff's mind didn't register what she saw. Crunched in front of the seat and under the steering wheel was a man—pointing a large caliber automatic pistol. Before either Tiff or Elliot could move, the man pulled the trigger. Elliot was immediately knocked back from the blast. He stumbled and fell to his knees as the man began crawling out.

"Paul!" Tiff yelled, as she brought her rifle up.

Three men with handguns jumped from bushes nearby and started running toward Tiff before she knew what was happening. When the fog cleared in her mind and she realized she was surrounded, she lowered her rifle.

The man raised his hand to the other three men so they wouldn't shoot. He finished stepping out of the Hummer and then took Tiff's rifle and her XDs. He then bent down and removed Elliot's Glock and picked up his rifle.

"Hello, detective," the man said.

Elliot winced as he looked up at the man. "Hello, Topper."

Without concern for what the men might do, Tiff dropped to her knees beside Elliot. She immediately placed her hand on his shoulder where blood oozed. "Paul!" she screamed. Elliot turned his head toward her. His eyes were glazed, but at least he was alive. Tiff got up, ran to the back of the Hummer, and returned with a medkit. She unzipped the bag and retrieved a gauze pack which she tore open. She placed the gauze against his wound and then lifted his shoulder slightly.

"Looks like the bullet passed through," She whispered.

"No shit," Topper said, as he towered over Tiff and Elliot. "It wasn't my intention to kill him."

Tiff looked up at Topper.

"I want your people to know what happened. They'll come looking for you."

Topper motioned to his three men. They stepped forward and jerked Tiff to her feet.

"Tie the bitch up, we're taking her in the Hummer."

Tiff struggled to stay next to Elliot, but the men dragged her toward the Hummer. Two held her while the third man rummaged in the back of the Hummer. He found some cord and wrapped it around Tiff's wrists pulled behind her back.

She kept her eye on Elliot who was pressing the gauze against the wound.

"Let them know where to find us, detective," Topper said in a calm voice. "We'll be waiting."

Elliot stared up at Topper but didn't say anything. Tiff kept her eyes locked on Elliot as the three men pulled her into the back of the Hummer where she could no longer see Elliot.

She then saw Topper slide into the driver's seat. He started the engine and pulled away.

The only thing Tiff could think about was Elliot lying on the ground bleeding, and she wondered if she would ever see him again. She wondered if she would see any of her friends again.

***

"Where the hell are they; I'm getting hungry," Chet said, as he looked out the hotel window.

"I hear them coming down the hall," Sam said, as he stepped to the door.

Sam opened the door and paused as his brain registered the scene. Elliot was partially bent over. His face grimaced with pain. And his left arm dripped blood.

Sam grabbed Elliot by his good arm and helped him into the room. "What the hell happened?"

Chet rushed into the hallway, looked up and down the hall, and then turned back into the room. "Where's Tiff?"

Elliot maintained pressure on his shoulder as Sam helped him sit on the edge of the bed. "They took her."

"Who took her?" Chet yelled.

"They call him Topper. He's number two with the Bloods around here. He works for a psycho they call Toothpick."

"Toothpick?" Sam asked.

"Yeah, they all seem to have a nickname," Elliot said. "Toothpick is actually fairly husky except for his skinny legs. Thus the nickname."

"Was she okay when you last saw her?" Chet asked.

"Yeah, they won't hurt her until they're done with all of us."

"Why did they take Tiff instead of just shooting both of you dead?" Sam asked.

"Because they know we'll come for her," Elliot replied. "They obviously want all of us."

Sam stood straight. "Payback."

Elliot grimaced with pain as he tried to move his shoulder. "Correct. Toothpick probably watched as we disrupted his plans today."

"Do you know where to find him?" Chet asked.

"I Do," Elliot replied.

Sam lifted Elliot to a standing position. "First thing is to get you to the hospital. You can tell us on the way."

***

"He's not going anywhere right now," the doctor said, as he put the finishing touches on the bandages to Elliot's arm. An IV line led from a bag of clear liquid down to Elliot's arm. "He's lucky there's no major damage."

Sam rubbed his entire face with his hand and then stared at Elliot. "Tell us again where we can find this Toothpick guy."

"Without me, you won't get within three blocks," Elliot responded.

"Clearly, you won't be going," Sam said.

Lieutenant Harvey walked up. "What happen?"

"Some guy named Toothpick happened," Chet said. "He shot Elliot here and took Tiff."

"Toothpick—the Bloods?" Harvey asked.

"That's the one," Elliot replied.

"Why did they leave you alive?"

"Because they want us all—the four of us," Elliot said. "They probably blame us more than any others for the massacre they suffered. They took Tiff knowing we'd come after her."

"I'll round up some crews and we'll take the mounted Hummers," Harvey said. "Captain Jeffries is supervising the load up but I'm sure he can spare some men for a good cause."

"If they see anyone other than us three, they'll kill Tiff," Elliot said. "The only thing we'll find is her dead body."

"It doesn't look like you're in any shape to travel," Sam said.

Elliot started to rise up as he reached for the IV needle stuck in his arm. "Watch me."

The doctor placed his hand on Elliot's chest and pushed him back down to the gurney. "If you try to move, you'll start bleeding again."

Elliot stopped struggling against the doctor and appeared to relax a bit.

"What about tomorrow morning?" Sam asked. "Your unit is supposed to pull out."

The doctor turned to Sam. "We need to play that by ear. Let's see how he's doing in the morning."

Sam patted Elliot on his good shoulder. "Rest easy my friend. We need time to figure this out, so you might as well remain here for now."

Chet stepped closer to the gurney. "Elliot, what kind of reception can we expect?"

"Toothpick will have enough men to do the job. But he's probably thin on manpower. He lost a bunch here. Plus, he needs men at the food distribution centers."

"How many?" Chet asked.

"He probably has ten or twelve with him. That includes Topper—the one who shot me and took Tiff."

"How much time do we have?" Harvey asked.

"They know I needed treatment. My best guess… if they don't see us approaching by tomorrow afternoon, they'll kill her and move on. Keep in mind—we've not been very good at anticipating Toothpick's actions." Elliot paused for a few moments. "There is one thing. He likes being up high so he can see the action."

"Okay, tell us again where we can find these guys," Sam said. "We need to make a plan."

"Toothpick knows I'll look for him in Trinity Heights, the high rise projects. That's his turf. He'll make himself easy to find. And of course, he'll be waiting for us to take the bait."

***

Sam, Chet, and Harvey stood next to a table in the open hangar pouring over a map.

Harvey jabbed his finger at a spot on the map. "Trinity Heights."

Sam leaned closer and examined the area on the map. The buildings appeared to be situated in a large open area surrounded mostly by parkland. "How many stories?" Sam asked.

"Four buildings," Harvey replied. "Each in the shape of a cross. Ten stories each. And each building has two entrances, one each on opposite sides."

Chet leaned closer to study the map. "Four buildings spread over several acres. No communications. They can't watch and report to Toothpick on every road approaching the area."

"And there are a lot of parks and wooded areas all around," Sam said. "Offers good access." Sam rubbed his face with his hand. "What we need is Intel," he mumbled.

"I might have the ticket," Harvey said, as he turned and walked to a nearby Hummer loaded with equipment. He pulled a large metal box from the back of the Hummer and set it on the ground. Sam and

Chet joined him and watched as Harvey bent down and opened the box.

When the lid flew open, Sam was looking down on a high-tech drone, painted black, along with all the necessary associated equipment.

Chet whistled. "Does this thing still work?" he asked.

"It was shielded. It works."

Harvey pulled the combat drone from its Styrofoam cutout. "They might see it during the day. But not at night."

"Infrared?" Sam asked.

"Yes. And plenty of range."

Harvey handed the drone to Chet and then reached back in the box. He came out with a control box that included a small monitor. "Pretty much self-contained."

Harvey flipped a switch on the control box and then pushed a toggle forward. The drone immediately came to life with propellers spinning and leaped up from Chet's hand. The drone came to a hover about five feet above Chet's head.

"She's quiet," Sam remarked.

"And fast," Harvey said, as he pushed two toggles. The drone raced out of the hangar and came to a hover over the center of the tarmac.

"There's no time like the present," Sam said.

Harvey nodded, looked back to the control box, and flipped another switch. The monitor on the control box emitted a dull green glow and displayed the ground directly beneath the drone.

"Just like night-vision goggles," Chet said.

CHAPTER 14

The room stank of body odor and flickered with the dull light of a single candle. Tiff was squared off against Topper as best she could with her hands tied behind her back. Her eyes were slits, teeth and jaws clenched, and the muscles in her neck, shoulders, and arms flexed. All she could think about was tearing Topper from limb to limb for shooting Elliot. She thought about Elliot lying in the dirt, blood oozing from his shoulder, and how he might be dead. She wasn't worried so much about her own predicament, just revenge.

Topper stood in front of her with two other men behind him. His eyes were wide with anticipation.

The only thing stopping him from pouncing on Tiff was the tall man standing to one side.

"Nobody touches her!" the man said. "She needs to be in one piece until I get my hands on the other three. Then, she's yours."

Despite the still dire circumstances, Tiff relaxed a bit. The corners of her mouth turned up slightly as she continued to stare at Topper.

Topper turned away and motioned for the others to do the same.

The man in charge stepped closer to Tiff. "They call me Toothpick."

Tiff said nothing.

"You killed my crew."

Tiff said nothing.

"You killed my brother."

Tiff looked up. "Your brother?"

"At the fence."

Realization spread over Tiff's face. She said nothing.

Toothpick stepped closer. "You're screwed," Toothpick said, as he cupped one of her breasts in his hand. "But not before we enjoy every part of your body." He slid his hand to the other breast and then down to her crotch. "Soon after your people come for you." His rankness was almost debilitating. Tiff turned her head away.

"They won't be coming," Tiff said. "I barely know them."

Toothpick removed his hand. "Detective Elliot is gonna come for you, and he'll bring the others. Right now, they're chilling on his wound. Once he's patched up he'll be along. If not tonight, certainly by tomorrow."

Tiff glanced out the window next to her into the pitch darkness outside. "How will they know where I am?"

"Detective Elliot will know. He's been here before."

"What if he brings more friends than you expect?"

Toothpick stepped back. "He won't. He knows I would just kill you before they get within a mile. It will be just the three of them."

Toothpick turned to Topper. "Give this bitch some water."

Topper retrieved a bottle from a half-empty case, unscrewed the top, and poured the water into her upturned mouth. He poured slowly at first, but then he upended the entire bottle. The water sloshed over her face and soaked her t-shirt. Her breasts and nipples became more visible. Topper licked his lips and winked.

Toothpick pointed up. "Go make sure the crew ain't lacking," he said to Topper.

Topper picked up an M16 style rifle leaning against the wall near the door and left the room.

***

Harvey pointed at the soft green image on the drone control box. "There's only one building with men on the roof."

Sam leaned closer. Green blobs stood out from the darkness of the building's roof around them. "I count four men... five, one more just came out from that door."

Chet looked up at Harvey. "Those extra men you mentioned?"

"I'll go and I'm sure I can get a few others," Harvey replied.

"We have an advantage... communication," Sam said. "We'll be able to coordinate."

Harvey pushed a toggle on the control box and the building image on the monitor left the screen. "Need to bring it back for recharge." He flipped a switch. "It will automatically come back home."

At that moment Captain Jeffries, with one arm in a sling, walked up. "I'm going to split the convoy going back. Half leaves with me first thing tomorrow morning. The other half, including the ambulance and the doc, can follow under your command." He pointed to Harvey.

"Thank you, sir," Harvey said.

"You'll have two mounted Hummers at your disposal. And there will be an extra transport Hummer for Sam, Chet, and Tiff that the colonel promised."

"Thank you, captain," Sam said.

"Least we could do. If I don't get a chance to see you again before we leave, you take care. I hope you make it to where you're headed."

Sam and Chet shook with Jeffries' good hand.

"You too," Sam said. "We appreciate your help."

Jeffries nodded at Sam and Chet and then turned and marched off.

"We need a plan," Chet said, as he turned back to the map table.

***

"Comm check," Sam said into his mini-mic, as he bounced around in the back of a mounted Hummer. Chet sat in the front passenger seat across from a driver. A gunner occupied the M2 turret.

"Lima charlie." Harvey's voice came through loud and clear in Sam's earpiece.

Sam's Hummer pulled to a stop next to another mounted Hummer in the heavy forest. The Hummers were nearly invisible in the pitch dark. Sam and Chet stepped out of one; Harvey and Sergeant Forsyth stepped from the other.

Harvey walked up to Sam and Chet. "We're a mile out and we have one hour to sunup."

"Elliot is going to be pissed," Chet said, as he shook his head.

"That's the third time you said that," Sam said. "We get it."

"The Hummers will wait here until we call them in," Harvey said, "if we need them. We're on foot."

Harvey stepped out followed by Sam, Chet, and Forsyth.

"We need to be in that building before the sun," Sam whispered to Harvey.

Harvey glanced at Sam, nodded, and kept his pace forward.

Twenty minutes later, they were at the edge of a clearing. Sam could see the looming dark hulks of the Trinity Heights buildings in the distance. There was no light from any of the windows which gave the buildings a sinister appearance. Sam thought Stephen King should consider these buildings for a backdrop in his next book.

Sam glanced over to Harvey and Forsyth as they slung their rifles over their back and drew their side arms. Each produced a suppressor from a pocket. Sam heard the sound of metal on metal as they screwed the suppressor to the barrels. Harvey swiveled his head for a final look,   popped up, and began low trotting across the open field toward the nearest building. Forsyth followed close behind. Sam and Chet stepped out on their heels. Halfway across the open field, Harvey and Forsyth split off. Each headed for opposite sides of the building. Sam followed Harvey; Chet followed Forsyth.

Fifty yards from the nearest corner, Harvey stopped and took a knee. Sam pulled up and crouched beside him.

In his earpiece, Sam heard Forsyth's voice squawk. "Alpha 1, fifty out. Two at the door."

"Copy," Harvey whispered. "Two more at my door."

Harvey looked around at Sam. "Ready?" he whispered.

Sam nodded.

Harvey keyed his mic and brought his pistol up. "Taking them out now." His pistol spit twice with reports louder than Sam expected. Both men at the door went down. Sam raised an eyebrow, impressed by Harvey's accuracy. Sam wouldn't want to compete in a shooting tournament against him.

Sam heard two muffled shots from his left and then Forsyth's voice. "Two down. Oscar mike."

"Copy," Harvey replied.

Harvey stood up and raced to the door followed closely by Sam. Both gang members were sprawled on the concrete. Dark viscous pools ebbed under their heads.

"Feels too easy," Sam whispered. Sam could just make out Harvey's head nod up and down in the dark as he reached for the handle on the glass door.

Harvey let go of the handle and stepped back to the concrete wall next to the door. Sam moved to the wall on the other side of the door.

Harvey whispered into his mini-mic. "Alpha 2. How's it look?"

No answer.

"Alpha 2?" Harvey whispered again.

Sam heard Forsyth's voice. "Two down. Ready for entry."

"Recommend maximum force," Harvey said into his mic.

***

From inside the lobby, Topper saw two flashes through the glass doors and his men outside fall to the ground. A few seconds later he saw the dark silhouettes of two men approach the glass doors from the outside. Topper elbowed the man standing to his left and right. All three raised their rifles and waited. The silhouettes suddenly backed away from the door and moved to the side, out of sight. Time passed in slow motion as Topper waited for the shadows to reappear. Thirty seconds passed — then forty-five, then sixty. Something wasn't right. Topper elbowed his men again as he started to step backward. Suddenly, a massive explosion, from down the hall shook the entire building. Topper dove behind a large potted palm tree just as a second explosion ripped through his lobby doors throwing glass, metal, concrete, and heat into the room. Deafened by the blast, Topper heard the muffled blasts from semi-automatic gunfire. He pressed his face deeper into the cold tile floor. And then all went quiet except for the muffled sound of boots crunching on broken glass.

Topper remained still as he tried to shed the fog from his brain. He heard muffled voices and more boots crunching on glass. He didn't feel any excruciating pain, so he rolled to his side and was about to get up when he came face to face with the barrel of an automatic rifle only inches from his nose. He froze.

***

"Two dead," Harvey said, as he moved through the lobby.

"I have one alive," Sam said, as he pointed his rifle at the man's head.

Sam heard Harvey speak into his mini-mic. "Alpha two, report."

"Entrance successful," Forsyth answered in Sam's earpiece. "Three dead."

"Two dead here, one alive," Harvey said. "Hold your position."

Harvey looked out the doorway for several moments and then walked over to where Sam stood. Harvey pressed the tip of his barrel into the man's temple. "Where's the girl?"

Sam saw a confused look on the man's face. "I don't think he can hear," Sam said.

Harvey bent down closer and pressed his barrel harder. "Where's the girl?" he yelled.

Sam saw the man's eyes focus on Harvey.

"He heard that," Harvey said. Harvey stood up straight and brought the barrel of his rifle to rest on the man's left knee. He pressed hard. "Where's the girl?" he yelled again.

The man winced as he stared at Harvey.

Sam jumped at the sudden blast from Harvey's rifle. Blood oozed from the kneecap as the man screamed in pain.

"Where's the girl?" Harvey yelled.

"Now he can't hear again," Sam said.

"He can hear enough," Harvey replied, as he moved the barrel of his rifle to the man's right knee.

"Top floor," the man mumbled through gritted teeth.

"Which room?" Harvey asked.

"Southwest corner," the man said, as he rocked back and forth holding his knee.

"How many men?"

"Two in the room," the man grunted.

"Alpha 2," Harvey said into his mini-mic.

"Copy," Forsyth replied in Sam's earpiece.

"Top floor, southwest corner room, two men reported. Expect more.

"Copy. Oscar mike."

"Copy," Harvey replied, as he started toward the stairwell door with his rifle shouldered.

"What about him?" Sam asked, pointing to the man sprawled on the floor.

Harvey stopped and looked back at the man on the floor who was grasping his knee with both hands as he rolled around on the floor in agony. Harvey brought his rifle down and fired one round. Topper fell back lifeless. A small amount of blood seeped from a hole in his forehead. "Desperate times," Harvey said, as he continued to the stairwell.

Sam paused for a moment, shocked at Harvey's brutality. He looked at Harvey and then back down to Topper.

"You coming?" Harvey asked.

"Right behind you," Sam replied.

Sam caught up just as Harvey opened the stairwell door and stepped inside.

"These shitheads killed a lot of my friends," Harvey whispered.

Sam nodded and stepped carefully up the stairs behind Harvey.

At each landing, Harvey opened the door, checked the hallways, and then continued up the stairs.

***

"Your people are on their way," Toothpick said to Tiff, who was still tied up but now sitting in a corner.

"You could always give up," Tiff said.

Toothpick moved over to the window and peered outside. The sky was getting light. "Not happening." Movement at the tree line caught his attention. He kept his eye on the spot. After a few moments, he saw a man step out wearing a red bandana around his arm, then another man, and another. Soon, there were twenty-two men low trotting across the open field toward the main entrance. Each carried a rifle.

Toothpick turned back from the window and looked down on Tiff. "Not happening," he repeated.

***

Harvey froze on the fourth landing and looked back at Sam. "Did you hear that?"

Sam cocked his ear. After a few seconds, he was about to reply when he stopped short and cocked his ear some more. "I heard it. Stepping on glass. They're moving up behind us."

"My thoughts exactly," Harvey said. "Let's keep moving."

Harvey stepped off at a faster pace. Sam followed. By the sixth landing, the sound of footfalls on the steps below was unmistakable. Sam detected a lot of feet and they were practically running. Harvey began taking steps two at a time. Sam remained close. At the tenth and final landing, Harvey stopped. He cracked the door and checked the hall. Nothing. "Alpha two, status?" Harvey said into his mic.

Forsyth's voice squawked. "Coming up on eight. Negative on any Hadji so far."

Harvey keyed his mike. "On ten. We have multiple bogeys coming up our six. Recommend you check your six and then charlie mike."

"Copy, alpha one."

Sam looked at Harvey. "Hadji?"

"Desert lingo for bad guy," Harvey replied. "Forsyth will continue with the mission. We need to hold off these guys coming up."

"Roger that," Sam said, as he stepped to the door and pulled it open a crack. "We'll need a back door."

He stuck his head out and looked down the interior hall. Gunfire erupted. Sam felt the whoosh of rounds before they started ricocheting off the wall and floor around him. He slammed the door shut. "We won't be going this way anytime soon."

Harvey motioned at the stair railing. "Let me know when they get to nine." He pulled his last hand grenade from his vest and put his finger through the trigger ring.

Sam moved to the railing and looked over the side. He could see men coming up on the eighth landing. One guy stuck his head out and looked up. He and Sam locked eyes. The guy smiled. "They're at eight," Sam said, as he jerked his head back.

Sam listened to the footfalls getting closer until finally, they were at the landing immediately below. He motioned to Harvey. Sam watched as Harvey pulled the pin and rolled the hand grenade down the stairs. Harvey dove to the floor and covered his ears with his hands. Sam followed suit and tried to sink into the concrete to get as low as possible. A few seconds later a concussion wave from the blast pushed against Sam's temples and he felt debris land on and around him. He opened his eyes. Thick white dust drifted in the air and settled on a bloody forearm only inches from his nose. The forearm wasn't attached to a hand or an elbow. Sam thought about what Chet and Tiff said about this trip starting to get real and he wondered if any of them would ever make it to Tennessee.

***

"Considering you guys don't have explosives, sounds like the homie team may not be doing so well," Tiff said.

"Shut that bitch up," Toothpick said to the only other man in the room. The man, covered in tattoos, and a gold earring in each ear, walked over and slapped Tiff across the face.

Tiff returned to a sitting position as best she could, considering her hands were still tied behind her back. The man returned to his position near the door.

Toothpick opened the only window in the room and looked out. The sun was up and the open field was empty of people. He walked to the opposite side of the room and picked up a coil of rope along with a short piece of two-by-four and returned to the window. He tied one end of the rope to the center of the board and then threw the coil of rope out the window. He placed the board across the window opening to secure the rope. He then drew a pistol from his waistband and walked toward Tiff.

***

Forsyth cracked open the door to the tenth-floor hallway. About halfway down, what would be the center of the building, he saw three men barricaded and pointing rifles in the opposite direction. Forsyth took the last hand grenade from his vest, pulled the pin, and rolled the grenade down the hall. Forsyth closed the door, covered his ears, and motioned for Chet to do the same. After the explosion, Forsyth cracked the door and looked out. The hallway was filled with smoke, debris, and a collapsed ceiling. One of the three men was sprawled on the floor not moving. The other two were covered with white powder and were trying to stand up.

Forsyth sprang through the door and rushed forward followed closely by Chet. Forsyth fired two bursts from his rifle. The two gangbangers fell back lifeless. Forsyth pressed on past the remains of the barricade toward the southwest corner of the floor.

Sam and Harvey stepped into view from the stairwell door at the other end of the hall and converged with Forsyth and Chet. The four of them hustled to the last room at the southwest corner of the building and stopped outside the door.

***

Toothpick pointed his pistol at Tiff's head and smiled. Tiff drew her feet close to her butt and curled into a ball. But she kept her eyes on Toothpick.

In her peripheral vision, she saw the tattooed man run to the window and take hold of the rope. He clambered through the opening and disappeared below the window sill. The two-by-four flexed slightly from his weight on the rope.

Toothpick glanced at the window. In that split second, Tiff shot both legs out and caught Toothpick in the kneecaps. Toothpick stumbled back but remained standing.

At that instant, the door burst open and Harvey rushed in. He immediately fired two rounds into Toothpick who fell to the floor at Tiff's feet.

Sam rushed over, placed two fingers on Toothpick's neck for a few seconds, and then pulled his knife. He cut the rope binding Tiff's hands and pulled her to her feet. "You okay?" he asked.

She hugged Sam and then pushed back nodding her head up and down. "Where's Elliot?"

Chet stepped forward. "We came without him; left before he could complain."

"He's back at the field hospital," Harvey said. "He'll be fine."

CHAPTER 15

Late the next morning, Sam, Chet, Tiff, and Elliot, with his arm in a sling, stepped from the field hospital just as Lieutenant Harvey pulled up with a transport model Hummer. They met Harvey as he hopped out of the vehicle.

"Compliments of Lieutenant Colonel Byers," Harvey said, as he waved his hand at the Hummer. "She's fueled, packed with MRE's, and the doc provided an expanded med kit that includes antibiotics, just in case. There's extra ammo. And there's the radio. Range is only ten clicks but it might be useful."

"We can't thank you enough," Sam said. "When this is over I'll make sure you get your truck back."

Harvey smiled and then looked at Elliot. "Captain Jeffries pulled out early this morning, and I'm about ready to head out with what's left of the convoy, where can we drop you?"

"Thank you lieutenant, but these guys are letting me tag along. I'll be going with them."

"Are you sure?" Harvey asked. "We're in no hurry, and we'd be glad to drop you anywhere and help get you situated."

Elliot glanced at Tiff and then back to Harvey. "Divorced, no kids. The only thing keeping me here was the job, and now that's gone. I might as well move on. Maybe I can help."

"The air force and army appreciate the help you gave us," Harvey said. "Maybe we did some good."

"Maybe," Elliot said.

Engines started and Harvey glanced at the line of Hummers behind him. "Looks like we're oscar mike. Good luck. You know where to find me if you're down around Valdosta."

Everyone shook hands and Harvey jogged off toward the lead Hummer.

"I guess we should stop by the room and load our gear," Sam said.

Chet slid behind the wheel, Sam took shotgun, and Tiff and Elliot crawled in the back.

***

Sam stared out his window as the Hummer crept along the broad highway. The light breeze coming through the opening did little to alleviate the sweat rolling down his neck. *Uncomfortable,* he thought, *compared to the air-conditioned relative luxury he took for granted only days earlier, but still light years better than what most were feeling these days.* The number of people leaving Atlanta had increased even more. Masses shuffled along with what they could carry and lined both sides of the road. Most looked dejected — probably not sure where they were going. They all looked up as the Hummer passed. Many waved for the Hummer to stop. Some even tried to block the truck with their bodies.

Chet slowed but never took his foot off the fuel pedal. When the people realized Chet wasn't stopping, they moved out of the way.

"I feel terrible for these people," Tiff said. "What will happen?"

"There's nothing we can do to help them," Chet said. "If they expect to survive they each must find a way."

"That seems cold," Tiff said.

Chet glanced back at Tiff. "It is cold. If the last few days have taught us anything it's that we're going to have to get downright frigid to survive."

"Some will have the drive," Sam said. "We need to make sure we're among them."

Everyone withdrew to their own thoughts.

Once they were through the metro area an hour later, Chet was able to maintain a moderate speed as he drove up Interstate 75.

"Tell me about this cabin of yours," Elliot said.

Sam glanced back at Elliot. "It's in the mountains south of Knoxville, not too far from Gatlinburg, just outside a small town called Townsend. It's a two bedroom with a detached garage and pump house sitting on ten acres. The nearest neighbor is half a mile away. There's a year-round stream that runs through the property."

"Sounds nice. Do you plan to just camp out until the lights come back on?"

"Well, Tiff has her Mom and Dad in Ohio. If she doesn't mind I thought we could stop by the cabin and then head on up to do what we can for her parents."

"I appreciate that," Tiff said.

"Is there anyone at the cabin now?" Elliot asked.

"Not supposed to be," Sam replied. "But who knows? I plan for us to go in quietly."

"At this speed, we'll be arriving in the dark," Chet said.

"We'll play that by ear," Sam responded.

"I know you guys arrived from down south with Harvey, but where are you from?"

"Daytona Beach area for me and Chet," Sam said.

"Orlando," Tiff said.

"And the cabin is a second home?" Elliot asked.

"Well, more of a bug out location," Sam said. "My brother and I inherited it from my parents. They both died in an accident when I was ten. My brother and I were raised by an uncle who is also deceased now. My dad actually built the cabin."

"Brother?"

"Yeah, lives in St. Louis."

"That place must be a real mess about now," Elliot said.

"No doubt," Sam said. "He has more in St. Louis to keep him there—wife, kids, wife's family. But who knows, they may all end up at the cabin at some point."

***

Several hours of creeping along put them past Chattanooga, and Chet was able to increase speed.

After a couple of those hours with not a lot of chatter from the back, Sam glanced in the rear and watched as Tiff put her hand to Elliot's forehead. "Elliot has a fever," she said. She then looked into Elliot's eyes. "You're shivering."

Sam checked the side mirror, glanced left and right, and saw they were on a deserted stretch of the highway. He motioned to the right. "Let's pull over for a while and get him some air and water."

Chet drove off the road, through a grassy area, and turned off the engine under the shade of a large oak tree. "Let's see what the doc provided for us in that med kit," he said, as he stepped out of the Hummer.

Sam followed. Chet opened the rear and extracted a large red nylon bag. He unzipped the bag and started rummaging.

"We have a couple of different antibiotics," Chet said. "Pills. The most powerful seems to be Cipro."

Sam stuck his hand in the bag and pulled out an IV kit. "We have a couple of IV antibiotics as well."

Tiff helped Elliot out of the Hummer, walked him over to the base of the tree, and sat him down. She walked back to the Hummer and then returned to Elliot with a camouflage poncho liner and a bottle of water. She wrapped the liner around Elliot's shoulders and gently laid him back against the tree. Elliot continued to shiver. She opened the bottle and had him take some sips. She then walked over to Sam and Chet. "Let's try the Cipro."

Chet dumped a pill into Tiff's hand. She walked over to Elliot and helped him swallow the pill with a few gulps of water.

"I'm thinking maybe we should stay here for the rest of today and tonight," Sam said to Chet.

"I was thinking the same thing," Chet said. "We'll see how he's doing in the morning."

Sam reached into the Hummer and pulled out four MRE packs. "He probably should eat something.

None of us have eaten much in the last couple of days."

Sam and Chet walked over to where Tiff sat with Elliot.

"We're thinking we should stay here for tonight," Sam said. "Give Elliot a chance to rest, eat, drink, and let the pills work."

Tiff nodded. "Good idea."

Chet started back to the Hummer. "Mosquitoes will carry us away. We'll need the tents."

"Actually, Tiff and Elliot can sleep in one of the tents," Sam said. "So he can lie flat. You and I can sleep in the Hummer. We'll be able to keep a better eye out that way."

Chet nodded as he pulled one of the tents from the back of the Hummer and started putting the tent poles together near Tiff and Elliot.

Sam opened one of the MRE's, sorted through the contents, and handed Tiff the peanut butter and crackers. "See if he'll eat something."

"You know, I'm right here, quite capable of understanding basic instructions," Elliot said.

"You need to eat something," Sam said.

Tiff spread some peanut butter on a cracker and handed it to Elliot. Elliot moved his head back and forth. "Not really that hungry."

"You need to eat something with that pill. Otherwise, it will do a number on your stomach."

Elliot took the cracker and nibbled at the corner while Tiff prepared another cracker.

Chet moved closer to Sam. "We have some people approaching."

Sam looked down the highway and saw two adults—a man and a woman—and two children, probably early teens. They weren't carrying a lot, and they did not appear to be armed.

"Great," Sam muttered.

The group stopped when Sam and Chet started walking toward them.

Sam put his hands up, palms facing the people. "We're harmless."

The man and woman visibly relaxed a bit and started walking to meet Sam and Chet.

"Are you military?" the man asked.

Sam glanced back at the Hummer. "Kind of. Where you folks headed?"

"Not sure," the man replied. "Not safe at home."

"Where's home?" Chet asked.

"This side of Cleveland… Tennessee, just down the road."

"Why did you leave?" Sam asked.

"Too many assholes with guns," the woman replied. "They are taking what little there is and shooting anyone who gets in their way."

"I have a sister in Chattanooga," the man said.

"The larger cities are even worse," Chet said. "Gangs."

The man winced and looked at his wife. "We have nowhere else to go."

The woman put her arm around her daughter. "Why isn't the military doing something?"

"What would you like the military to do?" Chet asked.

"I don't know… something!"

"We tried, in Atlanta," Sam said. "There are just too many people, too few resources, and way too many assholes with guns."

"Can you spare some water?" the man asked.

"Sure," Sam said, as he glanced at Chet.

Chet walked toward the Hummer.

The man pointed at the Hummer. "Does she work?"

"She does," Sam said.

Chet returned with four bottles of water which he handed out to the people.

The man looked up at the sun, removed his hat, and scratched his head with the same hand. "Hot one, even for August."

"It is," Sam said.

The man replaced his hat, took a swig from the bottle, and then screwed the cap back on. "I guess we should keep moving."

"Thanks for the water, mister," the youngest child said.

"Not a problem. You folks take care."

The family continued walking toward Chattanooga. Sam and Chet returned to Tiff and Elliot under the tree.

"What do you think?" Elliot asked.

"They're harmless... just a family on the move," Sam replied.

"I mean about staying here tonight," Elliot said. "Maybe we should move on as well."

"There's no telling what we'll find at the cabin," Sam said. "I think it would be better for you to rest up for tonight. Hopefully, you'll feel better tomorrow."

"I agree," Tiff said. "You need to rest. And you need to eat some more." She shoved another cracker with peanut butter at his mouth.

Sam looked at Chet. "No fire tonight. I think you and I should split staying awake."

Chet nodded. "Where's those MRE's?"

***

Sam was able to make out details in the landscape as the first rays of light filtered through the trees. He stepped from the Hummer and stretched. Chet stepped from the Hummer, yawned, and then headed off toward some bushes fifty yards away.

Sam turned his head to the tent at the sound of the zipper.

Tiff stuck her head out. "Morning."

"How's he doing?" Sam asked.

"Still some fever but not as bad," she replied. "I think the Cipro is working."

"He needs that bandage replaced."

Elliot crawled out. "Morning," he said.

"Morning," Sam replied. "How are you feeling?"

"Like crap," he said as he sat back against the oak tree.

"Well, at least you're talking, and you look better," Sam said.

Tiff proceeded to remove the bandage from his shoulder.

Sam knelt and leaned in to get a better look at Elliot's wound.

"The doc did a good job on the stitches," Sam said.

"The wound is a little red, but otherwise looks okay," Tiff said.

"Do you feel like traveling today?" Sam asked Elliot.

"I'm fine," he replied. "We need to get moving."

"We will," Sam said. "As soon as the nurse gets you fixed up."

Tiff washed the front and back of his shoulder with Betadine, applied a fresh dressing, and then helped Elliot put his arm back in the sling. Sam handed items to Tiff during the process.

"I need to visit the little boy's room," Elliot said.

"Do you need help?" Tiff asked.

"Yeah, do you need help?" Chet asked with a smirk as he walked up heading back from the bushes.

"No, I can handle it on my own."

"I'm sure you can," Chet said. He winked at Tiff.

Tiff frowned at Chet and then helped Elliot to his feet. He walked off toward the bushes.

"What's the plan?" Tiff asked.

"Break down the tent and get moving," Sam said. "We can eat something in the Hummer."

By the time Elliot returned, Tiff and Chet had the tent down and packed. Sam sat in the passenger's front seat looking at a map as Chet, Elliot, and Tiff settled in their seats.

"Which way?" Chet asked as he started the engine.

"I say we turn off at Lenoir," Sam said. "We can take country roads all the way from there. We'll be bypassing Knoxville."

Chet nodded as he put the Hummer into gear and pulled out on the road.

"I'm surprised at the number of people we're not seeing out here," Tiff said.

"They're not going to find a lot of food out here along this highway," Chet said.

"Makes sense," Tiff said.

Chet kept the Hummer at a moderate speed, weaving around stalled cars when necessary.

Sam focused on the map. "We're coming up on Cleveland," Sam said. "But we're fairly far to the west, so we should bypass a lot of whatever is going on in the city."

They cruised past both of the Cleveland exits with no problems. Chet pressed on.

"How are we doing on fuel?" Sam asked.

"A little more than half," Chet replied. "Maybe we should fill up while we have all these diesel trucks to choose from."

Tiff leaned forward in her seat. "And it will give us a chance to go potty."

Chet came to a stop next to several stalled trucks and everyone hopped out. Sam grabbed the siphon hose from the back while Chet poured one of the five-gallon cans of diesel into the tank. Soon, the tank was full, the fuel cans were full, and all bladders were empty.

Two hours later, Chet took the highway 321 exit at Lenoir, curved around the off-ramp, and then accelerated on the four-lane highway heading east. They passed several gas stations and fast food restaurants, but not a lot of people. The few people they did pass just stood gawking as the Hummer went by.

"Our turnoff is in Townsend," Sam said. "About twenty-five miles. Through Marysville."

"It's beautiful up here… and cooler," Tiff said.

"And the people are nice, or at least, they were," Sam said.

Chet glanced back. "They could all be zombies by now." He smiled.

"I'd like to stop in Townsend and get an idea of what's going on up here," Sam said.

"Think it's a good idea to stop with the Hummer?" Elliot asked. "Any type of authority will want to commandeer a running vehicle."

"I know the police chief," Sam said. "But you're right. We can park outside of town and I'll walk in."

"How about if we leave Tiff and Elliot with the Hummer," Chet said. "You and I can walk in."

"Even better."

Forty minutes later Sam pointed to the side of the road. "Pull off over here and into the forest a bit. The police department is about two miles down."

Chet slowed, pulled off, and drove into the forest a hundred feet. "We should be good here."

"How long do we wait?" Tiff asked.

"If we're not back in two hours, something's up," Sam replied.

"And then what?" Elliot asked.

"I'd recommend you wait until dark and then head in on foot," Sam said.

"Or we could just keep driving to Ohio," Tiff countered.

Sam detected a slight smile on Tiff's face. "Or you could continue to Ohio."

Chet threw Tiff a dirty look. Tiff smiled.

Sam and Chet exited the Hummer.

"Sidearms only?" Chet asked.

Sam thought for a moment. "Probably a good idea." Sam smiled as he glanced at Tiff. "We always have Tiff and Elliot for backup."

"Hurry back guys," Tiff said. "I'd like to get Elliot into bed."

Chet rolled his eyes.

"You know what I mean," she said.

"We know exactly what you mean," Chet said.

With a wave and a smile, Sam and Chet started off toward the road and quickly disappeared into the foliage. At the edge of the road they stopped and checked both ways. There were no people in sight. They stepped onto the road and started walking into town. Sam thought it was odd that there were no people around. Except for an occasional lifted blind in a window or the corner of a curtain pulled back slightly, Sam couldn't detect a sign of anyone.

"Seems pretty quiet," Chet said.

"Yeah," Sam nodded. He glanced around. "I can think of only one reason why at least some people wouldn't be out."

"Not safe," Chet said.

"Exactly."

CHAPTER 16

Two men standing and talking in front of the police department turned toward Sam and Chet as they approached. The bigger man—early thirties, toothpick in his mouth, and wearing jeans, a stained T-shirt, and a large automatic pistol on his side—stepped forward with his hand up. The other man—younger, also in jeans and a T-shirt—put his hand on the revolver holstered to his side.

"Hold up there, gents," the bigger man said.

Sam and Chet stopped, about ten feet back. "Looking for Chief Daniels," Sam said.

"You won't find him here," the bigger man said. "Who are you two?"

Sam raised his hand. "Sam. This is Chet."

"Howdy," Chet said.

"Where can we find Chief Daniels?" Sam asked.

The younger man snickered. "The chief met with an unfortunate accident."

The bigger man put his hand on his pistol. "Sam and Chet, what brings you to Townsend?"

"I own property around here."

"Really, whereabouts?"

"Around here," Sam repeated. "So, who's in charge?"

The bigger man shuffled his feet a bit. "I'm Dan Jones. This is Tony Smith. I'm in charge."

"Jones and Smith," Chet said. "You don't look like police officers."

"Self-appointed," Jones said. "How did you get here?"

"Walked," Chet said.

Jones pulled his pistol and pointed it at Sam and Chet. "Enough chit-chat. This is a gun-free zone. You'll have to give up your weapons."

Smith pulled his revolver and pointed it at Chet. "Starting with you."

Sam caught Chet's eyes. Chet shrugged his shoulders. They both raised their hands.

Smith stepped forward and removed their pistols from their holsters and their knives from their sheaths.

Jones motioned with his pistol. "Inside."

Sam and Chet walked forward with Jones and Smith following. Sam opened the door and stepped into the police department, followed by Chet and the two men. Sam immediately saw a large stain in the middle of the floor. *Could be blood*, he thought.

Jones pointed to a hallway. "Just walk straight back."

Sam and Chet, hands still in the air, did as they were told. The hall opened into a large room that contained two holding cages.

"Take a seat in the cage on the right," Jones said.

Sam and Chet stepped into the cage, lowered their hands, and sat on the metal bunk bed. Jones closed and locked the door.

"Now, where's this place of yours and how did you get here?" Jones asked.

Sam and Chet looked at each other and then stared back at Jones and Smith without saying a word.

"Look, this will go a lot easier if you just answer our questions," Smith said.

"Where is everyone?" Sam asked.

Jones holstered his pistol. "Those that cooperated are in their homes."

"And those that didn't cooperate?" Chet asked.

"In a hole," Smith answered with a laugh.

"So that's your choice," Jones said. "In your home or in a hole."

***

"Something's wrong," Tiff said. "It's been well over two hours."

Elliot's eyes blinked open, and he started to sit up. He winced and sat back in his seat.

"How are you feeling?" Tiff asked.

"I've been better, but I'll do."

Tiff opened the door to the Hummer and stepped out. "It's almost dark."

Elliot sat up again and winced. He paused a few moments and then opened his door.

"Where are you going?" Tiff asked.

"With you," Elliot replied.

"You'll just slow me down. Plus, someone needs to watch over the Hummer."

Elliot sat back in his seat. "You can't go alone."

"Why not?" Tiff asked. "They're probably just lost."

"If you're not back in a couple of hours, I'll be looking for you."

"Fair enough," Tiff said, as she checked the chamber on her XDs. She holstered the pistol and took a long swig from a water bottle. "I'll be back as soon as possible, hopefully with the guys in one piece."

Tiff made her way through the brush and stepped out on the highway. She looked at the last of the sun peeking through the leaves and started walking down the road. She kept her head on a swivel. There were no people about and all the buildings were dark.

Once in town, she moved from sign to sign. With very little light, she had to get close to read each one.

Finally, she found one that said *Police Department* with an arrow pointing to the right. She walked down the single lane drive until she saw a dim light flickering from the window of a building up ahead. A sign out front identified it as the police department.

There was a large building across the street, what appeared to be a school. The ground around the police department was completely open on three sides. The fourth side, the far side, had brush and trees to within a few feet of the building's wall.

Tiff took a knee behind a small bush so she could see the front of the police department and the light flickering in the window. After ten minutes with absolutely no activity, Tiff low trotted to the side of the building and ducked under the window with the flickering light. She popped her head up for a moment and saw several desks, filing cabinets, and a counter facing the front entrance, but no people. The light was coming from a hallway.

She stepped carefully as she inched her way along the wall toward the rear of the building. The elevation dropped away in the back. The windows were on the second level, well above her head. She noted some metal stairs leading up to a second-floor door and then continued to the forested side of the building. There were several windows on the far wall but all were dark. She crept forward and stopped at the southwest corner, the front of the building.

She took a step to round the corner but immediately jerked back. Standing on the sidewalk, less than twenty feet away, was a man visible in the moonlight who apparently did not hear her movement.

The man flicked a lighter and brought the flame to a cigarette wedged between his lips. Given the brief additional illumination, Tiff's mind registered only two characteristics: grungy T-shirt and a revolver in a holster on his side.

The man took long drags from the cigarette and stared up at the cloudless sky as Tiff considered the situation. Bad guy or good guy? Unknown. How many were in the building? Unknown. Were Sam and Chet even in the building? Unknown. Tiff decided to err on the side of caution.

She eased her pistol from its holster, stepped out from the building, and padded across the grass, almost on tiptoes. She was within five feet when the man whipped around, saw Tiff, and started for his revolver.

"Don't," Tiff said, as she shook her head side to side and pointed her pistol with both hands at the man's head. "Two fingers, take it out slow."

A sarcastic expression spread over Smith's face. "And if I don't?"

"I'll shoot you and move on to whoever's next," Tiff replied. "Your choice."

Smith's sarcastic expression faded. He flipped the cigarette away and then used his right thumb and index finger to extract the revolver from the holster.

"Toss it on the ground," Tiff said.

Smith complied. "Now what?"

"Turn around and down on your knees."

Smith took his time turning around. "This is not going to work out well for you lady."

"Knees."

Smith went down on his knees.

"How many are inside?"

Smith snickered. "More than you can handle."

"How many?"

Smith grinned as he shook his head. In the dim light of the moon, she could see his eyes wander from her eyes down to her breasts and then back to her eyes. He smiled.

Tiff walked up and smacked Smith on the side of his head with her pistol. He crumpled to the ground, out cold. Tiff holstered her pistol, grabbed Smith by the feet, and dragged him to the side of the building. She removed his shoelaces, rolled him to his stomach, and tied his hands and feet. She then tore the bottom half of his T-shirt off and used it to gag him. She threw his revolver into the bushes.

Tiff returned to the sidewalk and then hurried to the front, mostly glass, entrance. The inside was dark except for a faint, flickering light coming from down the hall. Tiff eased the door open, stepped inside, and paused to listen.

Tiff heard a man's voice from down the hall. "We've waited long enough. You either tell me how you got here or we take you out back."

Tiff then heard a familiar voice. "Like I said, we walked," Chet said.

"Have it your way," the man said. "Tony, where the hell are you?" he yelled.

Tiff heard footsteps coming down the hall. She stepped into the hall and saw a man silhouetted by the faint light from behind. She pointed her pistol at him.

"Tony is indisposed," Tiff said. "Now back up!"

Jones raised his hands and stepped backward. "Who are you?"

"A friend of the two you have back there," Tiff said. "Who are you?"

"I'm the police chief and you're in a lot of trouble."

"Bull shit! Back up!"

Jones backed into the room, lit by a couple of candles, and stopped in the middle of the floor.

"Uh-oh, he went and pissed her off," Chet said to Sam.

Tiff took careful aim at Jones' forehead. "Two fingers, remove the pistol."

Jones pulled the pistol from the holster and placed it on a desk nearby.

Sam and Chet stood in their locked cage and watched.

Tiff glanced at Sam and Chet. "You guys okay?"

"Yep," Sam replied.

Tiff looked back to Jones. "Keys!"

Jones hesitated a moment and then pointed. "They're in my pocket."

"Remove them… carefully."

Jones reached into his pants pocket and came out with a key ring full of keys.

"Place them on the desk and then step into the other cage," Tiff said.

"Where's Tony?"

"I said, in the cage!"

Jones stepped into the empty cage and pulled the door closed behind him. Tiff picked up the keys, moved to Jones' cage door while keeping her pistol pointed at him. She tried several keys until she found one that fit. She turned the lock and then tried the door to make sure it was secure. She kept her pistol on Jones while she walked to the other cage and handed the keys to Sam.

Chet looked at Sam. "This is getting embarrassing."

Tiff raised her eyebrows.

"I'd rather be embarrassed than dead," Sam said. He fiddled with the keys until he had the door open. "We owe you another one," he said, as he stepped out of the cage.

"You can pay me later," Tiff replied.

Chet followed Sam out of the cage. "What do we do with this guy and his friend?"

"The other one is out front, tied up," Tiff said.

Sam turned to Jones. "What happened to Chief Daniels?"

Jones sat on the bunk and said nothing.

Sam rummaged around the room until he found his and Chet's guns and knives. Sam walked over to the cage holding Jones and pointed his M&P. "What happened to the Chief?" Sam pointed his gun at Jones.

"We had a disagreement."

"What about his other officers… he had three?"

"Disagreement with them too."

Tiff moved closer to the hall and cocked her ear. "I hear voices."

"That will be *my* officers," Jones said.

Chet retrieved his Glock and took a position behind a desk.

Sam motioned toward a small hallway in the rear of the room. "There's a back door down this way."

Tiff followed Sam and Chet as they hurried down the hallway. They bunched together at a metal door at the end of the hall.

Sam pushed on the metal bar. "Locked." He still had the keys in his hand and fumbled with them trying to find the one that would open the door.

Tiff turned to face the holding room and raised her pistol expecting the men she heard to walk in any moment. She heard the keys jingle as Sam tried each key on the ring. Finally, she heard one slide into the lock. She turned back to Sam and Chet as Sam pushed the door open. Tiff followed Sam and Chet out the door to a metal landing. Metal stairs led to the ground, the same stairs she saw before. Sam closed the door and locked it with the same key. They ran down the stairs and trotted north across an empty lot to a line of trees. They took cover behind a clump of bushes.

"We'll have to deal with these characters eventually," Chet said.

Sam pointed to the silhouette of four men running down the side of the police department. They converged with two other men who had run down the other side.

"I don't think now's a good time," Sam said in a low voice.

"I second that motion," Tiff said. "Let's wait until they cool off some."

"And we're better armed," Chet added.

Sam turned and made his way farther into the trees. "This comes out on the highway," he whispered.

"Any sign they had a running vehicle?" Tiff asked.

"Not that we saw," Sam replied.

They came up on the highway and waited in the tree line long enough to make sure no one was around. Sam stepped out, followed by Tiff and Chet. They started walking west.

"Finding the Hummer in the dark could be a chore," Chet said.

"Just finding the spot where we pulled off could be a chore," Tiff added.

Twenty minutes later, they slowed to a crawl as they began searching for the spot where they pulled the Hummer into the woods.

"There's no way we can find the exact spot," Chet whispered. "Even with the moon, it's too dark out here."

"Keep looking," Sam said.

"Hey!"

Tiff jumped at the sudden voice from behind a tree.

"Dammit, Elliot…," Sam said.

"Sorry, you guys looked lost," Elliot said. "I thought you might have trouble finding the Hummer in the dark."

"Temporarily disoriented," Chet said.

"Thanks," Tiff said.

"How'd it go?" Elliot asked.

Sam stepped into the woods and stopped next to Elliot. "Not good. Shitheads have taken over the town."

"They killed the police chief and his three officers," Chet said.

Sam led the way through the woods. "If it wasn't for Tiff, we'd still be locked up… or dead."

"She saved your butts yet again?" Elliot asked.

"It's becoming a full-time job," Tiff said.

Sam stopped next to the Hummer. "Uh-huh."

Chet opened the driver's door and got in. "What now?"

"First, we get out of the mosquitoes," Elliot said.

Sam, Tiff, and Elliot got into the Hummer.

"I repeat—what now?" Chet asked.

"We can avoid the town," Sam said. "Side roads work their way around the south side. We'd have to do it without lights. Plus, we don't know what's waiting for us at the cabin."

"Wait here until morning?" Elliot asked.

"That would be my choice," Sam said.

Tiff snuggled closer to Elliot on the Hummer's rear bench seat and then slid her butt forward so she could rest her head on the back of the seat. She drifted off while the guys talked.

***

Squirrels rummaging in the leaves and barking at each other woke Sam. He opened his eyes to the light just starting to filter through the trees. He sat up in his seat and then poked Chet who was slumped against the door.

Chet opened his eyes, sat up straight, and put his hands on the wheel. "Where to?"

Sam opened his door and stepped out. "Let me make sure the coast is clear."

Sam stepped carefully through the woods. At the side of the highway, he scanned in all directions while he peed on the asphalt. He returned to the Hummer and slid into his seat.

He heard Tiff and Elliot move in the back.

"How's the arm?" Chet asked.

"I'm alive," Elliot replied.

Tiff sat up. "We need to replace that bandage before we start moving."

"Do it quickly. We need to be moving before anyone else," Chet said, as he stepped out of the Hummer. He walked a few feet away and relieved himself behind a bush.

Sam watched as Tiff grabbed the med kit from the back and went through the same routine as before.

"How's the wound?" Sam asked, as Chet got back behind the wheel.

"About the same, no worse," Tiff replied.

"There's no one about," Sam said. "We need to backtrack a bit and then we can take the back roads."

Tiff and Elliot opened their doors and stepped out. "Bathroom first," Tiff said.

With everyone back in the Hummer, Chet started the engine, put the truck in gear, and backed out the way he drove in. He backed onto the pavement, shifted gear, and then sped off to the west.

"There's a turn up here on the left," Sam said.

Chet slowed and turned down the road which was paved but barely more than a single lane. Sam gave directions as they slowly drove through thick forest and hills. There were no people or buildings along the side, just forest. Finally, they came up to an intersection and Sam stuck his head out the window to get a better look at the road sign. *Laurel Creek*. He motioned for Chet to turn left and then pointed to an almost immediate right. Sam glanced at the road sign as they rounded the corner. *Tremont Road*.

"The turn off for the cabin is about two miles up on the left," Sam said. "We'll pull off before that and go in on foot."

"This area is desolate now, it must have really been desolate when your father built the place," Elliot said.

"I was too young to understand much of anything back then but that's apparently what he wanted," Sam replied.

"Off the grid," Tiff said.

"That it is," Chet agreed.

"The last power line I saw was miles back," Elliot said.

"The cabin has a whole house generator," Sam said. "It runs on pretty much any kind of fuel. At least, it used to."

"Probably doesn't work now," Chet said.

"I didn't know they had those back then," Tiff said.

Sam glanced back. "My brother and I put it in about five years ago."

Chet motioned with his arm. "How much farther?"

"Pull off anywhere along here," Sam said. "The cabin is about half mile down."

Chet slowed, turned, and maneuvered around the trees until the Hummer could not be seen from the road. He clicked off the engine. "Honey, we're home."

Everyone got out and joined Sam who had walked a few feet away from the truck.

Sam motioned with his arm. "The cabin is that way."

"What about snakes?" Tiff asked.

"Oh yeah, watch out for snakes," Sam replied. "There are lots of them—copper heads and rattlers."

Sam watched Elliot take furtive glances around the area. Sam winked at Chet who glanced at Elliot and then smiled.

Everyone drank some water, grabbed their rifles, and then stood looking at Sam.

"Well?" Tiff asked.

Sam started walking, being careful where he placed each foot. The others followed keeping about ten yards between each person. Chet brought up the rear. They had walked about forty minutes when Sam raised his fist in the air. Everyone stopped. Sam hunched over and scurried back to Tiff. Chet and Elliot came up and joined them.

"The cabin is visible through the trees," Sam whispered. "Chet and I will go forward." He pointed at Tiff and Elliot. "You two stay back in reserve."

"You mean, in case we need to save your butts again," Tiff said.

Sam smiled. "That's right."

They all moved forward, using bushes and trees as cover. The tree line gave way to a small clearing beyond. Everyone took a knee. Sam scanned the area. The cabin, garage, and pump house sat in the middle of the clearing. There were no people in sight and there were no obvious signs that anyone had been there recently. Sam pointed at Chet and motioned for him to follow.

The two of them stood, shouldered their rifles, and dashed forward. The only sounds Sam heard were his and Chet's boots hitting the ground. Even the birds and squirrels stopped what they were doing to watch.

CHAPTER 17

Sam and Chet covered the open ground in seconds
and took cover behind the pump house. From the
pump house, Sam could see the back of the garage
and the back and north side of the house. There still
was no one in sight and no activity. In fact, the shovel
Sam forgot to put away the last time he was there was
still leaning against the north side of the house.

Sam motioned his intention to head for the garage
and then stood and raced off. Chet waited until Sam
plastered himself against the back of the garage and
then made his way to the southeast corner. Chet
rushed forward and joined him.

"I don't think there's anyone here," Chet said, panting.

"I think you're right."

Sam motioned again and then took off for the north side of the house. He came to a stop next to the only window on that side. Sam peered inside and saw no movement. He waved for Chet to move up. They both crept along the wall to the northwest corner of the house which gave them a view of the front entrance and the driveway.

"No tracks and no footprints," Chet whispered.

Sam nodded and then stepped on the front porch. Chet followed. Sam looked in both the front windows and tried the knob on the door. Locked.

Sam stood up straight and relaxed. "I think we're good."

Chet waved for Tiff and Elliot to join them. Tiff swept her head back and forth, keeping an eye on her surroundings, as she and Elliot walked to the house and joined Sam and Chet on the porch.

"Your dad must have liked wood," Elliot said. "The place is beautiful."

"Thanks," Sam said, as he dug into his pocket. He came out with a set of keys, inserted one in the door's deadbolt lock and twisted. The bolt clicked back. He then stuck a different key in the knob lock and turned. The door opened and everyone stepped inside.

"Excuse the mustiness," Sam said, as he stuck his head in each room for a quick inspection. "And the dust."

"Even if the generator works, I wouldn't recommend it," Elliot said. "Might draw attention to the cabin."

"Agreed," Sam said.

Tiff's shoulders slumped. "No shower?"

"There's a shower," Chet said. "You'll just need a bucket of water."

"Our water will come from the stream out back since the pump doesn't work," Sam said. "And we'll need to boil or filter before drinking."

Tiff, smiling, started for the front door. "Let's have a look."

Everyone walked out of the cabin, around the back, and continued toward the trees.

They had walked about fifty yards, with Tiff in front, when she glanced back. "I can hear the water."

A few more yards brought them to the edge of an embankment looking down on a crystal-clear, rocky stream, about fifteen feet wide and two feet deep in places. Tiff jumped down to the bank and stuck her hand in the water. "Chilly, but not too bad."

"It's okay this time of year once you're in there," Sam said. "I recommend bathing from a bucket."

"Of course," Tiff said. "Don't want to pollute the water."

Sam turned to the woods. "I'll get the Hummer."

"The rest of us can start hauling some water," Chet said.

***

Tiff put a bowl of rice on the kitchen table and then took a seat. "I think everything's ready."

Sam, Chet, and Elliot sat down and started spooning food onto their plates.

Chet was the first to take a bite. "Beans and rice have always been a favorite," he said, munching.

Elliot took a bite. "Just pretend the spam is steak and the canned green beans are fresh."

"It's better than MREs," Tiff said.

Elliot took a bite. "True," he mumbled.

Sam finished chewing. "About tomorrow…"

"I'm anxious to get started," Tiff said. "I'm worried about my parents."

"Do we need to leave someone here to watch the place?" Chet asked.

"I say we all go," Sam said. "The cabin has been okay this long—a couple of more days shouldn't matter."

"We get a good night's sleep and head out first thing," Elliot said.

Chet pointed to Elliot's sling. "How's your arm?"

Tiff spoke up. "I changed the bandage after we showered. It's no worse. He's feeling better, so the Cipro is working."

"How's the pain," Sam asked.

"Better," Elliot replied. "I can actually move my arm a little."

"Not too much... don't want to open those wounds," Sam said.

Elliot nodded. "Just wearing clean clothes again helps."

"I agree," Sam said.

Chet finished eating and slid his plate forward. "Tiff, you said your parents are in Lebanon, where is that in relation to Cincinnati?

"Ten miles northeast of the beltway."

"Two hundred miles straight up seventy-five," Sam said. "We should be able to do that in a day, easy."

"Lexington might slow us some," Chet said.

"Maybe, but the highway runs east of the main part of town," Sam said. "And then there's Cincinnati."

Elliot nodded, stood, picked up his plate, and took it to the sink. "I guess we need another bucket of water for the dishes."

Chet got up. "I'll get it." He walked toward the door. "In fact, we should put several gallons in the bathtub for flushing the toilet."

"Hold up," Sam said. "I'll give you a hand."

Tiff brought her plate to the sink and edged Elliot out of the way with her hip. "You can't wash with one arm."

"I knew there was something positive about getting shot," Elliot said.

Sam brought his and Chet's plate to the sink. "Two positive things."

Elliot turned to Sam and raised an eyebrow.

Sam thrust his chin toward Tiff who had her back to them.

Elliot smiled, nodded, and turned back to the sink.

Sam and Chet walked out.

***

Early the next morning, Sam was boiling water on a camp stove in the kitchen and Chet was sitting at the table when Tiff came in yawning. She wore a very short pair of cotton shorts and a cropped shirt that showed off her slim waist.

"Sleep okay?" Chet asked, with a smirk.

"Just fine," Tiff replied.

"And Elliot?

"He slept fine too."

Sam picked up the pot and poured the water into one cup. "Coffee? I had some instant in the cabinet."

"I think I'll pass," Tiff said. "I'm past the caffeine withdrawal and I don't want to get the addiction started again."

Sam set the pot back on the burner and handed the cup to Chet. "We need to head out as soon as possible."

"Eat, lock up, and we're out of here," Chet said.

Sam nodded. "Is Elliot up?"

"I'm up," Elliot said from the doorway. He was fully dressed in the tactical pants and black T-shirt from the night before.

"Coffee?" Sam asked.

"Nah, never really got into coffee," Elliot replied. "Weird for a cop, I know."

Tiff walked to the counter and started opening cabinets. "What do you have for breakfast?"

"Oatmeal," Sam said.

"Perfect," Tiff said. "I brought some raisins and nuts."

CHAPTER 18

Tiff stepped out of the front door carrying two backpacks and slung them into the back of the Hummer while Sam closed and locked the cabin door. They then joined Elliot and Chet already in the Hummer.

"Back the way we came," Sam said. "We can work our way around Knoxville and link back up with seventy-five the other side of Clinton."

Chet started the engine and pulled out.

"Stop on the road so I can brush away the tracks," Sam said.

Chet pulled out on the paved road and stopped. Sam got out, cut a small branch with his knife, and brushed his and the truck's tracks away so nothing was visible from the road. He waited until they were a mile down the road to toss the branch to the side.

Just before the first turn, two men came into view walking toward them on the road.

"That's my closest neighbor and his son," Sam said, pointing. "Maybe we can get the skinny on this place."

Chet slowed and came to a stop next to the men. Sam opened the door and got out.

He shook hands with the older man. "Hey, Dave."

He turned and shook hands with the younger man. "Bobby."

"Hey Sam," they both said, as they admired the Hummer.

"Where'd you get that?" Dave asked.

"Long story," Sam said. "Your old Chevy pickup should still work, why are you walking?

"It works fine," Dave replied. "Unfortunately, we lost it to the goons in town."

"You mean Smith and Jones?"

"Yeah, that's what they call themselves. They came into town three days ago with a bunch of their friends. Chief Daniels tried to keep them orderly, but he ended up losing his life instead."

"So they have a running vehicle?" Sam asked.

"They had one before, an old Ford. Plus, they now have my truck as well."

"Do they come out this far?" Chet asked from inside the Hummer.

Dave peered in the window.

"Oh, sorry," Sam said. "You remember Chet."

Dave stuck his arm through the window and shook hands with Chet.

Sam pointed in the back. "This is Elliot and Tiffany, two friends we're traveling with."

Dave waved. "Nice to meet you both." Dave turned back to Chet. "Not so far, but they do seem to be spreading out."

"Spreading out?" Sam asked.

"Everyone is supposed to centralize their food in town—for the good of the people," Dave said with sarcasm. "It's for the good of the goons."

"We're trying to round up some people to stop them," Bobby said. "You and your Hummer could help."

"We have an emergency to tend to in Cincinnati," Sam said. "It shouldn't take more than two or three days to get back. Can you hold off till then?"

"It's hard rounding up people on foot—only have us and John Williams so far."

"That's all?" Chet asked.

"Most people don't want to get involved. They're scared."

"I understand," Sam said. "Keep trying to round up more people and I'll get with you as soon as we return."

Dave's face drooped, and he stared at the ground.

"Two or three days," Sam repeated.

Dave looked up. "Okay, Sam. Hopefully, we'll still be here by then."

"I'm sorry Dave. This is something we just have to take care of."

"We understand," Dave said.

Dave and Bobby shook hands with Sam, waved at Chet, Elliot, and Tiff, and then continued walking.

Sam got back in the Hummer and closed the door. "Let's go."

Chet put the truck in gear and pulled away.

"I'm sorry Sam," Tiff said. "If you need to stay I can find another way."

"Or we could all just take care of the goons now," Chet said.

Sam did a full hand rub of his face. "Nah, we take care of Tiff's parents and then get back as soon as possible."

"And I'll be in better shape by then," Elliot said.

Sam nodded.

***

The drive toward Cincinnati was mostly uneventful. Sam spent a lot of the time staring out his window at the multitude of people walking along the highway. Each one, he noted, had an expression indicative of that person's place in the loss process. Some were still in denial. Those were the ones closer to home waiting for the power to come back on. It was inconceivable to those people that the power could be out for more than a few days. Even after the devastating destruction of a major hurricane in Florida, the power was always back on in a few days. After all, they would reason, the sun was shining as usual, the sky was blue—everything, except the lack of power, was normal. How could the lights not be back on soon?

And then there were the angry people. Those were the ones easiest to spot. Those were the husbands or wives stomping their feet and screaming at their spouse and the kids. They would lose their temper at the smallest things and throw or kick whatever was close. And those were also the looters, the ones who would throw a brick through a window, grab something, and run off.

Sam was surprised to see that even though it had only been a few days since the event, a lot of people had moved past anger. Those were the ones walking around with their eyes to the sky mumbling. Actually, they were talking to God. If only God would fix this mess, they would be a better person, they promised. They would stop their bad habits, go to church every Sunday, and give more of their time and money.

When that didn't work, people would understandably move to the next stage. And there were already some of those people walking around. Those were the ones shuffling their feet with their face to the ground, somber, dejected, and depressed. Those were the ones that probably would not make it very long.

Sam realized that many, including himself and Chet, had practically jumped to the last phase, by accepting the situation and making the best of it. Given the composition of those people, they could be preppers, those already well on their way to survival without invading other people's space, or they could be what Sam termed the gangbangers, goons, psychos, and shitheads. Sam, Chet, Tiff, and Elliot were in the prepper category, even if by accident. Just having the cabin, a vehicle that ran, and their guns and ammo put them way ahead of the vast majority of other people. The gangs in Atlanta and the goons in Townsend were at the psycho end of the scale. Of everyone walking around, the psychos, Sam knew, were the dangerous ones. Those were the people Sam would try to avoid if possible but kill if needed.

So far they had come close to killing people outside the psycho category only once, and that was today when they stopped to siphon fuel and refill their tanks, just north of Lexington. People crowded around the Hummer much faster than they anticipated. Chet had commented that they must have thought the military had arrived. But once they realized Sam, Chet, Tiff, and Elliot were not the military and were not there to help them, they instantly skipped forward or reverted back to the angry stage. Sam and Chet had just finished filling the tanks when the crowd of about thirty people—men, women, and children—pressed forward. Everyone yelled and screamed; some waved rifles and pistols in the air. They were rocking the Hummer back and forth and banging on the windshield making it difficult for Sam and Chet to get in and close the door. Things were about to get out of hand when Tiff stuck the barrel of her rifle out the window and fired several rounds in the air. That startled the crowd just long enough for Sam and Chet to hop in and slam the door. The crowd was resuming its rampage when Chet started the engine, slammed the gear shift, and slowly drove forward dividing the crowd like a herd of cattle. That was the first time Sam thought their expedition could actually be derailed. He hoped it was the last.

***

"Cincinnati coming up," Chet said. His voice brought everyone out of their reverie. "Which way?"

"East on the beltway," Tiff said. "Around to highway forty-two."

"What can we expect?" Sam asked.

"Don't have a clue," Tiff answered.

Chet continued weaving around stalled cars and disoriented people until he veered off on the two-seventy-five ramp. And then there was more of the same—stalled cars and disoriented walkers. It took well over an hour to drive the thirty-five miles on the beltway to the highway forty-two off-ramp. That's when things got dicey.

Sam tightened his grip on his rifle as he stared out the window. People were everywhere, running back and forth, screaming, yelling, fighting—it was complete chaos. Looting had obviously been rampant. Remnants blanketed the strip mall parking lots— glass, cardboard boxes, broken jars of food, all manner of appliances, stalled cars, and even a body lay scattered.

The only thing that stopped the bedlam, if for only a moment, was when people stopped to gawk at the Hummer as it passed. After the two seconds it took for the shock to dissipate, chaos resumed with renewed vigor—directed at the Hummer.

It was a stampede of people, a wall of human flesh, converging on the Hummer. This was much worse than Lexington. Body parts—hands, feet, and even heads—pummeled the truck.

Tiff and Elliot sat wordless, frozen by the scene. Their knuckles white from grasping their weapons.

Sam turned to Chet. "You need to punch it," he said.

Chet glanced at Sam. "The people—"

"Them or us," Sam said, cutting him off.

Chet tightened his grip on the wheel. The Hummer began to pick up speed. Amidst shouts and pounding, people reluctantly parted. And then there were gunshots. Several rounds pinged off the Hummer's metal skin.

Chet glanced at Sam who looked at the mass in front of the Hummer and then back to Chet. Sam nodded with a grim expression. Chet exhaled deeply and then pressed the fuel pedal more, and more. People bounced off the Hummer's front grille like stalks of corn at harvest. Finally, the view in front was more highway than it was people. Chet exhaled but kept the speed climbing as he avoided solid objects like vehicles, washing machines, and buildings.

Once they were in the open, Sam slammed his fist on the dash. "Shit!"

"Couldn't be helped," Chet said.

Sam slammed his fist again. "I can't believe people are this stupid," he shouted. "I wonder how many of them we injured."

Tiff leaned forward. "I had no idea it would be this bad," she cried out. "These are just regular people."

Elliot let go of his rifle and massaged her neck with his one good hand. Tiff turned to him, sunk her face into his chest, and wept. Elliot rubbed her back. "They're scared," he said.

Chet took a quick look back and then returned his focus to driving. "Your parents—"

"Her parents are okay," Elliot said, cutting Chet off.

Sam did a slow hand rub of his face and then just stared out the window.

Chet broke the silence. "I need some directions."

Tiff looked out the windshield. "First left after the creek, then the second right. The house is third on the left."

Once Chet turned off the main road, the number of people on the side of the road dwindled to almost zero. And there were no stalled vehicles. With Tiff giving directions with her hand, Chet pulled into the drive of a slender two-story clapboard house painted all white. *Probably built in the early nineteen hundreds*, Sam thought. There were several other similar houses in the sparsely populated community. Sam and Chet stepped out followed by Tiff and Elliot.

As Tiff hurried up the stairs to the porch, the front door burst open and a man, wearing shorts, sandals, T-shirt, a big smile, about Tiff's age, ran out. Before Tiff had a chance to react, the man slung his arms around her in a bear hug. Tiff returned the hug with much less enthusiasm.

"I can't believe you made it," the man said, having trouble controlling his exuberance.

"Taylor, what are you doing here?" Tiff asked.

Before he could answer, a man and a woman in their early sixties rushed out of the doorway with equal zeal and embraced Tiff in bear hugs of their own. Sam, Chet, and Elliot stood back, quiet, watching the reunion.

Finally, Tiff pushed back from the three, glanced at Sam, Chet, and Elliot, who still stood watching, and then back to the three who had greeted her. "Mom,

Dad... Taylor, this is Sam, Chet, and Elliot. If it weren't for these three, I wouldn't be here."

The older couple rushed forward, and each took turns hugging Sam, Chet, and Elliot. Taylor came forward and shook hands.

"We're Emma and Charlie Conway, Tiffany's parents," the older woman said. "This is Taylor Evans, Tiffany's fiancé."

CHAPTER 19

In unison, the cheerful expression on Sam, Chet, and Elliot's face instantly turned to one of confusion. Sam was struck by the *no doubt* tone in Emma's voice when she said *fiancé*. He was sure Chet and Elliot, especially Elliot, were thinking the same thing.

Sam caught Tiff's eyes and raised an eyebrow.

Tiff stepped in front of her parents. "Childhood friend."

"Nonsense," Emma said. "You two are engaged." Emma put her arm around Taylor's waist.

"We *were* engaged," Tiff said, exasperated.

Emma put her other arm around Tiff's waist, turned them both to the door, and walked them up the stairs. "You two can work that out later." Emma glanced back. "Sam, Chet, Elliot—come on in."

Sam and Chet exchanged looks and then started walking.

Chet swung his arm around Elliot's neck and started walking him forward. "Come on in."

Everyone took seats in the living room—Sam, Chet, and Elliot in separate chairs. Charlie and Emma on an old sofa. Taylor took a seat next to Tiff on an antique loveseat. Tiff shifted, trying to put some distance between herself and Taylor while her eyes pleaded with Elliot. Taylor missed the interaction or pretended not to notice.

Elliot smiled and looked at Charlie. "We came through absolute chaos a few miles down the road. How—"

"We can thank Taylor," Charlie interrupted. "He came over that first day and made sure we kept a low profile. No lights at night; no excess movement during the day."

"We're hoping the power will be back on soon," Emma said.

"Mom, the power isn't coming back on anytime soon," Tiff said.

"That's what I've been trying to tell her," Taylor said. "You know your Mom, ever the optimist."

Sam cleared his voice. "Unfortunately, Tiffany and Taylor are right. The power won't be coming back on."

"To survive, people will have to hunker down and deal with the reality," Chet said, scratching his beard.

"We've been getting water from the creek," Charlie said. "Taylor put together a makeshift filter out back. Made it from PVC, sand, and charcoal."

"And we still have plenty of food," Emma said.

"Won't last forever," Taylor said. "Eventually, the food will run out or we'll be overrun when people start ransacking."

"They've already started," Chet said. "They're just down the road."

Charlie looked at Emma with a worried expression and took her hand in his. "We've heard gunfire the last couple of nights."

"We'll be fine, now that our Tiffany is home," Emma said, smiling at Tiff.

Taylor looked at Chet. "Where'd you get the Humvee?"

"Long story," Chet said. "But I guess you could say we earned it."

"Getting up here hasn't been easy," Tiff said. "It's pretty much been a battle the whole way."

Emma stood up and started into another room. "Well, you are all welcome to stay here. We have plenty of room."

"We appreciate the offer," Sam said. "But we'll need to be heading back."

"Back where?" Charlie asked.

Emma turned back to the room. "You can't leave. You just got here."

"I have a cabin outside of a small town in Tennessee," Sam said.

"We have people ransacking there too," Chet said, "which is why we need to get back."

"We?" Taylor asked.

"Me, Chet... Elliot, and whoever wants to come with us," Sam said. "If we can stay the night, we'll head out in the morning."

"It's kind of important that we get back soon," Elliot said.

Emma returned to the sofa and sat down next to Charlie. "Can't you stay longer? I'm sure Tiffany would like it."

"I think we should go with them," Tiff said.

Emma, Charlie, and Taylor jerked their head to face Tiff.

"What do you mean, dear?" Emma asked.

"I mean this place isn't safe," Tiff said. "Actually, it's not safe anywhere, but at least Sam's cabin is isolated. There's water and food."

Charlie spoke up. "This is our home."

"It won't be for long when people realize you still have food," Chet said.

Sam edged forward in his chair. "Look, we're not trying to scare you. You just need to understand that this situation will continue for months, maybe years.

You can't last that long in this house. You have neighbors. Neighbors talk."

"People are hungry," Chet said. "They're desperate."

"What about the government, the military?" Charlie asked. "Won't they be spreading out to help?"

"What's that saying—democracy dies in the dark," Sam said. "It's from some judicial opinion I think and this situation is not what the judge meant when he wrote the passage. But it applies none the less. We're in the dark. Democracy has been suspended for the near future. This situation affects everyone, even the government. I'm sure the government will be jumping on the electrical grid situation as soon as possible and the military will do what they can to keep order and protect the country, but in the meantime, we the people are on our own."

"Look at it this way," Chet said, "in a single day the entire world has been plunged back to the eighteen hundreds. To survive we will need to fend for ourselves."

Taylor sat without saying anything.

"What about Taylor?" Emma asked.

"I have no problem with all of you coming," Sam said. "But I think that's up to Tiffany and Taylor."

Suddenly, awkwardness fell over the room, and everyone was quiet for several moments.

"Why don't we put some grub together and sleep on it?" Chet suggested.

Tiff jumped to her feet. "Good idea, it will give everyone time to think."

Chet got to his feet. "I'm going to pull the Hummer around back."

"Good idea," Elliot said. "I'll give you a hand."

Elliot got up and walked out the front door with Chet.

Sam got up and followed. "Need to get some things from the truck."

"Me too," Tiff said, as she followed Sam.

Sam glanced back and saw that Taylor got to his feet but stayed put as the four of them walked out the front door.

Outside, Sam and Chet hopped in the Hummer as Tiff and Elliot started walking around to the back of the house.

***

"I didn't know he would be here," Tiff said to Elliot in a low voice, as they ambled through the grass.

"I know," he replied. "Now what?"

"When I look at Taylor, the only thing I see is an abusive little man with a big ego," Tiff said. "He was an asshole when we were growing up and he's still an asshole."

"Why get engaged?"

"He can be charming, especially when my parents are around. After high school, he went away for a couple of years. Worked with an uncle out west or something. I got a job and started junior college. When he came back, he was super charming. I thought maybe he had changed, so I gave it a chance, mostly because of my Mom's urging. I agreed to marry him. Shortly after that the asshole that he was started showing his true self. I joined the Marines to get away from him."

"He and your parents act like you guys can continue where you left off," Elliot said.

"Not going to happen," Tiff said, as she placed her hand on Elliot's arm and stopped.

Elliot stopped, turned, and faced Tiff.

Tiff stared into Elliot's eyes. "Look, I'm not sure what you and I have, but I do know I want to find out where it goes. I seem to attract assholes like bugs to a bug light, but from what I've been able to tell so far you're different."

Tiff took Elliot's arm, turned him, and they resumed walking. "But no matter what happens between you and me, Taylor is never going to happen."

Elliot nodded his head and said nothing.

Sam and Chet pulled to a stop as close to the rear of the house as possible. Tiff turned to the Hummer and opened the rear hatch. She pulled packs from the back along with the rifles and some food items. Everyone picked up an arm full and headed for the back door. Neither Sam nor Chet asked any questions and Tiff offered no explanations.

***

Sam's eyes blinked open. He smelled bacon. Chet, in an overstuffed chair, and Elliot, on the living room floor, still slept. Sam rolled to a sitting position on the sofa, slid his boots on, and tied the laces. It was morning but still dark outside. A faint light emanated from the short hall that led to the kitchen. Sam got to his feet and tiptoed down the hall.

Emma was standing at the stove in front of a pan full of sizzling bacon. She turned each piece with a spatula. Several candles scattered around the room provided a dull light.

"Good morning," Sam said in a low voice.

Emma faced Sam with a smile. "Morning. Did you sleep okay?"

"Yeah, just fine."

Emma turned back to the stove. "I thought a good breakfast was in order."

"Gas?" Sam asked.

"Propane," Emma replied. "It's almost gone. I thought this would be a good time to cook the last of the eggs and bacon."

"We don't want to eat up your food, Emma," Sam said.

"Can't take it with us."

"So, you're going?"

"Charlie and I talked about it a good deal last night. We hate to leave, but you're right. We can't hold out here very long. We appreciate the invitation."

"Does Tiffany know?"

"She does," Emma said. "And she agreed to our only condition—"

"That Taylor joins us."

Emma turned the fire off, slid the pan off the burner, and turned to face Sam. "Right." His parents died in an accident several years ago. He has plenty of friends here but no family. Back when he and Tiffany were dating and then engaged, we became his family."

"I understand," Sam said. "Like I said, everyone is welcome."

"And she told us about Elliot," Emma said, "how they met in Atlanta and Elliot being a detective and all."

Sam raised an eyebrow. "Does Taylor know about Elliot and Tiffany?"

"He went to bed early," Emma said, "but these walls are thin. He knows."

Emma turned back to the stove and started breaking eggs into a bowl. "Can you wake everyone so we can eat," she said. "Tiffany is in the room to the right at the top of the stairs. Taylor is in the guest room to the left."

"Charlie?"

"Outside."

Sam woke everyone and then found Charlie sitting on the front stoop smoking a cigarette.

"Emma says it's time to eat," Sam said.

"I'm just taking some time to reminisce," Charlie said. "Tiffany was raised in this house. Emma and I have grown old here."

"You're not that old," Sam said smiling.

Charlie glanced at Sam. "Well, old enough." He got to his feet and flicked the cigarette away. "I guess we should eat."

Sam led Charlie back into the house.

Everyone was sitting around the kitchen table when Sam and Charlie walked in. Chet, Elliot, Taylor, and Tiff had already started digging in.

Emma pulled a chair back and motioned for Sam. "You're over here."

Sam took a seat and looked at Chet.

"Eggs, bacon, and biscuits," Chet said. "Who would have thought?"

Charlie took his seat at the end of the table and started scooping food to his plate. Emma sat at his side and did the same.

"You'll need clothes for the woods and the coming winter," Sam said to Charlie and Emma.

"They're going?" Chet asked.

"They decided last night," Sam said. "Probably couldn't sleep because of your snoring."

Chet paused between chews, thought for a moment, nodded, and continued chewing.

"We're good on clothes," Charlie said.

"What about guns?" Chet asked.

"Don't believe in them," Charlie answered, and then took another bite.

Sam and Chet stopped chewing and stole a quick glance at each other.

"I hunt with a bow," Charlie continued, "have since I was a kid."

Sam looked at Taylor. "Taylor?"

"Taylor's a black belt," Emma answered.

"We're likely to need help in the long-range department," Chet said, with a raised eyebrow.

"I've shot before, but I don't own a gun," Taylor replied.

"We'll need to find you a weapon," Sam said.

The last morsels disappeared. Emma stood and began collecting empty plates.

Tiff and Elliot had been quiet for the entire breakfast. Finally, Tiff pushed her empty plate forward and stood up. "Look, I need to clear the air."

Emma sat back down.

"Taylor and I were engaged once, but that ended years ago. I have no interested in resurrecting the past. I do have an interest in the future." Tiff's gaze drifted to Elliot. "Elliot and I have started something, and I intend to see where it leads. Period."

Tiff sat back down. Taylor got up and walked out of the room. Emma stood back up with the dishes and took them to the sink. Sam, Chet, and Charlie exchanged confused expressions. Elliot and Tiff stared at each other.

Sam stood and got everyone's attention. "I do need to warn you about one thing."

Taylor stepped back into the kitchen and leaned against the wall.

"My cabin is outside of Townsend, a small town in Tennessee. The cabin is isolated on ten acres in a very sparsely populated area with water and plenty of game. Unfortunately, a group of outsiders killed the police chief and his two officers and have pretty much taken over the town."

Charlie, Emma, and Taylor fixated on Sam's voice.

"I've promised to return and help eliminate this group."

"How big is the group?" Taylor asked.

"Six, eight, maybe more," Sam replied. "They are pretty well armed. And worse—Chet, Tiffany, and I managed to ruffle their feathers already."

Emma, with a worried look on her face, returned to her seat and took hold of Charlie's hand.

"I thought you should know what lies ahead," Sam said.

Chet cleared his voice and scratched his beard. "Look, surviving this thing will mean defending against those who will want your stuff. Sam's neighbor is rounding up men willing to help and is waiting for us to return."

"We have to take a stand," Sam said. "And this won't be the last time."

Emma took hold of Tiff's hand. "I thought this cabin would be safe."

Tiff patted her mother's hand. "This is not going to be a camping trip. We've had to battle our way from Florida. And it's only been a few days since this thing started. It's going to get worse. The cabin is our best bet."

"You won't survive here," Chet added.

Charlie stood up. "We need to get loaded and on the road."

CHAPTER 20

Sam reminded himself that the Hummer wasn't built for comfort as he slid into the cramped quarters. It was built for battle. Which meant the interior was mostly metal with a bit of cushion on the seats. And even though the passenger capacity of the transport model was eight, Sam and the other six occupants, along with their essentials, more than pushed the limits of available space. Even Chet, as the driver, and Sam, as the front passenger, in their individual seats, were crowded by equipment and provisions. Like Sardines. But the front was sheer luxury compared to the back. A bench seat separated miniature single seats to each side. Charlie, Emma, and Tiff, with Tiff on the right, occupied the bench. Elliot on the right and Taylor on the left occupied the miniature seats. Baggage occupied every other possible bit of space including the passengers' laps. Add to that stiff springs and they had the makings of an interesting trip.

Chet pushed the end of Charlie's long bow to the side so it wouldn't continue to gouge his hip, looked around the compartment, and chuckled. He then fired the engine, put the truck in gear, and pulled around the house to the front driveway. That's as far as they got.

Fifteen men and women stood in Charlie and Emma's driveway. Some had guns.

"Neighbors?" Sam asked.

"Yep," Charlie replied, as he shifted items off his lap, reached past Taylor, opened the rear door, and stepped out.

Elliot, Tiff, Emma, and Taylor scrunched forward in their seat.

Sam listened from the open window. "Why is the military helping you but not us?" asked a man in front of the group as Charlie turned to face them.

"George, this is not the military—these are Tiffany's friends."

The crowd mumbled amongst themselves for a few moments until a woman said, "Looks like the military to us."

Charlie approached the crowd with both hands raised. "I can assure you, this is not the military."

"Where are you going?" George asked.

"Tiffany's friends have a place in Tennessee they think will be safer," Charlie replied. "We're going there."

"What about us?" another woman asked.

Sam opened his door and stepped out. "Charlie and Emma's family has come together to survive. That's what you should do."

"Our families don't have a working vehicle or a safe place in Tennessee," George said.

Charlie glanced back at Sam and then faced the crowd again. "We have to do what we can to protect ourselves. All of you would do, should do, the same thing."

"We can't tell you what's best for you," Sam said. "Your best course will be different but, hopefully, just as effective."

George turned to the crowd. "Let's go home. We're not getting any help here."

The crowd turned and began shuffling down the drive and into the street. Sam and Charlie resumed their spots in the Hummer.

"Rowdy neighbors," Chet said.

"Good folks," Charlie corrected him. "Just scared like we all are."

Chet nodded and pulled out. He retraced his route which took them back to the scene of the previous day's melee. Sam surveyed the area as they approached. There was plenty of debris scattered about, but no people, dead or alive.

"I guess the rioters are sleeping in this morning," Chet said.

"How bad was it yesterday?" Emma asked.

"Bad," Tiff replied. "I'm just glad they're gone."

"Why do I feel like this is the calm before the storm?" Elliot asked.

Sam glanced in the rear and smiled at the stuffed conditions. He saw Tiff put her hand on Elliot's leg. Taylor looked away and remained quiet.

***

Five hours later, Chet pulled the Hummer to a stop in the same spot where they had first parked to approach the cabin on foot.

Sam twisted around in his seat. "We need to make sure the cabin is secure before we just drive up. How about if everyone stretches their legs here while Tiff and I check things out?"

"How far to the cabin?" Taylor asked.

"Half a mile," Sam replied. "If all is clear, one of us will be back to get you in forty minutes or so."

"And if it's not clear?" Charlie asked.

"If you hear gunfire, Chet will lead you through the trees. Take your directions from him."

Sam slapped Chet on the shoulder and then exited the Hummer with Tiff. Both carried their side arms and their rifles. They made their way through the brush and trees being careful not to make any noise. The Hummer was soon lost in the blur of green and brown behind them. Except for an occasional bird chirp or the rustle of a squirrel, the forest was quiet. Sam and Tiff continued until they were at the tree line between Sam's property and the forest. They took a knee behind a large pine.

"Seems deserted," Tiff whispered.

Sam nodded and was rising when he froze and then sunk back to his knee.

"What?" Tiff whispered.

"The shovel's missing," Sam replied in a low voice.

"Shovel?"

"There was a shovel leaning against the house. Now it's gone."

"Maybe Chet or Elliot moved it."

"No, it was there before. Now it's gone."

"Okay, now what?" Tiff asked.

Sam took a few moments to think while he continued observing the property. "Go back and let them know what's up. Bring Chet and Elliot back with you."

"And you?"

"I'm going to make my way through the woods, around the back, and to the other side. I should be back here by the time you return."

Tiff nodded and then started back the way they had come.

Sam moved from bush to bush stopping every ten feet or so to look and listen. He worked his way around until he had a clear view of the back of the property. The stream was to his rear; the clearing, pump house, garage, and the cabin were in front of him. Quiet. No movement. Sam continued through the trees until he was at the south side of the property with the south side of the garage and the driveway in view. Again, all was quiet. No movement. No signs of anyone having been there—except on the grass next to the driveway.

Sam saw the subtle imprint of vehicle tracks in the grass. *They had been here*, he thought. And they made the effort to not leave any prints in the dirt driveway. Jones and Smith knew the location of Sam's cabin. There were only two people who could have told them—his neighbors, Dave and Bobby.

Sam stepped from the trees and marched across the front of his property to the north side tree line. He arrived at the edge of the brush and saw Chet, Tiff, and Elliot creeping toward him through the trees.

"They've been here," Sam said, when they gathered together.

"How do you know?" Elliot asked.

"Vehicle prints in the grass," Sam replied. "We didn't drive in the grass."

"So Jones and Smith know where to find us," Chet said.

"But how could they know?" Tiff asked.

"My neighbors," Sam replied. "Let's head back to the Hummer."

Sam took off in a trot, dodging brush and trees. Chet, Tiff, and Elliot followed close behind.

They found Charlie, Emma, and Taylor leaning against the Hummer. Charlie puffed on a cigarette.

Charlie put the cigarette out against the Hummer's tire and then stepped to meet Sam. "What's up?"

"There's no one at the cabin, but they've been there," Sam said. He turned to Tiff. "Can you drive everyone to the cabin and get them settled? Chet and I will make our way over to Dave's place and check on them. They are pretty much the only ones who could have said anything."

"Mind if I tag along with you guys?" Taylor asked.

Sam nodded and then headed north through the woods with Chet and Taylor following.

They jogged dodging trees and bushes for a hundred yards before Sam veered over and crossed the paved road. He led the others immediately into the brush on the other side and then continued north for another hundred yards. They stopped and took a knee behind a large oak on the edge of a clearing. A cabin similar to Sam's stood in the middle of the clearing.

"What do you think?" Chet whispered.

"I think something's not right," Sam replied. He stood and started out across the clearing with his rifle shouldered. The others followed. Chet had his rifle shouldered. Taylor was unarmed.

Sam and Chet swept the surroundings with their rifles as they moved toward the cabin's front door. Well before they got to the porch Sam could see that the front door was smashed in. Sam motioned for everyone to slow as he crouched lower and approached the door. Sam stepped up on the porch followed by Taylor. Chet hung back and swept their rear.

Sam eased up to the doorway and peered inside. He saw tables, lamps, and chairs overturned but no people. Sam stepped lightly through the debris and made his way to the hall leading to the bedrooms, stopping every few feet to listen. He looked back at Taylor and motioned for him to wait by the door.

Sam continued down the hall to the first bedroom. The door was open. He glanced inside. No one there. He continued to the second bedroom, Bobby's room. The door was open a crack. Sam used the barrel of his rifle to ease the door back until it was fully open. No one was inside. Sam continued to the master bedroom, the only room left at the end of the hall. The door was open. Sam stepped through the threshold, swept his rifle back and forth, and then stepped back. Empty. Sam retraced his steps back down the hall, back into the living room, and then toward a second hall that led to the kitchen.

Sam could smell it before he got to the kitchen. Blood. He eased forward, rifle at the ready, and stepped into the kitchen. Dave and Tina, his wife, were at the table, both tied to their chairs, and both dead. They each had a bullet hole in their forehead.

Sam made his way back down the hall to the front door. He stepped outside and immediately dropped his chin to his chest.

"What is it?" Chet asked.

"Dave and Tina are dead," Sam said in a low voice. He raised his head. "Bobby's not in the house."

Sam raised his rifle and started walking around the side of the house toward the backyard. As soon as he rounded the back corner, he saw Bobby. He was tied to a tree. Head drooped. Naked. Black and blue masses covered his midsection and ribs. Sam raced over to Bobby and raised his head. His left eye was bloody and swollen shut but his right eye blinked open.

"He's alive," Sam said, as he rested his rifle against the tree and pulled his knife. Chet came toward the tree but kept his guard and his rifle up. Sam cut the rope and Bobby fell forward into Sam's arms. Sam eased him to the ground and rolled him onto his back.

Chet, still sweeping his rifle back and forth, glanced down at Bobby. "How bad?"

"He doesn't appear to be shot, but he's been beaten badly."

Taylor came over and kneeled next to Bobby. "Who did this?" he asked Sam.

Bobby moved his head slightly and gurgled, barely audible. "Jones and his thugs."

"Don't talk, just rest easy," Sam said.

"Mom and Dad?" Bobby gurgled. He raised his arm toward the house.

"Rest," Sam said.

Sam glanced at Chet and Taylor. "One of you needs to go for the Hummer so we can get Bobby to my cabin."

Sam looked back down at Bobby. Bobby's right eye was locked open in a permanent stare. Sam placed his ear on Bobby's chest for a few moments and then stood up. "He's gone."

"Jones is the guy you mentioned?" Taylor asked.

Sam retrieved his rifle and returned his knife to its sheath. "Yep."

"We need to get back to your cabin," Chet said.

Sam began walking in that direction. "I'll return with the Hummer and bury them."

"When do you think all this happened?" Taylor asked.

"Based on the level of blood congelation, I'd guess this morning," Sam replied. "The psychos could be back anytime."

***

Everyone converged on Sam, Chet, and Taylor when they stepped into the family room at Sam's cabin.

"What did you find?" Tiff asked.

"Dave, his wife, and son are dead," Sam said.

Emma brought her hand to her mouth in shock and immediately sunk her head into Charlie's chest. Charlie put his arm around his wife's shoulder and dropped his chin.

"Now what?" Tiff asked.

"Normally, I'd say that a strong offense is the best defense," Sam answered. "But we have three people basically unarmed and we can't leave them here alone."

Emma raised her head. "Will these thugs come here?"

"They will," Sam replied. "And the worst part is we don't know when."

"They've already been here," Chet added. "This morning."

"Do they know we're here?" Charlie asked.

"Probably not," Sam said. "So that gives us some time—a few hours to prepare."

CHAPTER 21

"I think you and I should go on a scouting mission," Chet said to Sam, standing next to the Hummer in the front yard.

"I agree," Sam said. He glanced at the sky. "It will be dark soon."

Chet nodded and then followed Sam back into the house. He gathered everyone in the family room.

"Chet and I are going to scout the situation," Sam said.

Tiff stepped forward. "Count me in."

"Me too," Elliot said.

Sam shook his head. "We can't leave the cabin undefended." Sam handed his rifle to Tiff. "I won't need this." Sam looked at Taylor. "You said you could shoot; can you shoot an AR?"

"I can shoot a rifle just fine," Taylor replied.

Sam nodded, stepped back, and then glanced at Tiff, Elliot, and Taylor in turn. "Three shooters and Charlie has his bow. That'll have to do." He glanced at Elliot and Tiff. "I'll leave it to you guys to work out the details."

"How long will you be gone?" Elliot asked.

"Hard to say," Sam replied. "If we're not back by morning, I would say there's a problem."

Sam scanned the room and saw that everyone was staring at him. "Don't worry, we'll be back." He motioned to Chet and the two of them walked out the door.

***

Tiff turned to Taylor. "We need some advanced warning of anyone coming down the road. You're the most logical among us."

"If that means standing out in the mosquitoes, I don't think so," Taylor said.

Elliot stepped forward. "I'll do it." He started moving to the door.

"I'm thinking a hundred yards down the road, in the woods," Tiff said.

Elliot looked at Tiff and then glanced at Taylor. "Exactly my thoughts."

Elliot grabbed a bottle of water and an MRE from the kitchen and then left through the front door with a rifle in his hand and his Glock holstered on his hip.

After Elliot had gone, Tiff turned to Taylor. She huffed, thrust Sam's rifle at Taylor, and put her hands on her hips. "Make yourself useful."

Taylor smiled for a moment until he realized Charlie and Emma were staring at him. He dropped the smile and with the rifle walked out of the room.

***

Sam pulled off the road and into the woods well before the town limits. He continued about fifty yards into the trees and cut the engine behind a large bush.

He turned to Chet. "Three miles into town on foot."

"Police station?" Chet asked.

"Yeah, the back way."

They took a long drink of water from bottles, stepped out, and closed the doors. Sam's M&P 9 rested in its holster on his hip; Chet had his Glock plus his rifle. They walked through the woods to the paved road and then single file along the side toward town.

Staying in the shadows in case anyone popped up, Sam led Chet down Chestnut, to Domar, and to the end of Middletown. Dark homes lined all these streets. There was no activity. The place was almost a ghost town.

Sam stopped in the shadow of a large oak and pointed to a dark line of trees ahead. "The elementary school is the other side of those trees," Sam whispered. He crept forward followed by Chet. A hundred yards later Sam could see the east end of the school. The station stood across the large parking lot on the northwest side of the school. Sam and Chet raced from the trees and pasted themselves at the northeast corner of the school. From this position, seventy-five yards out, Sam could see the entire front of the police station along with the twelve or thirteen men standing at the building's front entrance.

***

"Where is Taylor?" Tiff asked, as she walked into the family room. A single candle flickered in the room. The room's windows were covered with thick blankets.

Charlie was in the process of stringing his bow. Emma was putting arrows into a quiver.

"Haven't seen him since he left the room," Charlie said, as he finished stringing the bow and stood up straight.

"I've checked the rooms," Tiff said. "He's not in the cabin."

"One thing's for sure," Charlie said. "He's somewhere."

"He must be outside," Emma said. Emma stepped the few feet, opened the door, and looked out on the porch. "Not out here."

***

"Looks like they're getting ready for something," Chet said in a low voice, as he looked at the fifteen men in front of the police station.

Sam nodded. "I just hope they're not headed for my cabin."

At that moment, two men exited the front entrance and called for the men to group around them. Sam recognized Jones' voice but couldn't make out the words. Jones then pointed to the Ford and Chevy pickup trucks parked nearby. Jones finished talking, and the men started toward the trucks.

"I don't like it," Sam said.

"I say we start shooting," Chet said. "That will knock them off their plan, whatever it is."

Sam glanced at Chet, nodded, and pulled his 9mm. Chet took aim with his rifle. Just as the men were loading themselves into the bed of the two trucks, Chet opened up and emptied the entire thirty round magazine. When Chet paused to reload, Sam started pulling the trigger on his pistol.

Several of the men went down. The rest scattered, taking cover behind the trucks and the concrete pillars of the building's front entrance. They started returning fire in the direction of Sam and Chet, apparently aiming for their muzzle flashes. Rounds pinged off the side of the school building. Some chipped concrete from the northeast corner. Sam took off running back to the trees with Chet following close behind.

***

"Stop firing," Jones yelled. "They are not returning fire." Without leaving his cover he surveyed the area. Five men lay in the parking lot. He looked at Smith who was crouched behind the Chevy pickup. "Take two men and check on the wounded." Smith hesitated, glancing at the school building. "Move, now," Jones yelled. Smith pointed to two other men and the three of them hesitantly moved to check on the fallen while staying as low as possible.

Jones stepped from the concrete pillar and started pointing at men. "You three go left, the rest of you are with me." The seven men split off and began running toward the school.

***

After Emma closed the front door, Taylor stepped from the shadows on the side of the cabin. He looked at the rifle in his hand and then leaned it against the cabin. He then trotted down the driveway and out to the paved road. He didn't know exactly where Elliot would be lurking in the trees but he knew it was about a hundred yards down, probably on the right. Taylor hugged the right side of the road as he skulked along. When he got about seventy-five yards down, he entered the tree line. As silently as he could in the dark, Taylor stepped from tree to tree. Behind each one he paused for at least a full minute to look and listen. Ironically, it wasn't either of those senses that told him he was close to Elliot. It was his sense of smell. Peanut butter. Taylor took even more care with each step, sliding his toe between the leaves and sticks before he put any weight on that foot. He did the same with the next foot. Stealth was his only concern. He paused behind the next tree and listened. A faint sound came to him on the light breeze. The ruffling of plastic. *The MRE package*, he thought.

Taylor strained to peer through the darkness. A dark spot moved. And then he made out the outline of an arm and then a head. Elliot was still eating. Elliot was crouched, one knee on the ground, his body mostly concealed behind a tree. Taylor was amazed he had gotten this close without being detected, especially with Elliot being the big time detective and all.

With less than twenty feet between them, Taylor felt he could be on Elliot before he could even pull his pistol. But why not try for closer to increase the odds? Taylor placed a foot, wiggling his toe through the leaves and twigs, set his weight, and then placed his other foot. He took the same approach with the third step—wiggled his toe through the leaves and started transferring his weight. That's when the twig snapped. Barely audible, but enough.

Taylor saw the dark glob of Elliot's head twist in the direction of the sound. Taylor rushed forward closing the distance in less than a second. Without even seeing it, Taylor knew Elliot would be going for his pistol. A moment's hesitation was all he needed. Taylor was within three or four feet when he saw the glint from Elliot's pistol. It was coming up from his thigh, almost level, and pointed toward Taylor.

Taylor pivoted on his left leg and brought his right foot up and around in a move he had practiced a million times. The strike was instantaneous and precise. Elliot's pistol flew from his hand and skittered through the leaves on the ground.

Taylor recovered his footing, pivoted the other way, and smashed his left fist into Elliot's temple. Elliot went down on one knee keeping his eyes on Taylor. Elliot's eyes opened wider when Taylor stepped close enough to be recognized in the dark.

"Taylor—"

"That's right… Tiffany's fiancé."

"Just for the record, she thinks you're an asshole," Elliot said. "I tend to agree."

"She'll change her mind when you're out of the picture," Taylor spat.

"Not likely. She thought you were an asshole long before I came along."

Taylor stood up straight from his crouch and slowly began closing in on Elliot. He saw Elliot glance at the rifle leaning against the nearby tree.

Elliot dove for the rifle.

Taylor pounced. Long before Elliot even got close to the rifle Taylor caught him around the neck from behind with his right arm. Elliot struggled. He tried to punch with his one good arm, but Taylor easily dodged the blows. He applied pressure against Elliot's head with his left hand until he heard the loud snap of Elliot's vertebrae. Taylor relaxed his hold. Elliot's body went limp; his head drooped to one side at an odd angle. Taylor allowed Elliot to fall to the ground.

CHAPTER 22

"How much time do you figure?" Chet asked, breathing hard as he kept up with Sam running back the way they had come.

"It won't take them long to realize we're not there," Sam said, equally out of breath. "They'll go for the cabin."

"Tomorrow morning?" Chet asked.

"That would be my guess."

Forty minutes later Sam slowed to a trot as he began scanning the trees in earnest.

Chet jogged past him. "It has to be along here somewhere."

"I can't see shit out here," Sam said, still panting. "It all looks the same."

Sam stopped for a moment, cocked his ear. The sound of an engine at maximum rpm's suddenly screamed into existence, coming up fast behind them. They dove in unison for the brush along the road. Headlights flashed illuminating the entire area that a second earlier had been total darkness. Sam scrunched lower and began back crawling into thicker brush. He had just put his head down when the truck roared past. Sam lifted his head just enough to make out three men standing in the Chevy truck's bed, leaning across the top of the cab with rifles outstretched. "That didn't take long," Sam mumbled. He considered the fact that Jones looking in this direction meant that Sam and Chet were his first inclination.

With the truck down the road a half mile, Chet raised his head. "The cabin," he said.

Sam and Chet were half way up when they heard the truck screech to a stop. Sam heard the gears jamming and saw the headlights swing back and forth as the driver executed a three-point turn. The engine gunned, and the headlights swung forward to light the paved road in front of Sam. Sam and Chet dropped back to the ground. Sam scrunched even father back into the brush. At a time when he could be shot or worse, the only thing on his mind was snakes.

The truck headed back toward Sam and Chet, much slower this time. The men in the back scrutinized the side of the road with their rifles shouldered.

"We might be screwed," Chet said, just loud enough for Sam to hear.

"If we stay here, they'll see us for sure," Sam replied. "I say we run for the trees."

"Lead the way," Chet said, as he started to rise up.

Sam jumped into a crouch and trotted to the thicker brush of the tree line. Chet was right behind him.

"On the left up ahead," a voice yelled from the back of the truck.

The engine screamed, and the truck accelerated directly for Sam and Chet. The headlights caught them just before they entered the brush. A shot rang out and slammed into the tree next to Sam.

Sam crouched lower and trotted faster into the dark. Sam had gone a few feet when he ran headlong into a small tree. The trunk caught him in the shoulder. Sam thought back to his high school football coach, and the hours spent on tackling practice. He wasn't very good back then and hadn't gotten any better with time. Sam bounced back and then resumed his pace, now behind Chet. They both ran as fast as possible in the dark. Limbs snagged at their clothes and skin.

Behind them, Sam heard the truck skid to a stop and men piling out.

"An extra week's rations to the man who shoots the first one," a voice yelled. Sam recognized it to be Jones' voice.

Shots rang out and bullets smacked the trees and brush around Sam and Chet.

"Hard left," Sam whispered to Chet.

Chet veered to the left in front of a large oak tree. Sam followed on his heels. They both accelerated and were able to dodge most of the limbs for another fifty yards before they ran into a solid wall of brush. The limbs gouged and scrapped Sam's face, neck, and hands.

Sam dropped to his knees and pulled Chet's shirt until he too was on his knees next to Sam. In the almost pitch dark Sam could just barely make out the outline of Chet's face. Sam took deep breaths to get his breathing under control.

Sam heard the men running and yelling through the brush. They apparently had not seen Sam and Chet make that left since they continued forward a good fifty yards from Sam and Chet's position. Sam could tell by the sound of the men running that they were slowing. They finally came to a complete stop.

"We'll end up shooting each other out here," a voice yelled. Sam recognized Smith's voice.

After a long pause, Sam heard Jones reply. "Okay, everybody back to the truck."

A few minutes later, Sam heard the sounds of the men getting back in the truck. The engine turned over and caught into a low purr. Gears jammed, the lights flicked on, and the truck pulled away heading back toward town.

"Trap?" Chet whispered.

"Maybe," Sam replied. "At least they're not headed to the cabin. Let's wait here for a while."

The sound of the truck died off in the distance and the night time forest noises started up. Crickets began their incessant racket—a loud ratchety drone. Frogs began croaking to each other. Mosquitoes whined in and out of earshot. Sam heard Chet slap his neck.

"Bloodsuckers," Chet whispered.

"Just be glad we haven't been snake bit," Sam whispered back.

***

The front door of the cabin swung open and Taylor stepped in carrying Sam's rifle. He closed the door and then turned to see Tiff, Charlie, and Emma sitting in the family room. All three stared at him.

"Where the hell have you been," Tiff asked.

Taylor leaned the rifle against the door frame. "Thought I would take a spin around the property," he replied. "Seems clear."

Tiff stood up. She flexed her fists at her side until her knuckles were white. "You went out there without letting me know?" she asked.

"I didn't know I had to report to you," Taylor replied in a calm voice. He took a seat.

"That's why Elliot's out there," she said. "I thought you didn't like the mosquitoes?"

"I kept moving," Taylor said. "They never touched me."

Charlie stood up. "Okay, okay, everything's fine now," he said. "Let's get back to what we were doing."

"What were you doing," Taylor asked.

"Making a plan," Charlie replied.

Tiff paused a few moments, closed her eyes, and took a deep breath. She opened her eyes more composed. "At first light, we need you in the tree line on the south side," Tiff said. "Dad will be in the tree line on the north with his bow. I'll be in here with Mom."

"What about Sam and Chet?" Taylor asked.

"We stay flexible," Tiff replied. "But that's the plan if they are not back."

"What about Elliot?" Taylor asked.

"If he's not back by then, I'll go get him," Tiff replied.

Taylor didn't say anything. He just let his head fall back on the chair's headrest while he thought.

Emma got up and started toward the kitchen. "We should at least eat something."

Charlie followed Emma out of the room.

Tiff took a stern stance. "This is why I didn't marry you," Tiff said.

"What?" Taylor replied without raising his head.

"Your attitude."

"What about my attitude?"

"You're an egotistical asshole," she said firmly. "And I hate that sorry ass smirk of yours."

Tiff turned and marched out of the room. Taylor smiled as he closed his eyes and relaxed.

***

"How long's it been?" Chet asked in a low voice.

"Half hour or so," Sam replied.

"What do you think?"

"About what?" Sam replied.

"Trying to find the Hummer," Chet replied.

"I have no idea where the Hummer is," Sam said. "Do you?"

"Not really," Chet said, as he slapped the side of his face. "If they're back in the morning before we find the Hummer, we'll really be screwed."

Sam slapped his neck and then rubbed the mosquito bite. "If I were Jones, I would have left two or three men to cover the road. There's no way we can move through this shit without being heard."

"Yeah. Damned if we do; damned if we don't."

Sam and Chet were silent for a few beats, except for the slapping at mosquitoes.

"Actually, what I would do is bypass us first thing in the morning," Chet said. "Assault the cabin and then come back for us. He probably figures we left somebody at the cabin."

Sam stood up. "Okay, you convinced me, let's find that truck."

Sam took a step and heard the snap of a dead branch under his foot. They both froze. Even the crickets and frogs froze... for a few moments, and then they started up again. Sam took another step, being more careful with his foot placement. For several minutes they worked their way toward the road.

Sam looked around. "It's lighter than before," he said in a low voice. "The moon's out." Sam could see Chet's head nod up and down as they both continued making their way through the trees and bushes.

Sam stopped. "The road is right there," he whispered as he pointed.

They moved from tree to tree until they were finally behind a large pine at the edge of the low scrub at the side of the road. They both moved their heads side to side scanning the road for several moments.

"Anything?" Sam asked softly. Sam glanced at Chet and saw him shake his head back and forth.

Sam stepped from the tree. He saw the muzzle flash and heard the blast a millisecond after the round smacked the pine tree. He jumped back behind the tree just as muzzle flashes and blasts opened up from the other side of the road about fifty yards north of their position. Rounds whizzed by and impacted tree trunks and branches all around them. Chet raised his rifle.

"Don't," Sam said, as he put his hand on Chet's shoulder. "Let them think we're hit."

A few moments later the firing stopped. Sam and Chet both sunk to their knees and then went prone on their stomachs facing the shooters.

"I count three," Chet said softly.

"Yep. And they're moving toward us."

They both began to back scoot into the thicker brush behind them. They had covered fifteen feet when Sam rose to a knee behind a small tree trunk.

He pulled his 9mm and motioned for Chet. Chet got to his feet as Sam began to skulk from tree to tree parallel to the road, in the direction of the approaching men. Sam could see their silhouettes walking single file on the road toward where Sam and Chet had been. Sam and Chet kept moving, placing their feet carefully before taking a step. When they were thirty yards from their previous position, Sam stopped. Chet pulled up next to him. With the moon higher and lighter, they watched through the trees and brush as the silhouettes stopped out on the road directly in front of Sam and Chet's new position but at least twenty-five yards away. The men swept their rifles back and forth pointed generally at where Sam and Chet used to be. That's when Sam heard the truck engine, far off in the distance, coming back toward them.

Sam and Chet used the sound of the approaching truck to mask their steps as they slunk deeper into the trees. By the time the truck screeched to a stop, Sam and Chet were seventy-five yards away, in the thick trees and bushes. Sam could just make out the muffled sounds of the truck doors closing and voices, but not clear enough to make out what they were saying.

Sam and Chet stepped quickly through the darkness and brush when abruptly Sam stopped in mid-stride. He focused on the blob in front of them. There, before them, in the dull light of the moon, stood the Hummer.

"Son of a bitch," Chet said, as he continued forward and put his hand on the Hummer's hood. "Talk about luck."

Sam joined Chet at the Hummer. "That's one problem out of the way," he said. "How do we get past the other problem?"

***

"I'm getting worried," Emma said. "It's been a long time since they left."

"What time is it?" Charlie asked.

"Got to be after midnight," Tiff replied.

Tiff, Charlie, Emma, and Taylor sat around the kitchen table. Residue from MRE packages littered the table.

"I feel like I need to check on Elliot," Tiff said.

"I'm sure he's fine," Taylor said. "Probably sleeping." The corners of his mouth curved up into a slight smile.

Tiff stood up. "Don't care," she said. "I'm going to check on him."

Charlie stood up. "I'll come with you."

Tiff nodded, and they both headed out of the kitchen while Taylor and Emma remained at the table.

"What should we do?" Emma asked.

Tiff stopped at the doorway. "You might as well try to get some sleep," she said. "We'll have plenty of notice if anyone's coming this way."

Tiff and Charlie continued into the family room where Tiff retrieved her rifle and Charlie picked up his bow and the quiver of arrows.

They exited the cabin, walked down the drive, and up the paved road in front of the cabin about a hundred yards.

"Elliot should be along here," Tiff whispered. In a low voice, she called out for Elliot. A little louder, she called out again. No response.

"Where is he?" Charlie asked.

"Wish I knew."

"Where's he supposed to be?" Charlie asked.

"We talked about a hundred yards up, probably on the right, which would be right here," Tiff said.

She called out again even louder. No response. "Something's not right," she said, as she peered into the trees with the dull light of the moon. "He wouldn't have gone that far off the road, and there would be no reason to be anywhere but here."

Tiff waded into the short brush on the side of the road and swiveled her head back and forth. "Elliot, where the hell are you?" she yelled. When there was no response she stepped farther into the brush.

"We're not going to find him in the dark," Charlie said. "Maybe he really is asleep."

"He doesn't sleep that soundly," Tiff replied, and then paused to consider what she had said. She glanced at her Dad and then back to the tree line.

"I agree, something's wrong," Charlie said. "But we need the light of day to figure it out."

Tiff screamed Elliot's name, not caring who heard her. She listened a few beats but heard only the night sounds of the forest.

"Come on," Charlie said. "We'll find him first light."

Tiff took the few steps back to the pavement while looking over her shoulder. With her hand, she wiped the tear sliding down her cheek.

CHAPTER 23

Sam felt Chet's elbow poke him in the side as they reclined against a tree. "Are you awake?"

"Yep," Sam replied.

"It's getting lighter," Chet said.

Sam rotated his shoulders, stretched his neck, and then got to his feet. "I must have dozed. You?"

"Maybe," Chet replied as he got to his feet scratching his neck. "Tell me again why we didn't spend the night in the Hummer."

"Hear better out here."

Chet nodded and opened the driver's door. Sam went around to the passenger side, opened the door, and slid in the seat.

"I say we just punch it out of here," Chet said.

"Might as well," Sam replied. "If they're still on the road, they'll hear as soon as the engine turns over."

Chet closed his door and turned the key. The engine fired to life. Sam closed his door as Chet stomped the fuel pedal and wrenched the wheel to the left. The Hummer leaped into a tight turn mowing down some short bushes. Chet maneuvered the truck around until it was back on the original tire marks heading out of the woods. The Hummer dove through gullies and jumped over hills while plowing through the brush.

The Hummer tore through the tree line in the dull light of early morning and shot onto the pavement. Chet muscled the wheel to the right and slammed on the fuel pedal.

Sam unconsciously ducked expecting gunfire to pummel the truck's metal skin, but gunfire did not come. He gradually relaxed, raised his head, and looked to the rear. "The road's clear," he yelled over the roar of the engine. "I guess they regrouped back in town."

"Or they went on to the cabin last night," Chet offered.

A sickening feeling washed over Sam. "Or that."

Chet got the Hummer up to its sixty-five max speed as he ripped down the back roads toward the cabin. When they were within two miles Sam motioned with his hand to slow down. Chet let off the fuel pedal. The Hummer slowed to thirty.

"Drive in or walk in? Chet asked.

"If they're not there already I suspect we don't have a lot of time," Sam replied. "Drive in."

Chet kept his eyes forward and to the left while Sam scanned their rear and right side. The morning sun was beginning to shimmer through the trees to the east bringing more light to the surroundings.

About a hundred yards out from the cabin Sam motioned for Chet to stop. "Let's have a listen before we drive in."

Chet brought the truck to a halt in the middle of the road and killed the engine. They both stepped out and listened. Sam walked around to the driver's side of the Hummer and joined Chet. Birds chirped, squirrels rustled through the leaves, but that was it.

"I say we go on in," Sam said, as he stepped toward the rear of the truck. Something caught his eye in the woods and he stopped his motion to take a second look. Something white just visible through the brush. Sam took a few steps to the side of the road for a better look.

"What is it?" Chet asked.

"Not sure," Sam replied, as he stepped into the brush along the roadside.

Chet stepped to the edge of the pavement. "Probably just trash," he said.

Sam moved closer to the tree line. "Probably."

Chet scratched at his beard as he glanced down the road to the rear. "The shitheads could be on us at any moment."

Sam had moved into the tree line. "They may have already been here," he said.

"How do you know?" Chet asked.

Sam knelt down in the brush. After a few moments, he motioned for Chet to come over. "It's Elliot... he's dead."

Chet hustled through the brush and knelt next to Elliot's body. "That means they must have attacked the cabin last night." Sam detected a rare twinge of anxiety in Chet's voice and watched as he jerked his head around to scan the surroundings.

Sam examined Elliot's torso. "There're no bullet wounds."

"What?" Chet said, as he looked back down at Elliot.

"No wounds," Sam said, as he ran his hand over his chest and around his neck. His hand paused behind his neck. "His neck is broken."

Chet reached down and felt the vertebrae. He then glanced at the empty holster. "Where's his gun?" Chet asked as he stood up and looked around.

Sam glanced up for a moment while he continued to exam the body. "Looks like he was eating." He looked at the tree nearest the body and saw Elliot's rifle leaning against the trunk. "His rifle is here."

"Over there," Chet said. Sam watched him walk a few feet away and bend down. He stood up with

Elliot's pistol in his hand. He smelled the barrel. He then checked the magazine and the chamber. "His pistol hasn't been fired," he said. "Still has a full mag."

Sam stood up and looked around. "How the hell could someone get close enough to snap his neck without him getting off at least a shot?"

Chet stuck the pistol in his waistband and walked over to Elliot's rifle. He picked it up, smelled the barrel, checked the magazine, and the chamber. "Rifle hasn't been fired either." He started back toward the Hummer. "The cabin, brother."

Sam removed two extra 9mm and two 5.56 magazines from Elliot's pockets and then made his way back through the brush toward the Hummer. He handed the 9mm magazines to Chet.

***

Tiff blinked her eyes open and then leaped from the sofa in the still pitch dark room. She scurried to the window and pulled the blanket back. A sliver of dull light entered the room. She put her hand on the pistol still in the holster on her hip, picked up her rifle, and hurried to the front door.

Taylor, lounged in an overstuffed chair, opened his eyes and rubbed his face. "What's up?" he asked with a yawn.

"Going to check on Elliot—he's still not back."

"I'll come with," Taylor said. He got to his feet and picked up Sam's rifle.

Tiff opened the front door just as the Hummer pulled to a stop in front of the cabin. She walked over and met Sam as he stepped from the passenger seat. Taylor ambled up but stood well behind Tiff.

"Did you guys run into trouble?" Tiff asked.

"Yes," Sam replied. "It's headed our way, but we need to talk about something else."

"Can it wait?" She asked. "Elliot's not back and I'm on my way to find him."

Sam walked over and put his hand on Tiff's shoulder. "Already found him." Sam clenched his jaw.

Tiff gazed at Sam's eyes. "What... where—"

Sam raised his hand to cut her off. "A hundred yards down; he's dead."

"We didn't hear anything last night," she said. "How's that possible?"

Chet stepped up. "He wasn't shot."

Tiff glanced at Sam and then Chet with a questioning look. "If he wasn't shot—how then?"

"His neck was broken," Sam said. "I'm really sorry, Tiff."

Tiff took off running down the drive. Sam grabbed his rifle from Taylor and then followed Tiff down the drive and down the road. Tiff rushed through the brush at the side of the road to Elliot lying in sight. She dropped to her knees next to his body. Sam rushed up right behind her.

Tears flowed down her cheeks. "I don't get it," she said choking up. "Why would Jones kill Elliot and then not attack the cabin?"

"I don't think it was Jones," Sam replied. "He was busy most of the night with Chet and me back in town."

Tiff looked up at Sam. "Who then?"

"I don't know," Sam answered. "All I know is someone was able to approach Elliot in the dark and disarm him before he could get a shot off."

Tiff shook her head back and forth as she looked down at Elliot.

"Tiff, I'm sorry about Elliot," Sam said. "But Jones is on his way and we need to get ready."

Tiff stood up and wiped her tears with the back of her hand. She paused a few moments with her head down. Then she looked up and started walking out of the brush. She stopped when she got to the edge of the road and looked back at Sam who was following close behind. "We need to bury him."

"We will, but right now we need to get ready for Jones and his band of shitheads," Sam said.

Sam stepped up on the pavement and then began jogging toward the cabin. Tiff sauntered a few steps and then started jogging behind him.

Charlie, Emma, Taylor, and Chet were standing next to the Hummer when Sam and Tiff ran up.

"Chet told us what happened to Elliot," Charlie said, as he and Emma wrapped their arms around Tiff.

"That's just it, what did happen?" Tiff mumbled.

"We'll figure it out, but right now we need a plan," Sam said. "Jones will likely be arriving any time and I don't expect him to drive up to the front door."

"He's probably working his way through the woods as we stand here," Chet added.

Sam glanced around the compound. "We'll be sitting ducks if we stay in this cabin," he said. "They'll burn it while we're in there. We need to meet them before they get to the cabin."

"What do you have in mind?" Charlie asked.

Sam glanced at the bow in Charlie's hand. "What kind of range do you get with that thing?"

"I can hit most things at a hundred yards," Charlie replied. "Not too good beyond that."

Chet scratched his beard while Sam did a full hand rub of his face.

After a few moments, Sam looked at Charlie. "Okay, you and Chet take a position up the road a hundred yards in the trees on the left side. Whether they drive in or walk in you should be in a good spot to come up behind them. You'll need to load up on ammo and arrows."

Charlie and Chet nodded.

"What about me?" Tiff asked.

Sam walked to the Hummer and retrieved Elliot's rifle. He handed the rifle and the 5.56 magazines to Taylor and then pointed to him and Tiff.

"How about if you two wait at the rear of the property, down by the stream? Whether they come from the north or south, you'll be able to flank them. Expect them from the north but stay alert."

Tiff and Taylor nodded.

"And me?" Emma asked.

Sam turned his attention to Emma. "If you're okay with loading magazines, I'd like to have you in the cabin with me."

"I can do that," Emma said.

"Okay, load up with ammo, water, and something to eat," Sam said. "It might be a long day. And then take your positions. I'll put the Hummer in the garage."

"How many are coming," Tiff asked.

"From what Chet and I saw, they started out with fifteen last night. We were able to drop that to ten. But there could be more."

As everyone turned away to head into the cabin, Sam took a long look at Taylor. Taylor glanced back at Sam and caught his gaze. The corners of his mouth turned up with a smirk just before he turned his head back to the cabin. Sam clenched his jaw and kept his gaze on Taylor as he walked away.

CHAPTER 24

Tiff and Taylor hunkered down at water's edge behind the embankment. From their position, Tiff could see the clearing north of the cabin and pump house along with the tree line.

"Are you going to say something?" Taylor asked.

Tiff focused on the clearing. "First of all, keep your voice down," she replied in a low tone. "Beyond that, what would you like me to say?"

"I can tell you're upset," Taylor said. "Look, I'm sorry about Elliot."

Tiff jerked her head toward Taylor. "Are you? Really?" She jerked her head back to the clearing.

"Of course, he seemed like a nice guy," Taylor said.

Tiff glanced down the embankment. "We need to move farther north, more into the tree line." She got to a low crouch and started moving north along the embankment.

Taylor followed. "You act like it's my fault or something," he said.

Tiff stopped, turned, and looked straight into Taylor's eyes. "Shut the hell up and pay attention. Got it?" she said in a low but stern voice.

"Got it," Taylor said.

Tiff turned and continued down the embankment. They settled into a spot twenty yards farther up, just beyond where the tree line met the embankment. A large dead oak, probably taken down by a storm, had fallen across the bank giving them partial cover from the south and from the other side of the stream. Tiff and Taylor nestled into the natural cubby-hole provided by the tree trunk and the embankment. She raised her head above the embankment and surveyed her field of fire. From here she had a better view into the woods and she could still see the clearing leading up to the cabin. She motioned for Taylor to turn around and keep his eyes toward the trees on the other side of the stream. Taylor spun around, resumed a sitting position, and leaned his back against the embankment.

Tiff took a water bottle from a canvas bag, unscrewed the top, and was in the process of raising the bottle when a twig snapped in the distance, from the woods in front of her. She peeked over the embankment but saw nothing. She screwed the cap back on and replaced the water bottle. Taylor started to spin around. Tiff stopped him with her hand and then motioned with her fingers to keep his eyes on the other side of the stream.

***

Charlie peeked around the tree trunk. "Movement," he whispered.

Chet glanced at where Charlie was looking and then peered around his own tree trunk. No movement. "You sure?" he asked in a low voice.

"I think so, but now it's gone."

Chet scanned the trees and brush on the other side of the road. Something caught his eye. "Shithead due east moving toward the cabin."

"Shithead?"

"Bad guy," Chet replied.

Charlie looked due east. "Got him. Now what?"

"We wait until they are past us," Chet replied.

Chet continued his survey of the trees. He spotted three men skulking through the brush. He was wondering where the rest of Jones' men were when he heard the snap—from the forest behind him.

Chet caught Charlie's attention with a slight hand motion. Charlie glanced over and was about to say something. Chet put his finger to his lips and then pointed to their rear. Chet dropped to a squat, then to his knees, then prone on the ground. Charlie did the same. Chet then crawled to the nearest bush behind him and slowly separated the branches and leaves. About thirty-five yards out, Chet saw three more men creeping from cover to cover. He looked back at Charlie who was on the ground in front of his original tree. Chet figured Charlie would not be able to crawl with his bow and quiver of arrows without making noise so Chet turned and crawled to Charlie.

"Three men," Chet whispered. "Thirty-five yards out."

Charlie nodded.

"Can you take them with your bow?"

Charlie nodded and started to rise up. Chet stopped him with his hand.

"We need to wait until they are a little past our position," Chet said.

Chet checked the forest on the other side of the road. After a few moments, he had the three men in sight. They were still moving toward the cabin. That made six he had been able to spot so far.

After a couple of minutes, Chet crawled back to the bush and looked through the branches and leaves. The three men he saw before were much farther down, almost fifty yards out. Chet motioned for Charlie to join him.

Charlie crouched low and stepped carefully holding his bow in one hand and the quiver of arrows in the other. He joined Chet at the bush. Chet gave hand signals to indicate the relative position and distance. Charlie then moved to the closest large tree.

Chet watched as Charlie put his right arm through the quiver strap and then raised the strap over his head to position the arrows on his right hip. He pulled an arrow, placed it on the bowstring, and set the shaft in the slot.

Chet moved to an adjacent tree and brought his rifle up pointed in the direction of the three men. He then motioned for Charlie to proceed.

Charlie pulled the arrow back and paused for a moment while he took aim.

***

The north side of the cabin had only one window. Sam knelt at that window, in the family room, with the blanket pulled back just enough to give him a view of the clearing and tree line to the north. He took his time and focused on the details about every five degrees of the hundred or so degree arc. Nothing. He looked back at Emma in the dull light, standing in the middle of the room wringing her hands together. Finally, she unclasped her hands.

"Sorry, never been very good at waiting," she said. "And I'm worried about Charlie."

"Chet knows what he's doing," Sam said. "Charlie will be fine."

"What can I do?" Emma asked.

"How about if you check the view from the bedrooms and kitchen," he said. "Let me know if you see any movement."

Emma left the room.

Sam resumed his scrutiny of the north side through the window. After a few minutes, Sam saw a man run to a tree at the edge of the woods. And then another man hustled to an adjacent tree.

"Emma," he called out.

Emma hurried into the room.

"I have movement on the north side—two men so far," he said. "I need you to stay low, as low to the floor as possible. These walls won't stop rifle bullets."

Emma got down on her hands and knees and then all the way to a prone position in the center of the room. Sam brought his rife up, moved the blanket to the side with the tip of the barrel, and rested the muzzle brake on the window sill. With the window casing raised a few inches, Sam was able to aim the rifle without any obstruction.

He looked through his magnified sight and placed the red dot on the arm of the first man, partially visible behind the tree. Sam couldn't see the man's face but could tell from body movements that he appeared to be talking to someone to his right. Sam swung his rifle to the left and picked up the second man behind the adjacent tree. He swung the rifle farther left and picked up a third man behind a small bush. Sam then swung the rifle back to the first man. His arm and left thigh were visible.

Sam debated on whether to take the shot. He knew Tiff was on their left flank and Chet might be on their rear. But what about the other men? There should be at least ten men. Sam controlled his breathing and lightly massaged the trigger with his finger.

In his peripheral vision, he saw movement to the left. He glanced up from the rifle sight and saw the second man dart from his tree. He raced toward the pump house. Sam swung the rifle around, but too late to get the man in the magnified sight. Sam swung the rifle back to the first man. He was still behind the tree. Sam saw him motion with his hand. Sam swung his rifle to the left just in time to see the third man leap from the bush and run toward the pump house. Through the magnified sight, Sam led the man just a bit with the red dot and squeezed the trigger. Without ear protection, the blast was deafening. Sound became muffled. Sam saw the runner crumple to the ground about halfway across the clearing. Sam swung the rifle back to the first man. About four inches of his shoulder and an inch of his head were exposed from behind the tree. Sam immediately placed the red dot on the man's shoulder and squeezed the trigger again.

Sam saw wood splinter from the tree but couldn't tell if the man was hit.

***

Charlie let the arrow go a split second before he heard a gun blast from the cabin. The arrow left the bow on a trajectory that would intercept the closest man in the center of his back—but only if he kept the same pace. He didn't. The man stopped at the sound of the gunshot and jerked his head to his left. The arrow sailed past an inch in front of the man's chest. Charlie instantly brought another arrow up, pulled the string to its full stretch, and let go while the man stood frozen apparently wondering what just flew past. He didn't wonder long. The second arrow found its mark in the man's temple. He crumpled to the ground.

Charlie brought a third arrow up, placed it on the string, and pulled back. He took aim at the next closest man who had turned at the sound of his friend hitting the ground. Charlie released the string. The arrow flew silently until it came to rest in the man's chest. The man stood stunned for a moment before he finally collapsed to the ground.

With the gunfire and hearing his two friends fall to the ground, the third man ducked behind the nearest tree. He jerked his head around in all directions, apparently not sure from where the arrows came.

Charlie let loose a fourth arrow just as the man caught sight of Charlie standing to the side of the bush. The arrow sunk into the tree trunk with a loud *thunk*. The man glanced at the vibrating shaft and then brought his rifle up, pointing it toward Charlie.

***

Tiff saw the man crouched on the north side of the pump house, a second man on the ground in the clearing, and the third man standing behind a tree north of the clearing. Sam's shot splintered wood but missed the third man.

Tiff was in a perfect position to flank the man at the pump house and the man in the woods. Tiff glanced at Taylor and saw that he had turned around, his head above the embankment looking at the clearing. He wasn't watching their rear. That's when she heard the sounds from the woods behind them, on the other side of the stream. People were running through the woods.

Tiff spun around and scooted up to the tree trunk. Four men were sprinting through the woods toward the stream a few yards south of Tiff and Taylor. The man in the lead was Jones. Apparently, he had not seen Tiff and Taylor. Tiff dropped her head below the trunk to wait for the men to reach the stream. Then they would be in the open where she and Taylor could cut them down.

Tiff sensed Taylor moving to join her at the tree trunk. A moment later blasts of gunfire opened up next to her. Her hearing went muffled and hot brass from Taylor's ejection port pelted Tiff in the head and neck. Too late to do anything about it, Tiff peeked above the trunk and saw that all four men had taken cover behind trees well back from the stream. Despite the threat from the men, she was more pissed at Taylor for being such an idiot. If he had waited a few more moments, the men would have been in the open.

The four men began returning fire. Taylor ceased firing and rolled up into a ball behind the tree trunk. Rounds whizzed over Tiff's head and also slammed into the trunk in front of her. The dense wood absorbed the bullets, but Tiff and Taylor were completely pinned down. They both buried their face in the sand and scrunched their bodies as close to the tree trunk as possible. Tiff realized that the four men could keep up the rate of fire while they walked right up and shot Tiff and Taylor at point blank range. Tiff had nowhere to run. Taylor had managed to turn a tactical advantage into a death trap.

Tiff raised one eye above the bark for a split second, long enough to see that the four men had apparently read her mind. One man was working his way north through the woods and another was moving south while two remained to keep Tiff and

Taylor pinned. They intended to flank her and Taylor from the north and south. She thought of Sam and Chet. But Chet was too far away, and Sam was in the cabin. And neither knew how much trouble Tiff was in. If the man at the pump house decided to attack from the west, it would all be over in less than a minute.

***

Sam heard gunfire from the stream just before the man behind the pump house brought his rifle around and opened fire on Sam's window. The first round hit the window frame and shattered the glass. Sam dropped to the floor and looked back at Emma to make sure she was flat on the floor. He motioned for her to crawl closer to the wall, but she was frozen stiff. She had her eyes clamped shut and her hands over her head. Sam then heard a second string of gunfire coming from the north side of the clearing. Obviously, he had missed the man in the woods.

Bullets ripped through the cabin's north wall and shattered nick-knacks and pictures on the opposite wall. Each hole left a shaft of light. Sam crawled to the center of the room, grabbed hold of Emma, and dragged her with him across the wood plank floor to the kitchen. Sam shoved her against the far side of the refrigerator.

"Don't move from this spot," he said. "I've got to get outside to do any good."

Emma curled into a fetal position on the floor and nodded her head.

Sam checked to make sure he had his pistol holstered and extra magazines for it and his rifle. He then crawled to the kitchen door and reached up to turn the knob. He pushed the door open with his elbow, stole a glance outside, and crawled over the threshold.

Once outside he was better able to hear the gunfire still coming from the stream mixed in with the continued fire from the north side of the clearing, which actually sounded like it was getting closer. Sam figured the men were working themselves closer to the cabin.

Sam crawled across the slate stone patio and took cover behind his brick barbecue. He came to a kneeling position behind the barbecue and brought his rifle around the corner. The pump house filled the lens of his magnifier. He swung the barrel through a ninety-degree arc but no one came into view. He then scurried back to the cabin wall and inched his way toward the northeast corner. He glimpsed around the corner and saw the two men walking toward the front of the cabin while continuing to fire through the walls.

Sam brought his rife up, captured the first man in his sight, and fired three quick rounds. The man spun around and spilled to the ground just as Sam moved his sight to the next man. Sam recognized Smith.

Three more rounds and Smith lay sprawled on the ground.

***

Just as the man aimed his rifle at Charlie, Chet stepped from behind the tree, rifle shouldered, aimed. The man's smile turned to a frown as he caught sight of Chet. Three rounds found their mark in the man's center mass. The impact punched him backward and to the ground before he could pull the trigger on his rifle.

"Check these guys to make sure they are down and out," Chet said, as he started trotting toward the gunfire coming from the cabin and the stream.

Charlie nodded as he moved forward.

Chet scampered across the road, into the forest on the north side of the cabin, and then from tree to tree. As he worked his way to the clearing, he saw three men lying in the grass a few yards in front of the cabin. Sam had apparently taken them out.

The only gunfire came from the stream—Tiff and Taylor. Chet veered to the left and dashed from tree to tree as he worked his way toward the water and the sound of gunfire. If he continued in the due east direction he'd come out about fifty yards north of where the clearing met the stream bank.

Chet stopped at the tree line and took cover behind a large oak. Down the embankment, he could see two men firing on Tiff and Taylor who were pinned behind a fallen tree trunk. Bullets splintered the wood as Tiff and Taylor hugged the ground unable to get a shot off.

Chet was about to raise his rifle when he caught movement in his peripheral vision to his left, across the stream. A third man was working his way around to flank Tiff. As soon as the man stepped down to the stream bank, Chet brought his rifle up and pulled the trigger three times. The man dropped his rifle, grabbed at his stomach, and fell face first into the water.

The two men firing at Tiff paused for a moment and caught sight of Chet. They turned their rifles and fired just as Chet ducked behind the oak tree.

***

When Tiff heard the gunfire from her left flank, she tensed her body and waited for the rounds to rip through her flesh. After a few moments with no bullet holes in her torso, she glanced to her left and saw Chet duck behind an oak tree. The two men across the stream resumed their fire. Tiff saw the rounds hit the trees around Chet and realized they were shooting at him, not her. Tiff took the opportunity to throw her rifle barrel over the top of the tree trunk, take quick aim, and pulled the trigger continuously until her thirty-round magazine was empty. She ducked behind the trunk to slap a new mag into the rifle. She glanced at Taylor. He was wrapped in a fetal position with his arms around his head. His rifle lay in the dirt.

That's when she heard gunfire from the south along the stream. She peeked one eye over the tree trunk toward the south and saw Sam in the brush on her side of the stream about fifty yards down. The fourth man lay prone on the opposite bank.

Suddenly, except for the ringing in her ears, everything was quiet in Tiff's muffled world. She scanned the opposite forest where the two men were shooting at her. They were out of sight. She then looked down at Taylor who was still curled in a ball. She kicked him in the ass. "Asshole," she mumbled.

CHAPTER 25

Sam crossed the stream and stopped for a moment to check the man sprawled on the bank. He was dead. Sam entered the tree line and began working his way toward where the two men had been firing at Tiff and Taylor.

He saw Tiff stand with her rifle shouldered. She swept the rifle back and forth in a one-hundred and eighty-degree arc which covered the entire tree line on the opposite bank. She stepped over the tree trunk and moved toward the water line.

Sam then saw Taylor stick his head above the trunk but didn't move from there.

Sam came up to the spot where the two men had been firing at Tiff. Chet stepped from the brush at about the same time. Behind a bush, both the men who had been firing at Tiff were on the ground. Neither moved. Both were riddled with bullet holes. Blood stained their clothing.

"Both dead," Sam yelled.

Chet moved closer to Sam. "Charlie and I got three in the woods, you got three by the cabin, and we have four here. That makes ten. I think our work is done."

"Mostly," Sam replied, as he started toward the stream.

Tiff stood at the stream's edge as Sam sloshed through the water toward her. Taylor walked up and stood by her side.

Sam motioned to the cabin and then looked at Tiff. "You might want to check on your Mom. She's okay but the cabin got shot to hell and she's probably worried about you."

Tiff nodded, turned, and started off. Taylor turned to follow her.

"Taylor, hold up a minute," Sam said.

Chet sloshed through the water and joined them. "We'll need a shovel for these guys."

Sam nodded. "Taylor and I will be with you shortly.

Chet glanced back and forth between Taylor and Sam who were each staring at each other. Chet walked away toward the cabin.

"What's up?" Taylor asked.

"These guys didn't kill Elliot," Sam said. There was no doubt in his voice or his meaning.

Taylor said nothing. He just stared into Sam's eyes with a slight smirk on his face.

"That doesn't leave too many suspects," Sam continued.

Taylor studied Sam's face for a few moments and then turned and walked off without saying a word.

Sam's eyes followed Taylor as he walked away. Sam climbed the bank and followed. Sam saw Chet approaching across the clearing with two shovels in hand. Taylor passed him without a glance. Chet stopped, eyed Taylor, and then resumed walking toward Sam.

Sam met Chet and took one of the shovels. "We bury Elliot first and then Dave, Tina, and Bobby."

Chet nodded and fell in behind Sam. Charlie exited the cabin and walked to meet Sam and Chet.

"I'll give you guys a hand," Charlie said.

"Appreciated. How's Emma?" Sam asked, as Charlie fell in beside them.

"Shaken, but she'll live. She and Tiff are trying to clean up the cabin."

"Taylor?" Sam asked.

"Taylor…. he's being very quiet," Charlie replied.

Sam nodded as the three walked into the garage and got into the Hummer. Sam fired the engine and then backed the Hummer out.

***

It was late afternoon when Sam and Chet leaned their shovels against the wall in the garage. It was a tight fit in there with the Hummer. Sam looked at his dirty hands and then at the dirt smudges on Chet and Charlie's face.

"We should wash up before we go in," Sam said.

"Lead the way," Charlie said.

Sam led the two men toward the stream. They passed a single mound in the clearing at the edge of the tree line, near the stream.

"Too bad about Elliot," Charlie said. "Tiff sure seemed to like him."

"He was one of the good ones," Chet said.

Sam said nothing.

At the stream, the three men washed their hands and faces and then stood up facing the opposite bank. Four mounds were visible a few feet inside the brush.

"What about the town?" Chet asked.

"I guess we should let them know their new police chief is dead," Sam said. "Tomorrow."

They turned toward the cabin and saw Tiff standing next to Elliot's grave. Sam, Chet, and Charlie joined her there.

"If Jones didn't kill Elliot, who did?" Tiff asked, as she continued to stare at the grave.

Nobody said anything.

"Jones and his men were tied up with you guys in town," Tiff continued.

"We were hiding in the woods for several hours and he wasn't on the road when we came out early this morning," Sam said. "I suppose they had time."

"Neither of his weapons had been fired," Chet reminded everyone.

"Doesn't make sense," Tiff said. "No way Jones could have found Elliot in the dark, in the woods, and got close enough to break his neck without a shot."

"Maybe he just tripped in the dark," Charlie said.

"Tripped in the dark and his pistol ends up twenty feet away," Chet said.

"Was Taylor with you the whole time last night," Sam asked.

"You think Taylor killed Elliot?" Charlie asked.

"He did go out alone," Tiff said. "He said he was keeping watch from outside."

Suddenly her jaw tightened, her eyes narrowed, and her fists clenched. She spun on her heels and marched toward the cabin. Sam, Chet, and Charlie followed.

"Wait, you can't possibly think Taylor had anything to do with this," Charlie said.

Tiff ignored him and burst through the kitchen door. Emma was sweeping glass into a pile.

"Where's Taylor?" Tiff demanded.

Emma stopped sweeping. "He was in the other room."

Tiff marched forward, followed by Sam, Chet, Charlie, and Emma.

Taylor was not in the family room. Tiff checked the two bedrooms and the bathroom. She returned to the family room and shook her head.

"Look, we don't know that Taylor had anything to do with it," Sam said. "Probably just a coincidence. Maybe Elliot did trip in the dark."

At that moment the sound of the Hummer's engine turning over caught everyone's attention. Sam slapped his pants pocket where he normally kept the keys. "Keys are in the truck."

Everyone raced out the front door and around to the left toward the garage.

The engine revved. Sam heard the gear selector shift. Just as Sam approached the open garage doors, the Hummer rolled back until Sam heard the right side scrape the garage doorjamb. The truck stopped.

"Not that difficult to drive," Sam said loud enough for Taylor to hear.

Taylor shut off the engine, opened the door, and stepped out. "Lousy visibility." He walked to the truck's right side, inspected the damage, and rubbed the side of the Hummer. "Not that bad."

"Where were you going?" Tiff asked.

"Just backing the truck to the front door," Taylor said. "We never finished unloading the food and stuff."

Tiff glanced at Sam. Sam raised an eyebrow and shrugged his shoulders.

"Good idea," Chet said, as he slipped into the driver's seat. "I'll back it out."

Chet started the engine and backed the Hummer up to the front door. He killed the engine and hopped out. Sam popped open the rear hatch and started handing items to everyone standing around. Sam handed Tiff two cases of MRE's.

Tiff took them with both arms. When she turned toward the cabin door, the bottom of the first box came open and twelve individual MRE packs fell to the ground.

"Shit," Tiff said.

Emma stepped to help pick up the packs. "Tiffany, your language."

"Sorry, Mom."

Taylor joined them. He folded the bottom of the box so it would stay shut and then helped replace the MRE packs. Everyone else continued shuttling items into the cabin while Sam handed them out. Emma stood, grabbed two bags of rice from Sam and headed for the cabin.

Taylor stood and handed the now refilled MRE case to Tiff, placing it on top of the box she held in her hands.

Tiff suddenly stopped and scrunched her nose. She dropped both boxes on the ground and stepped up to Taylor just as Chet came out of the cabin. Tiff stuck her head close to Taylor's chest, and then his arm, his right arm. Then she stood up straight and stared at Taylor's face.

Taylor stood with a confused expression. "What?"

Tiff didn't answer. She just stared at Taylor.

"What is it?" Sam asked, as he and Chet stepped closer.

"Eucalyptus," Tiff said, calmly.

"What is eucalyptus?" Taylor asked.

"Bug repellent," Sam said, as he turned to face Taylor. He bent forward, closer to Taylor's arm, and inhaled through his nose.

Taylor jumped back. "What is happening to you people?"

Sam straightened and then glanced at Chet.

Chet stepped up to Taylor and bent closer.

Taylor jumped back again. "Get the hell away from me," he yelled, just as Emma and Charlie came out of the cabin.

Chet nodded to Sam.

"What is going on?" Emma asked.

"These people have suddenly gone bonkers," Taylor said.

Sam glanced at Emma and Charlie. "Eucalyptus," Sam said. "Bug repellent. There's only one person in our group who used the stuff."

"Elliot," Tiff said.

Taylor shrugged his shoulders as though wrongly accused of something. "So what, I borrowed some."

"When?" Sam asked, as he stepped closer to Taylor.

"Look, you people stay the hell away from me," Taylor yelled, as he backed up.

Sam, shaking his head in disbelief, took two steps toward Taylor. As fast as a rattlesnake, Taylor pivoted on his left leg, brought his right foot up close to his left knee, and sprung it forward catching Sam in the midsection. Sam bent over expelling all the air from his lungs, staggered back, and then went down to one knee. Chet started toward Taylor who brought his fists up close to his chin and spread his legs apart in a fighter's stance.

Three loud blasts startled everyone, everyone except Taylor. He just fell backward, full length, and thumped into the dirt driveway. Everyone turned to look at Tiff.

She stood stoically as she stared at Taylor's dead body on the ground. Her XDs 9 in her hand hung to her thigh. Smoke wisped from the barrel.

Emma put her hand to her mouth, ran over, and knelt beside Taylor. There were three bloody holes—two center mass and one in the forehead. She stood up, tears running down her cheek, and turned to Tiff.

"Why?"

She said nothing. She just holstered her pistol, turned, and walked across the clearing toward Elliot's grave.

Sam stood trying to get his breath back and watched Tiff walk away. He then turned back to Emma. "Elliot was the only person we know who used eucalyptus. He obviously used it last night to keep the mosquitoes at bay. Taylor had the opportunity last night and he certainly had the motive. Elliot's neck was broken. Taylor was trained to do just that. When he did so, some of Elliot's bug repellent rubbed off on Taylor. He killed Elliot."

"But she didn't even give him a chance to explain," Emma said.

"For her, the evidence was overwhelming."

"Now what?" Charlie asked.

Chet let out a slow exhale. "Now we have another body to bury."

"And then what?" Emma asked.

Sam walked over to Taylor and stood looking down at his body. "We start surviving."

A REQUEST FROM THE AUTHOR

Thank you for reading *Solar Plexus*. I hope you enjoyed the story as much as I enjoyed writing it. I do have one request. I ask that you please take a few moments to enter a product review on your Amazon 'Orders' page. Independent authors depend on reviews to get their books noticed. And reviews also help make my future books better. A few moments of your time would be much appreciated. I look forward to reading your thoughts. —**Victor Zugg**

ABOUT THE AUTHOR

Victor Zugg is a former US Air Force officer and OSI special agent who served and lived all over the world. Given his extensive travels and opportunities to settle anywhere, it is ironic that he now resides in Florida, only a few miles from his hometown of Orlando. He credits the warm temperatures for that decision.

Check out the author's other novels—*Near Total Eclipse (Solar Plexus 2)*, *Surrounded By The Blue*, and *From Near Extinction*.

Made in the USA
Middletown, DE
06 September 2020

18953672R00208